ALSO BY TINA FOLSOM

Yvette's Haven

Scanguards Vampires #4

Tina Folsom

Yvette's Haven is a work of fiction. Names, characters, places, and incidents are the products of the author's imagination and are used fictitiously. Any resemblance to actual events, locales, or persons, living or dead, is entirely coincidental.

2011 Tina Folsom

Published in the United States

Cover design: Elaina Lee
Cover photo: www.bigstockphoto.com
Author Photo: © Marti Corn Photography

Printed in the United States of America

PROLOGUE

Haven was the first one to hear his mother's alarmed cry. Immediately, he seized his younger brother Wesley by the collar of his polo shirt, making him squeal in protest.

"Let go of me, Hav. I wanna play."

Haven ignored his eight-year-old brother's objection and slammed his hand over his mouth. "Shut up," he ordered, keeping his voice low. He could sense his mother's mounting fear, despite the fact that he and Wesley were in the den and their mother's panicked scream had come from the kitchen where she was mixing potions.

"Someone's in the house. Keep quiet." He gave his brother a stern look. Wesley's eyes widened in fear, but he nodded nevertheless. Haven took his hand off Wesley's mouth and was rewarded with his brother's silence.

Anticipating something just like this, his mother had drilled a strict protocol into him and his brother: hide and keep quiet. As much as Haven wanted to obey his mother, her scream had torn through his gut; he'd be a coward if he didn't help her. He was tall for his age, almost a man. Being abandoned by their father less than a year ago had forced him to grow up fast. He was the man of the house now. It was up to him to help his mother.

"Go get Katie and hide under the stairs." Their baby sister was sleeping in the downstairs bedroom, rather than in the nursery upstairs, so she could be heard if she woke. She wasn't due to be fed for another two hours, and hopefully that meant she'd remain asleep.

Wesley took off, running down the hallway, his sock-clad feet making no sound on the hardwood floor. Haven mustered all his courage and crept toward the kitchen door.

"You know you have to sacrifice one of them, so who's it gonna be?" a man hissed from inside the kitchen. The malevolence in the stranger's voice was unmistakable, and a cold shiver slithered up Haven's spine like a snake.

"Never," Haven's mother answered, a flash of white light accompanying her words. He knew if she was using magic so openly on the intruder it meant he was a preternatural creature: not human.

Shit!

A burglar Mom would have no problem dealing with, but this was different. That's why she needed his help, whether she'd forbidden it or not. She could ground him all she wanted later, but he wasn't going to stay away and hide like a spineless weasel. Wesley could take care of Katie by himself, but Haven was old enough now—eleven to be exact—to help his mother defeat an attacker.

Haven inched forward and glanced around the door frame into the well-lit kitchen. Aghast, he pulled back.

Double shit!

Without a doubt, her attacker was a vampire—top of the food chain. His fangs were extended and pushed past his open lips, his eyes glaring red like a car's taillights in the night. While vampires weren't immune to witchcraft, Haven's mother was merely a minor witch with no powers beyond her potions and spells. She'd never mastered control of any of the elements: water, air, fire, and earth, as others of her kind had. She was nearly defenseless.

The tall, slim vampire had his hand clamped around her neck even as her lips moved as if trying to cast a spell. But no words issued from her throat. She struggled in his hold, her eyes darting to her side, searching desperately for a means of escape. There was no way out—no way she could free herself if she couldn't utter a spell to make the vampire release her. And even then . . .

Haven knew what he had to do. Summoning all his courage, he rushed through the door and charged for the kitchen counter where an assortment of kitchen utensils stood in an earthen jug. He reached for the wooden spoon and broke it in half.

At the sound, the vampire snapped his head toward Haven and flashed his fangs in irritation. A warning snarl ripped from his throat. "Big mistake, little boy, big mistake."

Nobody called him little and got away with it.

A choked gurgle came from his mother. She blinked her eyes at Haven, intent upon sending him a message despite her obvious distress. He understood her all too well, but he wasn't going to flee. She wanted him to save himself. But he was no coward. How could she even think that he would run and leave her in the hands of this monster?

"Let my mother go!" he demanded from the vampire and lifted his hand holding the makeshift stake.

Haven charged toward the vampire, letting out a warrior cry like he'd seen in the Westerns he loved to watch on TV. Before he reached the bloodsucker, the vamp dropped his hold on his mother and tossed her against the stove, the sound of her back connecting with the metal oven door blasting a wave of fury through Haven. Faster than his eyes could follow, the vampire was on him and gripped his wrist, holding it immobile.

Haven clenched his teeth and kicked his leg against the massive creature's shin, but to no avail. A growl issued from the vampire's mouth. Behind him, Haven caught sight of his mother getting up, moaning in pain. But her face looked determined, and her lips mouthed a spell.

"Night bring day, day bring night, help the small, and . . . "

The vampire twisted Haven's wrist, wrenching the stake from his clenched fist. It clattered to the floor, rolling out of reach. Then the vampire released him. Spinning around, he reached into his jacket and pulled out a knife. "You stupid witch!" he snarled. "I was gonna let you live."

Undeterred, Haven's mother continued chanting, " . . . tall, and give them might . . . "

Haven launched himself at the vampire from behind, trying to wrestle the knife from his hands, but his opponent jabbed his elbow into the soft muscles of Haven's tender stomach and shoved him to the floor. When Haven looked up, he only saw the flick of the vamp's wrist as he released the knife to find its target.

A startled shriek interrupted his mother's chants. The knife had hit her in her chest. As she tumbled to the floor, blood staining her white apron, Haven scrambled to get closer, but the vampire blocked his approach.

"Haven," his mother's strained voiced cried out. "Remember . . . to love . . . "

"No! You bastard!" Haven screamed. "I'll kill you!"

But before he could do anything, the cry of a baby filled the house. Katie.

The vampire's head spun toward the hallway. Then a self-satisfied grin spread over his mouth. It did nothing to alleviate the ugliness of his visage. "Much easier," he proclaimed. "As if I wanted to burden myself with the likes of a troublesome little boy."

"No!" Haven screamed, realizing he was going after Katie. The vampire had said that all he needed was one of them.

The vampire stampeded out of the kitchen and down the hall. Haven ran after him, picking up a broom that leaned against the wall. He cracked the handle over his knee and gripped the shorter end like a stake.

When he reached his brother's hiding place beneath the stairs a few seconds later, the bloodsucker was already pulling Wesley from it, and Katie's wails mixed with Wesley's panicked squeals.

"Help! Haven, Mom, help me!"

The vampire yanked the little bundle that was Katie from Wesley's arms and pressed her to his chest, while he held Haven's struggling little brother off with one hand. Wesley's attempts at boxing the vampire in the stomach were futile—his tiny fists did no damage to the creature.

"Stop, you little idiot."

Neither Wesley nor Haven listened to the vampire's command. Instead, Haven jumped, his makeshift stake in his raised hand, but the bastard turned too fast. He slammed Wesley against the wall and raised his arm to fend off Haven's stake, holding Katie higher with his other arm. Haven was no match for the supernatural creature, even with his fierce determination to save his sister.

The vampire kicked him against the wall, the impact knocking the wind out of Haven. Pain seared through him, reminding him that he was only a human without any skills to fight the powerful bloodsucker.

"I mean you no harm. I'm only taking one of you." There was a flicker of something in his eyes, almost as if he regretted what he was doing. "To keep the balance."

A second later, he was gone. The front door was left ajar, darkness intruding on Haven's devastated home, the chill and fog taking hold where warmth and love had lived earlier.

Wesley moaned. "Mom, help us."

Haven crawled the few feet that separated him from his bother. How could he possibly tell Wes what had happened to their mother? And Katie, what was going to happen to Katie?

"Mom can't help," Haven whispered to his brother, ignoring the pain in his ribs as best he could. It was nothing compared to the pain he felt in his heart. He looked at Wesley and saw tears of realization run down his cheeks. Haven couldn't cry; instead, his heart filled with hatred: hatred for everything magical, everything preternatural, everything not human. Because, despite not knowing what the vampire had wanted or why he'd killed his mother, Haven suspected it had to do with her magic. There could be no other reason. He'd not been here to rob them of any of their worldly goods. *To keep the balance*, he'd said. The balance of what?

Haven stared at his brother and squeezed his hand. "I will find him, and I will kill him and all vampires that cross my path. And we'll get Katie back. I promise you."

And he wouldn't rest until he'd fulfilled his promise.

1

It was a trap—how big a trap, Haven could have never guessed.

After receiving Wesley's text message to meet him at the abandoned warehouse in one of the less fashionable neighborhoods of the city, he'd cased the area and determined that at most one or two assailants were waiting for him. Piece of cake, he'd figured.

It wouldn't be the first time he freed his little brother from the greedy clutches of a loan shark or other minor con artist he'd gotten himself in trouble with. Whatever the amount of money they wanted to extort from him for the release of his brother, they'd never see a penny of it. His concealed Glock would guarantee that.

The door to the warehouse was unlocked. He pushed it open and eased inside, taking in the musty scent of the building. It mingled with a strange mixture of herbs, conjuring up images of Chinatown with its foreign smells and tastes. The long corridor ahead of him was dark, the single light bulb hanging overhead covered in cobwebs and dust. There was nothing inviting about the place.

Any further explorations were cut short when a cold blast of air came his way. An instant later, Haven felt a force like a tidal wave press his six-foot-two, two-hundred-pound frame of solid muscle against the wall. Despite his strength and training in all types of hand-to-hand combat, he couldn't push against the invisible foe.

Shit!

This time he wasn't dealing with some low-life criminals.

Haven didn't like the feeling of helplessness that spread through his body as the assault by the force field continued. As a tough-as-frozen-shit bounty hunter, vulnerability wasn't a word in his vocabulary. And he wasn't going to add it now. His slate for *V's* was full: vampire, vermin, vulture. No space for vulnerability. Leave that to the people at *Webster's*; maybe they had use for the word.

And if he ever got out of this mess alive, he'd skin his brother, but not before he'd beaten the dog snot out of him.

"I see you got my text message," a female voice commented calmly. A moment later, she stepped into view. She was beautiful; long red hair cascaded around her face and over her shoulders. Her cheekbones were high, her skin pale, and her lips plump. At first sight, the woman was every man's dream and Haven bet that whatever predicament Wesley found himself in, it was because this woman had short-circuited his brain—making sure he had to use the one between his legs instead. Haven wasn't quite as susceptible to beautiful women as his brother was. He'd never allowed himself to have his head turned like that. And he wasn't as gullible as his little brother. No, he was tough as nails and unwavering as steel, and somehow he'd get out of this.

Haven gritted his teeth staring into the icy-blue eyes of the devilish beauty. "What did you do to my brother, witch?" Since she hadn't introduced herself, it was fitting enough to call her by her *profession* rather than her name. And of her profession he was certain: the force she was using against him wasn't something a physicist could explain. It was magic. And he recognized magic when it bit him on the ass.

"You make it sound like a four-letter word."

"Isn't it?"

She shook her head disapprovingly, her copper curls bouncing around her shoulders. "The name's Bess, not that it should matter to you. I would have expected more respect from the son of a witch. Don't you respect your mother's craft?"

The memory of his mother bit hard into his gut. He rammed it back, trying to stave off the emotions that came with it, emotions which he'd tried to suppress ever since her brutal death. He wasn't going to allow this damn witch to weaken him by dredging up things that should stay well hidden. "Leave my mother out of this. Now, where's my brother, and what do you want?"

"Your bad-boy, bounty-hunter attitude doesn't work on me, so leave it at the door and come in."

Haven glared at her and clenched his jaw.

"Unless you don't want to see your brother again. I can just leave him tied up and let him rot."

Suddenly, the pressure on his chest eased, and he was able to pry himself off the wall. He shook off the remaining feeling of claustrophobia and reached into his jacket. The thought of killing her was foremost in his mind, but without knowing whether she kept Wesley somewhere in this warehouse, he couldn't let the bullets do their job. Not yet, anyway.

"And take your hand off your gun."

It didn't take being a witch to know what his hand was reaching for. Haven snorted. "Get on with it. Where's Wesley?"

Bess walked into a fairly spacious room, a living room of sorts. He followed her. Several pieces of mismatched furniture filled the space. Rugs were spread over the concrete floor, and heavy drapes of thick velvet hung over the windows. Add the bookcase filled with old books and jars of ghastly looking herbs and animal parts, and the room had a decidedly gothic look. Not his choice of abode anyway.

In his eight years as a bounty hunter, working for different bail bondsmen along the way, Haven had seen his fair share of weird, so nothing surprised him. But even without that, he wouldn't have been surprised by her decorative choices. She was right; he was the son of a witch, and as such, he'd seen enough. More than he'd ever wanted to see—or know.

Haven shook off the memories. "Where's Wesley?"

The witch took a seat on one of the overstuffed sofas and pointed toward an armchair. "Somewhere safe. Sit."

"I'm not your dog." Witch or not, he didn't like being ordered around.

"I can turn you into one if you like."

Grunting his disapproval, he let himself fall into the chair, creating a dust cloud around him. "I'm sitting."

The witch let her gaze travel over his body. Uneasiness crept over him; he didn't like being studied as if he was some piece in an exhibition. Or worse, a subject in an experiment.

"Your brother is nothing like you. He seems much more . . . gentle. Not as—"

"I'm sure you didn't invite me for a psychology lesson; besides I don't appreciate the kind of invitations you send out." Why hadn't he guessed that his brother hadn't sent that message? Maybe because it had originated from Wesley's cell and sounded just like him: desperate for help and riddled with mistakes. His brother couldn't spell for shit; Haven hadn't questioned its authenticity.

"Would you have come if I had sent a polite letter? Anyway, pleasantries aside, we have business to discuss."

Haven raised an eyebrow. He had no business with a witch. Despite the fact that his mother had been a witch, neither he nor his brother had inherited any of her powers. It had never bothered him because the way he liked to kill his victims was close up so he saw the fear in their eyes when they realized he'd won; he had no desire to strike from a distance using magic. And his victims had always been vampires—not that he had any qualms about adding a witch to the bunch. Whoever threatened him or his family would be dealt with swiftly. In a deadly kind of way.

"What is it you want from me in exchange for my brother?"

"You catch on fast. Given your somewhat unorthodox profession, what I'm asking will be just another day in the office for you."

He hated being played with, and the cat-and-mouse game in which she was engaging him was his least favorite pastime. "Spit it out."

"There's a girl, a young actress. I would like you to bring her to me."

"Given that you managed to get me to your lair without any trouble, I don't see why you can't get her yourself."

Bess pursed her lips. "Ah, that's where the little problem starts. See, the girl has a bodyguard." The witch gestured with her hand. "Something to do with the paparazzi." She rolled her eyes, her disdain for celebrities openly showing in their cold blueness.

"And you can't get past the bodyguard? You used your powers to immobilize me. What's the guy made out of? Steel?" Something stank. And it wasn't the incense that was burning in the room, robbing it of oxygen.

"Unfortunately, her bodyguard is a vampire."

Haven listened intently now. Things had just started getting interesting. He leaned forward in his chair, intrigued by her words.

"I see I have your attention now. You could kill two birds with one stone: free your brother by bringing me the girl and kill the vampire as a bonus. It's a win-win situation."

Win-win, but for whom? "Are you trying to tell me that you can't defeat one measly vampire?" Haven knew for a fact that witchcraft worked on vampires just as well as on humans. And by the looks of it, this witch appeared strong enough to fight a vampire with her spells and potions and the way she was seemingly able to control at least one element: air. He'd felt it used on his own body earlier. A witch who controlled the elements wasn't to be trifled with.

"I could, if I got close enough. However, vampires can sense witches from afar. I'd never get close enough to work my magic. That's why I need a human; you'll be able to approach him without drawing any suspicions to you."

She dug her hand into the pocket of her cardigan and pulled out a little vial. It was filled with a purple liquid. "Once you're close enough, you'll smash the vial, and the gas it produces will render the vampire unconscious within seconds. And you know what to do then."

Stake him.

Haven grinned despite himself. While he didn't like the idea of being ordered by a witch, who held his brother captive, the thought of being handed another vampire to kill was appealing. Ever since his mother's death, he'd searched for the one vampire who'd killed her and kidnapped his baby sister. He hadn't found him yet, but he'd killed plenty of other vampires since.

However, the thought of handing over an innocent human to this witch created an uncomfortable knot in his stomach. "Who's the girl?"

The witch made a dismissive hand movement. "Nobody to concern yourself with."

Haven shook his head. "What do you want with her? If she's *just* an actress like you say, why would you be interested in her?" There was plenty Bess wasn't telling him. Maybe he shouldn't dig too deeply, maybe he should just take the assignment and get his brother out of her clutches. But he still had a smidgen of a conscience left.

"It doesn't concern you," she snapped and rose. "Get me the girl, or I'll crush your brother."

"And where is my dear brother?" he asked casually. Once he knew where she was keeping him, he could figure out a plan for how to free him without doing her dirty work for her.

"Even if I tell you where he is, you won't be able to free him. His cell is protected by invisible wards. You won't be able to break through them."

If Haven knew one thing about witchcraft, it was that once a witch died, all her wards and restraining spells would dissolve as well. Now *there* was an idea in the making. "So, he's here then," he hedged and watched her face for any affirmation of the truth of his statement. He wasn't an excellent poker player for nothing.

Her left eyelid twitched, and he followed the direction. He almost didn't see the door; it blended well into the bookcases next to it. When he looked back at her, he noticed how her lips had pressed together into a thin line.

Haven tilted his head toward the door. "I see."

"It'll do you no good. He's too well protected. You'll never break through the wards."

He didn't have to. If the witch was dead, there'd be no wards.

"Fine. We'll do it your way." He rose from his chair and turned slightly, attempting to conceal the movement of his right hand. He was a fast draw and had won plenty of competitions against the best in the field. Bess was as good as dead.

Haven slipped his hand inside his jacket, wrapped his fingers around the gun's handle and pulled it from its holster.

"Ow!" he yelped, releasing the weapon from his hand a moment later and dropping it onto the carpet where it made a muffled thumping sound. Shocked, he stared at the angry red skin of his palm. The gun had turned sizzling hot in his hand. "What the *fuck?*"

"It's better that you learn right now that there's no crossing me. Either you do what I say—or your brother dies."

Haven glared at her and recognized the impatience in her eyes. He swallowed his own anger, forcing himself to calm down. Losing his head now would not serve Wesley. He had to push his pride and scruples aside. Only his brother mattered. Wesley was all that was left of his family.

For now, he needed to keep a cool head.

"You win. What's her name and where do I find her?"

2

Yvette moved behind the privacy screen in Maya's exam room and ripped off the paper gown. How she hated these examinations, but in order to get what she wanted, she put up with them.

"It's consistent with the lab results," Maya explained from behind her desk. "There's nothing wrong with your uterus or your tubes."

"And the eggs?" Yvette asked as she shimmied into her entirely too-tight leather pants, sucked in a breath, and zipped up. She slid her toes into her black stilettos. Most other women would have broken their ankles twice over if they had to walk in her penny-diameter heels, but she felt powerful in them. Besides, a well-placed kick with her heels could do serious damage to any aggressor.

"As fresh and viable as the day you were turned."

Yvette pulled her black top over her head and walked around the screen, looking at Maya, who was rifling through the lab file. Over the last few months, she'd undergone test after test to help Maya figure out why vampire females were infertile and what it would take to change that. She couldn't deny Maya's dedication to the project, despite the fact that the two of them hadn't exactly started out on the right foot.

After Maya had been turned into a vampire against her will, Gabriel, Yvette's boss, had fallen hard for her. Yvette had her own eyes set on him at the time, and the fact that Maya had just swooped in and snatched him up within a week of meeting him had hurt.

But none of their earlier disagreements were evident now. Maya, who'd been a doctor before she was turned, had become a champion for her cause: to find a way for vampire females to become pregnant. But so far, all tests had resulted in a dead end; none of them indicated a reason for the infertility.

"Then I don't get it. I always assumed that my eggs died when I was turned. But if my eggs are intact, why haven't I gotten pregnant?" She'd had plenty of unprotected sex over the last decades, not just with vampire males but also with humans.

Maya motioned toward the chair in front of her desk, and Yvette sank into it. "You mean, apart from the fact that you haven't been with a man since we met?"

That got Yvette's hackles up, even though she *had* put herself on the shelf over the last few months. But that wasn't Maya's business. It was easy for Maya to talk: she had a man who loved her and was totally hot for her no matter what time of day or night. All *she* had were unsatisfying one-night stands, and she hadn't even bothered with those in the last few months.

"That's beside the point. I had lots of sex with virile men who, I know for a fact, have gotten other women pregnant. It's just been a little slow lately." Who was she kidding? She hadn't been interested in anybody after Gabriel had bonded with Maya. Not that she was jealous or anything—the two were really suited for each other—but she avoided men, afraid to fall for the wrong guy again.

"Listen, Yvette, we're at the very beginning of this. I don't want you to lose heart. Just look at what we've already discovered: your uterus is built the same way as a human's, which means the turning didn't change that. That's a good thing. Your fallopian tubes are clear and unobstructed, and your ovaries are stocked with viable eggs. The lab confirmed it."

She tossed Maya a hopeful glance. "What happened with the donated sperm?"

"Good news actually." Maya shuffled through her papers and pulled out one sheet. "Here's the latest result. Bringing donated sperm in contact with your eggs resulted in a fertilized egg in the test tube. So there's—"

"But my body won't keep the egg. Is that it?" Just like the other miscarriages. Yvette pushed the memories away. She didn't want to be reminded of those times. Nobody knew about her past. And she wasn't going to talk about it now. If Maya knew about the miscarriages she'd had as a human, she would have never even tried to help her. She would have considered Yvette a lost case and stopped wasting her time on this futile undertaking, but Yvette couldn't give up despite the obstacles.

Maya could never find out. But Yvette remembered everything: the pain and the disappointment—as well as her broken heart. She'd been married. Robert had wanted a family: her and kids, a dog and cat, a white picket fence surrounding their trim little yard . . .

What he'd gotten was a wife who couldn't hold onto the life that was inside her. The first pregnancy had started well enough. He'd been ecstatic. He'd told everybody that she was expecting. Every day he'd showered her with flowers and other little trinkets. But one day, at the beginning of her second trimester, she'd started bleeding. She'd miscarried. Robert had been disappointed, but he'd said they'd try again.

He'd been supportive then. Her husband had comforted her. Yvette had gotten pregnant again six months later. But it all had ended the same way. In her third month, she'd lost the baby. This time, her husband wasn't as understanding. He'd accused her of deliberately jeopardizing the pregnancies.

Which was ludicrous. It hadn't stopped him from leaving her, however. She wasn't important enough to him. All he wanted was a child. And she couldn't give him that, so he stopped loving her. She didn't want that to happen again; she hadn't let a man that close in a long time. With the next man, she wanted to know that she could give him everything he wanted. Then there would be no reason for him to leave her—and she didn't give a rat's ass about whether the man was human or vampire.

"Yvette?"

Yvette looked up and saw Maya's concerned face. "We'll have to be patient. You're healthy, and there's no apparent reason why you can't get pregnant. I'll just have to figure out what happens in a female vampire's body after conception."

Yvette rose and ran her hand through her short, spiky, black hair. "I know. It's just . . . well, I'm just impatient." And damn it if she didn't feel a tad bit guilty about having kept her prior medical history from Maya, but she couldn't divulge that information—or the pain and hurt that was so closely associated with those events. Nobody needed to know that as a woman she was a failure. It was enough that she faced the cold truth every day. And the truth was she wasn't woman enough to give a man everything he wanted. Not as a human, and certainly not now as a vampire.

"I'll do everything I can."

"Thank you." With a last nod to Maya, she strode out the door and took the stairs to the main floor of the Victorian mansion, relieved to leave the examination room behind her.

After bonding a few months earlier, Gabriel and Maya had bought a large, old Victorian home on Nob Hill, not too far from Samson's house. Ah, Samson. Scanguards' founder. He was another one who'd found love and happiness—with a human woman, a woman who was expecting their first child. Envy sliced through her like a knife. It wasn't a child she craved, but the love of a man. And how could any man truly love her for eternity if she couldn't give him everything he wanted? If she couldn't satisfy his every need?

"Just the person I wanted to see," Gabriel's gravelly voice greeted her as she reached the foyer.

Yvette looked at her boss. As was the case so often, he was dressed in black jeans and a white shirt. His long brown hair was tied back in a simple ponytail. He wasn't even trying to hide the long scar on his face, which stretched from the top of his right ear to his chin. It gave him a dangerous look. Yet underneath it all, he was handsome and kinder than anybody could imagine. Which couldn't be said for the man who stood next to him: Zane.

Just like her, Zane was one of the bodyguards employed at Scanguards, the security company owned by Samson Woodford. Zane was as tall as Gabriel, but his head was shaved bald, and apart from one single time, Yvette had never seen him smile or laugh. To say that Zane was brutal and violent would be a gross understatement; yet, at the same time, he was family, just like the rest of the vampires who worked for Scanguards. They were the only family she knew. The only one she was likely to ever have.

"What can I do for you, Gabriel?"

"Everything okay?" he asked and motioned downstairs, indicating Maya's medical practice.

Yvette's spine stiffened. "Sure, why wouldn't it be?"

"Good, good."

"Listen, Gabriel, I don't think we need to get Yvette involved," Zane interrupted, his feet impatiently grating against the wood floor.

Gabriel cut him off with an impatient hand movement. "We've discussed this. You won't use mind control on our client. I won't allow it. If she's afraid of you, it's better we assign somebody else."

Yvette raised an eyebrow. A client Zane was protecting was afraid of his—or if she heard correctly, *her*—bodyguard? Well, that certainly wasn't anything new. "You have an assignment for me?"

"Yes. The agent of a young actress has approached us to protect her while she's on a publicity tour here in the Bay Area. She's had some threats against her, the usual stuff any movie star deals with, probably some obsessed fan or some jealous actor or actress, or who knows, some disgruntled crew member. I originally assigned Zane, but it turns out the girl is intimidated by him."

"Go figure," Yvette muttered under her breath. Zane shot her a furious glare which didn't bode well for her immediate future.

"I could easily influence her, and she won't even realize that she can't stand me," Zane offered. She knew her fellow bodyguard well enough to know that he didn't give a rat's ass about whether somebody liked him or not—more often *not*—but that his ego was bruised because he'd been taken off a job. Zane wasn't a quitter. A lot of bad things could be said about him—hell, Yvette had a whole litany of things she could rattle off right now—but she had to concede one thing: he was loyal and determined to a fault.

"You won't use your powers on her. There's no need; Yvette can take over your job, and I'll assign you to somebody else."

"Fine by me," Yvette answered. "Any other things I should know?" She ignored Zane's grunt.

"Her name's Kimberly Fairfax. She's young, early twenties, an up-and-coming actress. Her latest movie has just hit the theatres, and it's making a big splash. There are bound to be lots of crazies around who think themselves in love with her. Just watch her back for stalkers and keep the paparazzi at bay. She isn't used to all the attention yet."

"No problem. When do I start?"

"Tomorrow night. There's a premier party at The Fairmont. I'll send a briefing to your iPhone. Good luck."

"Sounds good. Check in with you tomorrow."

Yvette walked to the door, the prickling tension at her nape telling her Zane was following.

"I'm out of here," Zane grumbled.

"Zane," Gabriel warned, the single word heavy with reprimand.

"What?" Zane didn't break his stride.

"Are my orders clear?"

With an answer more grunt than word, Zane stopped next to her and reached for the knob. Yvette was faster and opened the front door. Then she stopped in her tracks. There on the steps, a golden Labrador lay on his haunches. The moment he saw her, he rose and wagged his tail.

"Your dog?" Zane asked from over her shoulder.

"No. He's been following me for four months. I don't know what he wants." It wasn't entirely the truth. Yes, the dog had been following her ever since she and her colleagues had rescued Maya from the clutches of a rogue vampire several months earlier. What Yvette didn't reveal was that she'd begun feeding the stray.

"Looks like he's yours," Zane observed.

Made sense. Ever since she'd let the dog into her house on Telegraph Hill, the beast really thought he belonged to her.

"What's his name?" Zane continued undeterred, obviously enjoying her discomfort.

"Dog." At hearing her say his name, the dog's ears perked up and his tail went into overdrive. Damn, he even listened to her.

"Yep, definitely yours. Enjoy." And Zane was gone, striding down the dark, deserted street and disappearing into the shadows.

Yvette looked at the dog, whose intelligent eyes seemed to ask her a question. He tilted his head and looked as if he smiled. Could dogs smile?

She caved. "Fine, we'll go home."

3

Yvette heard the flap of the doggie door slap against the wooden doorframe and opened her eyes. Installing the door so the dog could go into the garden whenever he pleased had been a blessing; however, it was also a curse. Now that stray *really* thought he belonged here. How she'd ever get rid of him, she really didn't know. He'd even started barking at the mailman as if the poor postal employee was encroaching on his territory.

"Hey, dog," she greeted him as he jumped on the bed. One thing she'd definitely not do was to give the beast a name. Once he had a name, he would never leave.

"Is it sunset yet?" It was an idle question; the dog wouldn't answer her, nor did she actually need him to. Her own body had already told her that the sun had set over the Pacific Ocean and it was time to get ready for her assignment.

Yvette stretched, then put her hands onto her head. As every night upon waking, the short, spiky haircut she showed to everybody was gone, replaced by long, dark tresses. During her restorative sleep, her hair grew back to the length it had been the day she was turned. At first, she'd kept her hair long, but over the years, she'd decided that she didn't like the look anymore. She looked too female, too vulnerable.

She walked into her bathroom and picked up the scissors lying on the vanity. Even without a mirror, she'd learned over the years how to cut her hair. She took a bunch of it in her left hand, cutting with the scissors in her right. Instead of discarding the hair in the trash, she placed it in a plastic bag which was marked *St. Jude's Hospital— Cancer Department*. Let somebody else have long hair. She didn't care for it.

When the weight of her hair lifted from her head, she felt as if the pain of her past was lifting with it. It felt the same every time she woke. The long hair reminded her of her life as a human, of the husband who'd loved to bury his face in her long tresses when they'd made love.

Robert. His face wasn't as clear in her mind anymore as it had been in the first years after they'd separated. Almost fifty years had passed since. While her memory of his face had faded into the distance, the desire for a child hadn't. Or rather what a child represented.

Yvette placed her hand on her flat stomach. While human, a life had grown in there, not just once, but twice. She'd felt like a woman then, a woman who could give her husband what he desired above all. During those brief months of her pregnancies, she'd felt loved, not just by her husband, but also by the child inside her.

Crazy. Yvette shook her head and continued cutting her hair. She'd been devastated when she'd lost the second baby, and Robert hadn't been there to comfort her. He'd blamed her. For a year, she'd lived as if in a trance, taking whatever drugs she could get her hands on. The numbness the drugs had produced had prevented her from taking her own life. But then, one night, she'd woken up in a stranger's home, stoned out of her skull. He'd asked her if she wanted to live forever and enjoy sex without consequences. *Sure*, she'd joked, still riding on a drug high.

She'd struggled against his bite at first, but then she'd allowed death to take her, hoping the next life would be kinder. Only when she'd woken again had she realized what had happened to her. The stranger had turned her into a vampire—an *infertile* vampire, a fact she'd had to come to terms with the hard way.

As a human, she might have had another chance at a child and at making a man happy, but as a vampire, no such hope existed. And men were men, no matter what shape or form they came in. They fucked her, and she fucked them. But when all was said and done, even her sire had given her the marching papers. *Too clingy*, he'd called her. *Too needy*.

Not anymore. Now she was as tough as any vampire male, and nobody would ever see otherwise. The fragile woman inside was dead to the world.

Just like Gabriel had told her, the girl Yvette was to protect was young. What he'd neglected to mention was that Kimberly was also extremely beautiful. A twinge of jealousy hit Yvette the moment she set eyes upon her charge. This girl had everything: a thriving career, beauty, and a human body to bear children. Life was cruel. She wished now that Gabriel had let Zane use mind control to make the girl forget about her dislike for him. Yvette really didn't need a constant reminder of what she couldn't have. She would have much rather protected some wealthy, overweight executive with a bad haircut, body odor, and a beer gut.

Her consolation was that the assignment would last only a week before Kimberly would return to Los Angeles to work on her next movie.

"This is so much better," the girl blabbered. "Frankly, that other man, Zane, or whatever his name was, he was really strange. I didn't like him at all. The way he looked at me, I tell you, he made me really nervous. And I really don't get nervous. Normally. The one other time I really got nervous was when I had to audition for . . . "

Yvette tuned out Kimberly's chatter and looked out of the tinted window of the limousine. This was just peachy. Not only did Kimberly have everything humanly possible, she talked constantly. She only hoped the girl didn't actually expect her to listen to her chit-chat and respond. She swore she'd make Gabriel write a big bonus check for this one.

" . . . so I said to him, 'back at the orphanage we had that game . . . '"

Yvette offered a fake smile and nodded as if listening intently while she scanned the goings-on outside. The limo was stuck in traffic on California Street and was slowly inching its way up toward the Fairmont Hotel.

" . . . thought I was only nineteen, when I'm really already twenty-two, but it didn't matter, because they wanted somebody mature for the role . . . "

No waterfall could have produced a steadier gush than the stream of words coming from this airhead's mouth. Yvette gave her another sideways glance. Perched on the comfortable leather seat, Kimberly wore a pink evening gown. It suited her. Her wheat blond locks fell over her naked shoulders and looked perfectly natural. Only the faint smell of chemicals, picked up by Yvette's sensitive nostrils, hinted at the fact that blond wasn't Kimberly's natural hair color.

For the first time in a long time, Yvette was wearing a dress. It irked her, but Kimberly had insisted, saying that if she showed up in a pant suit, she'd stick out like a sore thumb, and everybody would think she was CIA.

So Yvette had rummaged through her closet and found a little black number that would do the trick. It was an old halter dress with a plunging neckline and a naked back. If anybody gave the dress a closer look, they'd notice it was vintage. Well, they hadn't called it vintage when she'd bought it back in the 60s. Why she'd held on to the useless thing she hadn't worn in nearly fifty years, she didn't know.

She should have given it to Goodwill years ago. It wasn't like she'd worn a dress or a skirt in the last few decades; leather pants were her favorite attire. Coupled with the same high heels that adorned her feet now, she was always ready to kick ass in her leathers. In the halter dress, albeit a black one—the only color she felt truly comfortable in— she felt uneasy. As if she was faking it. And maybe she was. For the sake of her client, she had to pretend that a dress was a perfectly normal piece of clothing for her, when inside it made her feel vulnerable. And on display.

"Ma'am," the driver interrupted her thoughts. "Don't think we get far. Cable car seem broken and block road."

Instantly alert, Yvette peered out through the tinted windows, scanning the street ahead for any immediate dangers. "Wait here," she instructed Kimberly and stepped out of the car. She looked up the street and realized that the next intersection was blocked by the cable car coming up from Powell Street. Nothing looked out of place. She'd gotten used to the fact that the old cable cars broke down from time to time.

The Fairmont Hotel was only a block farther. Glancing up and down the street and assessing the passing pedestrians quickly, she determined that everything looked as it should. Foot traffic was light. Yvette dipped her head back into the car.

"We'll walk from here. It'll be fine."

"Are you sure?" Kimberly asked, her voice faltering for the first time.

Yvette offered her hand to the girl and pulled her out of the car. "I'm sure. Let's go. You don't want to be late for your own party." She slammed the door shut, then tapped on the passenger window, keeping her other hand on her charge's arm. The driver lowered the window instantly. "I'll call you when we're ready to be picked up."

The hill was steep, but Yvette knew there was a side entrance to the hotel which was halfway up the block, and within seconds they reached it. She preferred side entrances anyway—it was a better way to escape attention, and for certain the front entrance of the hotel would be teeming with autograph hunters and photographers.

"Here." She ushered Kimberly through the side door and along a narrow corridor until it widened into a large opulent foyer, attesting to the hotel's turn-of-the-century roots.

Yvette's eyes scanned her surroundings. Waiters and waitresses passed through the area as did well-dressed people. She noticed the stares Kimberly received and knew that people recognized her. Whispers drifted to Yvette's ears as they passed.

When she found the hall in which the premier party was to take place, she noticed the security at the door and let out a sigh of relief. At least the movie studio had provided some additional security to screen the arriving guests and check IDs.

Yvette flashed her Scanguards ID.

The guard nodded then beamed at Kimberly. "Miss Fairfax, may I just say, I really liked your movie. You're so talented. Do you think I could have an autograph?"

He reached into his jacket pocket, putting Yvette on instant alert as she shifted into fighting stance, ready to strike him down. When he pulled out a postcard with Kimberly's face on it, Yvette relaxed marginally.

"Of course," Kimberly cooed and autographed the picture before turning to the door.

The hall was filled with several hundred people. By the looks of things, no expense had been spared. The room was decorated with still shots from the movie, overblown images of Kimberly and her male costar, Timothy Huntley, a twenty-something hotshot too handsome for his own good, and champagne fountains all around.

Waiters circulated with *hors d'oeuvres* and trays with different beverages. Yvette declined the offer of a drink at the same time as Kimberly snatched a glass of champagne off one of the trays.

"Aren't you having any?"

"You forget I'm on duty." Besides, champagne wasn't her preferred drink. While she could imbibe liquids if she had to, she liked something much darker and richer altogether.

"Yes, but don't make it look like that. Mingle. I don't want people to know I have a bodyguard. It looks so desperate. People might think I'm too high and mighty; I want to be seen as approachable. People should love me."

Yvette refrained from rolling her eyes and shrugged. "Let them think what they want. I'm here to protect you."

"I'm grateful, really I am, but I need a little space."

Yvette swallowed her next remark. "Fine." She could observe from afar. With her superior vision and hearing she could tune into any conversation in the room and scan for anybody approaching Kimberly. So when her charge stepped away from her to greet one of her many friends, Yvette didn't pursue; instead, she stood to the side where she could watch the happenings in the ballroom.

The elegance of the people in the room was stunning. Everyone had outdone themselves, almost like at the Oscars. For the first time, Yvette was grateful for Kimberly's insistence that she wear a dress. Comparing her outfit to that of the other women in the room, she realized she fit in. At least nobody would take any notice of her.

Slowly, her eyes scrutinized the crowd, intent on ferreting out anyone who could become a danger to Kimberly, when something in the corner of her eye caught her attention. She turned her head. The man who'd just entered the room and now looked around as if searching for somebody didn't fit in. Even though he wore an elegant suit, he looked as if he'd squeezed himself into it against his will. He looked more rugged than handsome, and his broad frame spoke of strength and power. Not an actor, definitely not.

His dark hair was a little longer than was currently the fashion, and his shirt was open at the collar, even though it appeared he'd worn a tie earlier. In fact, the item in question bulged from his jacket pocket. Not a movie executive either—he'd be used to wearing ties.

His face and neck were tan, as were his hands. Even the skin which was exposed at the top of his shirt was dark, indicating that he spent a great deal of time outside. He was no paper pusher and certainly no accountant either. Yvette let her gaze sweep over him once more, then zoomed in on his hands. Scars. Lots of them: cuts, bruises, and burns. A stuntman, possibly. He didn't quite fit in, even though at the same time he belonged.

Kimberly's movie was an action flick—with her being the proverbial damsel in distress—and there'd been more than one scene which needed a stuntman to stand in for the hero. Yvette had yawned during the entire performance at the theatre and was glad when the pointless movie had ended. This could easily be the guy who'd doubled for the male star. Even though it seemed impossible to hide his bulky muscled body and make anybody believe he was the young hero in the film. He was at least ten years older—somewhere in his early thirties—and much more mature than the lead actor. Yvette figured graphics and airbrushing could do a lot to make people believe anything. In any case, she'd have to check him out more thoroughly to make sure her assumptions were right, merely for Kimberly's safety's sake of course, and not her own inexplicable curiosity about the man.

When she raised her gaze to study his face, his piercing blue eyes greeted her. How long had he been watching her?

4

Haven exhaled. The woman was stunning. An actress for sure, even though he'd never seen her in a movie. What else could she be with that porcelain skin and the short black hair that was styled back away from her flawless face? Her high cheekbones accentuated her green eyes, and her red lips were so plump and kissable, he felt his cock ache at the thought of her mouth on—

Haven tried to shake off the erotic vision tumbling through his mind. He wasn't like his brother, who fell for every pretty face without thinking. But as he swept his gaze over her perfect body, appreciating the lush curves hidden under her black dress, he wondered why he'd ever faulted Wesley for his weakness. Right now, he was feeling the same kind of weakness he'd always chastised his brother for.

Haven's cock expanded under his entirely-too-tight formal suit which he'd rented at a tuxedo store down the street. It wasn't like he was ever going to wear that kind of wardrobe again. There was no point in buying such a useless garment. But as much as he tried to concentrate his thoughts on his unusual attire, they instantly drifted back to the beauty across the room and to the way she made his cock throb with lust.

Clearly, that's all this was: lust. His life had become too single-minded over the years—only concentrating on hunting vampires and searching for his sister—and he hadn't allowed himself to enjoy the company of women for too long. He didn't like being distracted by them. He had no time for family and love when all he wanted was to restore the family he'd lost.

It shouldn't matter to him that this stranger, who didn't shy away from the intensity of his gaze, inspired all kinds of desires, none of which were suitable for display in a public ballroom with hundreds of guests watching. The images currently charging through his mind were more suitable to a dark hallway closet where he could press the woman against a wall and fuck her until he'd slaked his lust and felt normal again. Already now, he knew it would take more than just one quick fuck. Maybe he'd have to have her under him for a few hours to get this feeling out of his system. And if she was any good, well, he could spare a whole night, but only after he'd taken care of what he'd come for. That didn't mean he couldn't go over there and get her phone number though.

Before he could change his mind, Haven walked up to her, only stopping when he was a foot away from her. To his surprise, she didn't back away but stood her ground: the sign of a confident woman. And why wouldn't she be confident? With her sultry looks, she could have any of the men in this room panting at her feet. Licking them even.

"I'm Haven." He turned on his charm and started counting. Thirty seconds was all he would need to get her number. And not a fake 5-5-5 number either.

"Odd name."

He inhaled her scent. She wore barely any perfume. It rather seemed as if her skin smelled of oranges. He didn't know of any commercial perfume of that scent. "My mother was into odd things."

She nodded as if she knew what that meant. "You were working on the movie?"

Was she trying to figure out if he was a big producer who could help her career? He wouldn't give her that satisfaction. No, when she submitted to his touch, she would do so because of *who* he was, not *what* he was. "Stuntman," he lied. It was a job unimportant enough for a woman like her, yet would show off his physical prowess. And being a bounty hunter wasn't that much different from being a stuntman. Only that danger was more up close and personal, more of a surety. For him, no safety nets existed. No ambulance was waiting when he got injured. No crew stood by to help him out if he got in too deep.

She gave a satisfied smile, her eyes traveling over his body. And damn it if he didn't love the way she licked her lips at the same time. "I figured."

Was it getting hot in here? "And you?"

"I'm not a stuntman," she purposefully misunderstood his question. It didn't matter. He didn't really care what she was. All he cared about was *where* she'd be very soon: under his body.

"Didn't think so." He swept an appreciative glance over her body, lingering on her round breasts for longer than necessary. When he met her eyes again, the knowledge that he'd been assessing her female assets was on her face, yet she didn't pull away or look at him with disgust.

"You think you've got what it takes?" The words rolled off her lips in a seductive sweep. Her pink tongue emerged, moistening her lips. "Many have tried. None have succeeded."

Fuck, the sight of that tongue did things to him. His body temperature spiked several degrees. He tugged at his shirt's collar, realizing he'd already taken off his tie earlier. He couldn't very well take off his shirt. "I'm willing to give it a shot."

Now it was her turn to look up and down his body. It didn't escape him how she held her gaze at his groin, assessing its ever-growing package. And he wasn't going to hide it from her. Might as well make sure she knew what she was in for.

"It might just do."

He'd never met a woman who'd so openly propositioned him. Or was she merely responding to his offer? It didn't matter. All that was important was that they were in the midst of negotiating the terms of their sexual encounter. The *whether* had already been confirmed. Now it was only a matter of figuring out the *when* and *where*. As well as the *how long*.

Haven took one step closer, bringing her flush to his body. A drop of sweat trickled down the back of his neck and disappeared under his shirt. Could she feel his heat the way he felt hers? He dipped his head to her ear. "Oh, it'll be plenty, I promise you." He could barely suppress the urge to press her against the nearest flat surface and hike up her dress, free his cock, and plunge into her.

"Don't make promises you can't keep." Her husky voice in his ear made him almost delirious. Damn, she could turn him on as if he were a light switch.

"Name the time and place," he gritted out, barely holding onto his control. Another few seconds of this and he'd do something that would get them both thrown out and arrested for committing a lewd act in public. Or whatever the police called it these days.

"By the way you're panting right now, I'd say immediately, but then you wouldn't get to imagine what it's like to fuck me, would you? And I wouldn't get to imagine what you're doing while you're imagining it and waiting for it. So, here." She shoved a business card in his pocket. "Call me once you've taken care of that hard-on in your pants, so you'll last longer than ten seconds when we fuck."

A moment later, he stood there alone. She'd disappeared into the crowd. Thunderstruck by her blunt words, he couldn't help but applaud her. She'd taken charge the way a man normally would, and while he hated bossy women, he couldn't stop his cock from expanding even farther. She would probably kick his ass in more ways than one, but he wasn't backing down from the challenge she'd just handed him.

Haven reached into his jacket pocket and pulled out the card she'd given him.

Yvette. Then a local number. That's all it said. No address. Nothing.

The woman had class.

***

Yvette fanned herself as she watched her charge from afar. During the entire exchange with Haven she hadn't forgotten about her job for a single second. It hadn't stopped her from getting all hot and bothered though. She'd tried to play it cool, slipping into her well-worn seductress suit, a cloak she'd worn for too many years. It had always served her well to keep men at bay. Most men had shied away from her dominant personality, just like she intended.

Not so Haven; the man was up for the challenge. Was *she*? Yeah, she'd had sex a few months ago—not that she could even remember the guy's name. What were one-night-stands for? And that was exactly what Haven would turn into: a one-night stand. It would probably be best if she just fucked him where she felt more anonymous. Certainly not her place, and if she could choose, not even in a bed.

A quick, frantic fucking over a table would do the trick. Nothing more intimate than that. To allow a man like him any closer would be dangerous. Sure, he was human, and she could take him in an instant. Not even his bad-boy-stuntman attitude would be much of a challenge for her. No, the challenge lay in those blue eyes that had tried to look deep into her. And when he'd stepped closer and whispered into her ear, his scent had wrapped around her and blanketed her with a wave of desire she couldn't explain.

She would have to watch herself with this man—before he got too close.

Yvette was grateful when her attention was suddenly captured by the man speaking to Kimberly. He'd just placed his pudgy palm on the girl's arm. Bad move. Inhaling as she approached, Yvette scented perspiration coming from her charge. Kimberly felt uncomfortable. Time to run interference.

"Kimberly, there's somebody who's asking for you," Yvette said as she approached and took her arm. Then she turned to the heavyset man, gave him a big smile and batted her eyelashes. The man's face flushed. "Excuse us for a moment, would you?"

Before the man could even protest, she'd ushered Kimberly off to another corner of the ballroom. "Who was that?" Yvette needed to know whether he could be the threat they were trying to protect Kimberly against.

Kimberley gave a dismissive wave with her hand. "Oh, that's Charles. He's the nephew of the producer—and a total bore. If you hadn't rescued me, he would have killed me with boredom. Really," she rattled on, her normal self again, "I could barely get a word in edgewise."

Join the club. "Yes, totally annoying, isn't it?" Yvette had a hard time keeping all sarcasm out of her voice.

"You have *no* idea. What do some of these people think? They don't listen. They constantly talk as if they're the most important people in the world. It's just so tiring. Can you imagine being stuck with somebody like that for longer than ten minutes? I thought I was dying right there."

Poor little rich girl. "Thank God you have me to rescue you," Yvette interjected, trying not to roll her eyes. No way would Zane have been able to suffer through an evening like this without killing somebody. She suspected he'd purposely intimidated Kimberly to be let off the hook. Maybe he'd even used mind control on her to plant the idea in her mind that she wanted him gone. And Gabriel had fallen for the trick and promptly assigned her. Damn, Zane was way too smart an asshole.

"I need another drink. Do you want some?"

"Still on duty, remember?" Yvette forced a smile. She could think of better things than spending the next couple of hours babysitting a spoiled little brat who'd never been told to shut up. Her only consolation was that she could tune out the inane chatter of the people around her and let her vampire senses alert her to the things she needed to know. It kept the rest of her brain free to pursue its own diversion. And the only worthwhile diversion she could think of right now was recalling the way Haven had looked, felt, and smelled. And imagining what he would feel like when he was underneath her, naked, panting, and begging for release.

5

Whoever the stinking vampire was who was protecting Kimberly Fairfax, he was good. Haven hadn't spotted him yet. That was another reason why he hated vampires: they were too stealthy.

It didn't matter. Haven knew that eventually Kimberly would leave the party with her bodyguard by her side. He was prepared for the encounter: a stake was tucked away in the inside pocket of his suit, and the witch's potion was readily accessible in his right jacket pocket. And just to be sure, he'd packed something else to defend himself: a strong silver chain with small weights on each end lay in his other pocket. Should everything else fail, he could throw it around the vampire's neck; the burning metal would sear into his skin, temporarily distracting and disabling him, and give Haven sufficient time to either deploy the stake or the potion.

Over the years of hunting vampires and looking for his baby sister, he'd learned an awful lot about the bloodsuckers—mostly about how to hurt or kill them. Their flesh sizzled and burned when it came in contact with silver, and no matter how hard they tried, they couldn't break the metal. What made being prepared for a vampire difficult was that neither he nor his brother had inherited their mother's ability to recognize a vampire by the aura that surrounded him.

Despite his lack of powers, Haven prided himself in having eliminated over two-dozen vampires over the years. None of the kills had brought him any further in his search for the vampire who'd abducted his sister; nevertheless, he'd taken their lives. Hell, they were dead already. How he *despised* those creatures who took from humans without concern, without mercy. So he'd shown them no mercy either. He'd become ruthless in killing vampires. Every time he turned another one to dust, his need for vengeance was stilled for a short while. But it never lasted long.

Haven assured himself that once he found his sister, he'd find peace and could finally think of a normal life, but until then, revenge was what drove him.

Waiting in the dark of an entryway, Haven bided his time. The sound of a door opening made him turn his head. Kimberly was unmistakable in her pink dress and blond locks. She exited the building and walked into the dark alley with another person. Haven had made sure it would be dark by opening the access panel to the streetlamp the previous night and cutting the wires inside.

Despite the darkness, Haven recognized the other person's face. He took a surprised, involuntary breath: Yvette was by Kimberly's side. Was it a coincidence? Maybe the two had been working on the movie together. He craned his neck to look for her bodyguard, but nobody else came out. The door fell shut behind them, the sound echoing against the high walls, mirroring the hollow sound in his heart.

Haven cursed silently as he watched the two women approach a dark limousine. Now that he observed them closely, he noticed how Yvette scanned their surroundings, how she barely listened to Kimberly's chatter and instead seemed to evaluate each entryway and each passerby.

Under the sexy halter dress that fit her like a second skin, her toned body was tense and on guard; he could see it in the way the muscles in her upper arms flexed. Had she sensed him yet?

Shit! This wasn't what he'd expected. Had the witch gotten it wrong? Was the girl not protected by a vampire bodyguard after all?

He'd spoken to Yvette inside the ballroom, and nothing in her demeanor had suggested that she was anything but a beautiful woman. He'd felt the heat her body had emanated, the passion radiating through her, and it had ignited his own body. How could he have reacted to her like that if she were a vampire? All he'd ever felt for vampires was disgust and hatred. It was impossible that his body got it wrong, that it would react to a despicable creature like it had.

But the more he watched, the more the telltale signs of a vampire were there: the fluid grace with which she glided down the street; the sharpness of her eyes that seemed to register everything around her; the way she seemed to pick up every sound, just like she did now when she lifted her head upwards to look at a window which somebody had just closed. Oh yes, she was alert. And it could only mean one thing: she was Kimberly's bodyguard. She had to be the vampire the witch had spoken of.

And damn it to hell if he didn't feel a twinge of regret at what he had to do. If she was the bodyguard vampire, she had to die, attraction or not. He shouldn't feel the scruples that started bubbling up in him at the thought. He'd never before had doubts about what he needed to do. His mission had always been clear: to kill every vampire he came across until he found the one who'd robbed him of his sister.

Swallowing his misplaced scruples and trying to bury them in the deep, dark recesses of his mind, Haven stepped out of the entryway he'd been hiding in and slowly walked toward the two women. He plastered a fake smile on his face and raised his hand in greeting. "Miss Fairfax, an autograph please."

Yvette's face showed only momentary surprise when she recognized him, then went back to her indifferent and businesslike mask. Haven's gut twisted. He forced himself to think back to the day his mother was murdered, knowing the hatred he felt for vampires would help him carry out his task and forget the other side he'd seen of Yvette: the sensual woman ready to meet him for some uninhibited fucking.

Kimberly smiled broadly as she stopped and waited for Haven to come closer. Yvette bent her head to Kimberly's ear and spoke a few words. Haven only picked up the tail end of it. " . . . stuntman from the movie set?"

When Kimberly gave Yvette a confused look and shook her head, he knew his time was up. Yvette would know that he didn't belong to the crew and had lied to her. But he didn't need much time. He was only a few feet away when Yvette issued her order.

"Get in the car, Kimberly, now!"

But Kimberly didn't move. She simply gave Yvette another confused look. "But he only wants an autograph. You shouldn't be so rude to—"

Yvette shoved her aside toward the limousine, her body now in attack stance. "NOW, Kimberly!"

Then Yvette jumped toward him. Haven barely had time to react. The sultry seductress from earlier was gone. What was left was a lethal fighting machine. If he'd ever had any doubt that she was a vampire, it was erased on impact—no woman could be this strong.

Yvette knocked him to the ground with one blow. He landed hard on his back. But he was no pushover. He captured her legs between his and twisted, bringing her down onto the pavement. But he hadn't counted on her agility. Like a gazelle, she jumped up and kicked him in the side just as he'd risen from the ground. Her karate kicks were high and graceful. A seam along her thigh ripped several inches of her dress as she kicked higher, allowing her more movement. And hell, if he didn't have to admire the way she fought with those powerful and sexy legs.

In the background, he heard Kimberly scream. If he didn't make this quick, the girl would attract attention and summon help.

Haven reached into his inside pocket and pulled out the stake.

Yvette's eyes narrowed as the combatants circled each other. "I would have let you impale me with your dick, but not with that thing."

Her words threw him off guard. Count on her to fight dirty. Bitch. "There's no way in hell I'll dirty my cock by sticking it into you." His cock called him a liar.

He saw the anger in her eyes, but there was something else in there too. Had his remark hurt her feelings? Haven shook off the stupid thought. As if vampires had feelings. Cold-hearted bastards—and bitches.

Yvette attacked, more forcefully this time. They dealt each other blow after blow. Her kicks to his lower half were taking their toll. Unfortunately, he couldn't get close enough with his stake to do any damage.

Another painful kick in the gut, and he faltered. She slammed him against the car. Haven squeezed his hand against his gut to ward off the feeling of nausea. His hand felt the little vial the witch had given him. He snatched it from his pocket and turned just as Yvette grabbed his neck.

"Take that, bloodsucker!" he pressed out, threw the vial to the ground and smashed it with his shoe.

Instantly, pink vapor billowed from it. Yvette's head snapped toward it, but already her movements slowed.

"Shit!" she yelped, her eyes darting to the side. "Kimberly!"

The girl was only a couple of feet away from them, still standing frozen in the same place where the attack had begun. With visible effort, Yvette released him and reached for Kimberly, clamping her hand over the girl's wrist before she collapsed on the pavement, pulling Kimberly with her.

"Yvette!" the girl screamed.

Great, now the starlet went into hysterics. How he hated that.

"Shut up!"

The girl's screams simmered down to a whimper as she shook Yvette, trying to wake her.

Haven looked down at Yvette, who lay motionless on the ground. He knew she wasn't dead, merely unconscious. Now was the time to kill her. He gripped his stake tightly and rolled the smooth wood between his fingers. Then he knelt down beside her and turned her onto her back. He shouldn't have done it. He should have just slammed the stake into her back.

Kimberly's kick into his side hit him by surprise. "Leave her alone!"

Haven tossed her a pissed off look and grabbed her ankle in the same instant, making her lose her balance and tumble against the car behind her, jolting Yvette, whose hand was still around Kimberly's wrist.

"What part of 'shut up' did you not get?"

In response to his unspoken threat, her eyes turned into those of a frightened doe.

Well, at least the girl could act. But damn, if he didn't hate frightening innocents. If his mother were alive, she'd beat the crap out of him for that.

Haven focused his attention back on the unconscious Yvette. What he saw in her face were the flawless features of the woman who'd seduced him so thoroughly in the ballroom hours earlier, the red lips of the woman who'd challenged him, the glorious curves and luscious breasts of the woman who had so blatantly offered a night of sex.

His hand shook for the first time when holding a stake. He'd never had any qualms about killing a vampire, so why could he not bring his hand to descend and drive the stake into her heart?

Instead, he rose and looked at Kimberly, who'd braced herself against the car's trunk, frightened and crying. Haven looked around.

They were still alone in the alley, and the driver's door of the limousine was open as if the driver had abandoned the car in the middle of the fight. Just as well.

"Let's go. You're coming with me!" he ordered.

He grabbed the girl's arm and tried to pull her toward the front of the car, but there was resistance. "I said, we're going."

"I can't," Kimberly wailed.

Haven looked back and noticed how Kimberly tried to loosen Yvette's hand from her wrist but couldn't pry her fingers apart. He stopped and took Yvette's hand, but his attempt was as fruitless as Kimberly's. Like a vice, Yvette's fingers had locked around Kimberly's wrists and had frozen in place.

"Shit!"

"What's happening?" Kimberly cried. "Help! Somebody help me!" Frantically, she looked around the alley, but there were no other passersby. It wouldn't stay that way, Haven was sure. He had to get the hell out of there quickly.

"Get in the car, now! And not another word!"

He hated what he had to do now. If he could have left Yvette right where she was, at least he could have put a lid on that chapter of his life, but circumstances were what they were. He had two choices, neither of which looked the least bit appealing. One of them he'd already tried and failed: for whatever reason, he couldn't stake her. Which only left one other option.

Haven ushered the girl toward the car door and lifted Yvette's limp body into his arms, carrying her and placing her onto the back bench of the limo as Kimberly stepped inside. He could only hope that she stayed unconscious for the length of the car ride, otherwise he'd have to fall back on option one. Of course, if she remained unconscious when he brought her to the witch, it meant he'd have to carry her again and feel her body close to his. And that presented a whole other issue: one his brain wanted to avoid and his cock looked forward to.

"One more scream, and you'll end up like her."

With frightened eyes, Kimberly nodded, one arm wrapped around her waist, the other stretched out toward Yvette. "Why won't she let go of my wrist?"

Haven didn't know for sure, but he figured it had something to do with her vampire powers. "Hate to break it to you, kid, but your bodyguard's a vampire."

6

"You idiot, you should have killed her immediately!" Bess hissed, her mouth distorting into an ugly grimace.

Haven was back in her makeshift living area, back amongst the disgusting smells and sights of her witchcraft.

"In front of the girl?" he asked, knowing it was a weak excuse. But he couldn't admit to her that he'd had scruples about taking Yvette's life. If only he hadn't met her and spoken to her at the party, he would have never developed a conscience about it. But now? Damn it, how could he kill her now?

"She'll get over it. Do it now while she's still out."

Haven shook his head, his mind frantically scrambling for another excuse. "We don't know what'll happen. Her hand is still attached to the girl. What if it affects Kimberly? What if she gets injured or killed? I'm assuming you want the girl alive . . ."

"Mmm." The witch's face distorted, frown lines building on her forehead.

Good, she was contemplating it. As farfetched as his statement was, maybe Bess was too superstitious to take any risks. He sure didn't want any more blood on his hands than he already had. Not even the blood of a vampire. It was bad enough that he'd delivered both of them to the witch. Once he had his brother back, the two of them could figure out how to free the innocent girl before the witch could harm her. As for Yvette? He had no clue what to do about her. Nor should he even waste a single thought on her.

"Fine," she finally agreed.

Haven let out a relieved breath. One hurdle was jumped over. Now to the next one. "Good, so you have everything you want."

"Indeed."

"Now, give me back my brother, and we'll be out of your hair."

And back again as soon as we can figure out how to wrench Kimberly from your evil clutches.

She gave him a smile. "As you just said, I now have everything I want."

Her measured speech caught his attention. Something wasn't right. Suspicion made the little hairs on his arms stand up.

"Kimberly, your brother, and you. All three of you."

Haven swallowed hard, not liking where the conversation was going. "You gave your word."

"I lied."

He took a step toward her, ready to throttle her. With her hand raised, she pushed an invisible shield toward him, holding him in place. God, how he hated witches! At least with a vampire he could engage in hand-to-hand combat. He hadn't planned on fighting her this time around. All he'd figured was to try and get his brother out, then come back in full force as a team. One of them would distract her while the other attacked. On his own, he knew he had no chance. He was powerless against her magic—as the son of a witch, he knew just how powerless.

"Give me back my brother and let us go!"

"Sorry, can't do that. I need all three of you."

He hated being outgunned. "You fucking bitch!"

She made a dismissive hand movement. "You can call me all you want. I really don't care what you think."

"What do you want with us?" Maybe if he could find out what was going on, he could figure out a way to escape and get his brother out alive.

"Now that would be telling, wouldn't it? I'm not in the sharing mood today. But I'm grateful—that's why I'll let you keep your stake when I lock you up with the vamp."

Double-shit!

As soon as Yvette woke, she would attack him. And then he would have no choice but to kill her after all.

"You can't do that!"

"Really? Watch me."

"Listen, the bitch is going to kill me." Of that he was certain. Then he ventured a guess. "And I figure you want me alive." He sure hoped so; otherwise, wouldn't she have killed him already?

"True, but as a big, bad bounty hunter and vampire slayer I count on your ingenuity. You might just have to kill the vamp before she kills you."

Manipulative witch!

That's what she was doing, getting him to do her dirty work for her. By locking him up with Yvette, she was forcing him to kill the vamp bitch to save his own hide before she took a bite out of it. Now he hated her even more.

"I've done everything you asked."

"I'm sorry. Did you want a thank you? Here you go: thank you!" Then she pushed more power against him, pressing him against the wall behind. "Time to join your friends."

Less than a minute later, she forced him into a large, sparsely furnished room. Three cots were lined up along one wall, a few pillows and blankets strewn about, a small fridge and table with a few chairs in another corner. An open door in the opposite corner showed a rudimentary toilet and a small sink.

Kimberly lay on one cot and Yvette on the one next to her, her hand still clamped around Kimberly's wrist. She was still unconscious. Kimberly was curled up in a ball, crying. He searched the rest of the room.

"Where is Wesley?" he yelled.

"You'll see him when I'm done with him," Bess answered from the other side of the already-closed door.

Kimberly jerked up from her supine position and pressed herself against the wall behind her. "You!"

He shrugged. "Well, honey, looks like we're all in the same boat now." And he'd been the one who'd delivered them both into the hands of the devious witch. Which meant he was the one who was responsible for getting them out.

"You bastard! You kidnapped me. Get out! I don't want to see you here. Leave me alone!" Kimberly tossed her head in Yvette's direction, her look weary.

"I can't do that. I'm imprisoned just like you."

"That's a trick! What do you want? Money?"

He ignored her question. "Listen, we have to work together now to get out of here."

Kimberly shook her head. "Why should I trust you? You got me in here in the first place. You attacked us, and you took out my bodyguard."

"Your bodyguard is a vampire."

She glanced at Yvette once more. "Yeah, you said that in the car already. I heard you. There's no need to try to confuse me. I'm not a dumb blonde, you know. I'm not even blond. Vampires don't exist, so I don't know what you're playing at. I want to go home now."

Haven sighed. He'd have his work cut out. "We all want to go home. But that's not going to happen right now. So, listen, here's the deal . . ."

***

Zane used his key to Gabriel's house when nobody responded to his knocking. It appeared that the doorbell had still not been repaired. He stomped into the foyer and listened for voices. The house was quiet except for the muffled voices coming from the basement where Maya had set up her medical practice a few months earlier.

He hated to intrude, but what he needed to report was urgent.

He slunk down the stairs as stealthily as always. It had become such a habit that even now, when he was visiting his boss's house, he approached silently as if closing in on prey. It was strange how some habits were so ingrained in his psyche that even consciously he couldn't rid himself of them. He knew it creeped his colleagues out. But hey, everybody had a reputation to uphold.

Zane heard the voices clearly now. They came from Maya's examination room.

"No, this is the foot, and that's the umbilical cord," Maya explained.

Great! That meant Delilah and Samson were here for Delilah's ultrasound. He should have guessed. Delilah was now seven months pregnant, and when he'd seen her last week, she'd looked like she was ready to drop the baby right there and then.

"She looks big," Samson commented.

"She is. So, would you guys please tell me how you know it's a girl? I don't recall ever telling you the sex," Maya said.

The smile in Delilah's voice was evident when she responded. "She talks to me. I think she's got a gift."

"Telepathy?" Maya asked.

"I think so."

"Congratulations! That'll make a lot of things easier for you. Every mother will envy you for understanding your child even when it can't talk yet. I suppose she hasn't yet told you when she's ready, has she? I think you might deliver earlier than with a human pregnancy. All signs point to it."

"Just as well," Delilah answered.

"I know it's hard on you." Samson's voice was comforting, and Zane shook his head. He just couldn't wrap his mind around how all these badass vampires turned into pussies once they were bonded. What a crock! Sure wasn't gonna happen to him.

"I'm not worried about myself. I'm worried about you. You barely feed from me lately."

Delilah did have a point. Samson was looking a little worse for wear these days, and Zane had suspected that he'd lowered his intake of blood. As a vampire blood-bonded to a human, he could only drink from his mate, and it appeared that he wanted to be mindful of Delilah's pregnancy. It was different for vampires blood-bonded to other vampires as was the case with Maya and Gabriel. While they could feed off each other, one partner had to keep feeding off human blood in order to maintain the strength for the pair.

"I'm fine, sweetness."

Before he hurled over all that lovey-dovey swill, Zane knocked on the door and entered.

"Sorry to intrude."

Samson instantly covered Delilah's bare belly with a blanket and rose to block Zane's view of his wife. "You'd better have a good reason for barging in here."

Vampires and their possessiveness about their mates—God, how he hated that. "I do. Where's Gabriel?"

"Meeting with the Mayor," Maya responded as she switched off the ultrasound machine and tucked away her instruments.

"Call him. We have a situation."

"What's going on?" Samson was all business now, and despite his tired look, there was determination in his hazel eyes.

"Yvette didn't call in."

"Did you page her?"

"No answer."

"Her cell?"

"Goes straight to voicemail."

"Have Thomas see whether he can activate the GPS chip in her cell remotely."

Zane wasn't a novice; he'd already called Thomas on his way over. "He's already working on it."

"Good."

"Her client didn't show up at her hotel either."

"At least that probably means they're still together." Samson ran his hand through his thick, dark hair. For a moment, Zane was distracted. He missed having hair and being able to ruffle it. When he was human, he'd been shorn bald for the experiments they'd conducted on him, and since his hair hadn't yet grown back when he'd been turned into a vampire, he was stuck forever with a head like Yul Brynner. Yeah, life sucked that way.

"The limousine they were supposed to take after the party has disappeared too."

"You think the driver could have abducted them?"

"I wouldn't eliminate that possibility."

"Let's see whether we can get a location on the limo. Find out if it was equipped with Lo-Jack and we can track it that way. If not, have the boys comb the city for it," Samson suggested. "I'll go talk to Gabriel and have him mount an all-out search. It's not like Yvette not to respond. Something is fishy."

"I agree."

As much as Zane couldn't stand the prickly bitch, Yvette was part of his family, the only family he had. And he'd move heaven and earth to keep his family together. He wasn't going to lose this one too. He'd had to watch his first family perish under horrendous circumstances. It had cut too deep, the pain still fresh even after over sixty-five years. "I'll check out her house in the meantime."

7

The first thing Yvette felt when she woke was long hair caressing her neck and shoulders. It instantly told her that she'd been out for more than two hours, the minimum hours of restorative sleep needed to make her hair grow back. The second thing she noticed was the fact that her hand was clamped around somebody's wrist.

Still slightly out of sorts and dizzy, Yvette forced her heavy eyelids open and shot up from her supine position, releasing Kimberly's wrist with her next breath. Her sudden movement made her vision blur, and she took a second to steady herself. Blood thundered through her veins, the noise no less jarring than a passing freight train, swallowing any other sound in the room.

Yvette took a breath, filling her lungs with air, but her brain couldn't process the scents that assaulted her—an aftereffect of whatever had knocked her out, for sure.

Yvette glanced at Kimberly, who immediately backed away from her, frightened and intimidated.

Were her eyes glowing red or her fangs showing? She slid her tongue over her teeth, realizing to her relief that her fangs hadn't descended involuntarily; however, how would she explain her suddenly long hair to her? "Are you okay, Kimberly? Did he hurt you?"

The girl shook her head. "You're a vampire. I didn't wanna believe it." Her tear-stained eyes were wide with fear.

Shit! How had she figured it out? Yvette's mind worked overtime, trying to piece together the memories of the fight with her attacker. Had she shown her fangs during the fight? Yvette shook her head and looked down at Kimberly's wrist where her hand had left a red imprint. It was a survival mechanism: a vampire could lock hands around an object to hold on to it, freezing it into place if channeling all energy to it. If knocked out by any unknown force, it would ensure not being swept away or taken to another location. In this case, it had made sure that

Yvette couldn't be separated from her charge. How she would explain this to Kimberly, she didn't quite know.

"I'm so sorry. I didn't mean to hurt you, but I *did* need to protect you."

Kimberly continued shaking her head, as if denying it would magically make it not true, not real. Reality sucked, but Yvette didn't have the luxury of believing it could be undone. The girl had already seen too much; it was best to come clean right now. Or maybe she should wipe her memory right now, make her forget what she'd seen—but only if she couldn't handle the truth.

"Listen to me. I'm still here to protect you, no matter what. What I am doesn't matter. I won't hurt you."

The girl sniffed. Where had all her bubbly personality gone? Right now, Yvette wouldn't mind her endless chatter; at least, it would tell her that her charge was all right. She sucked in a deep breath, trying to think clearly of how to assure her that she was no threat, when an all-too-familiar scent tickled her nostrils.

Yvette shot up from the cot and lunged at the person leaning against the wall over her left shoulder: Haven, the fucking asshole who'd attacked them. She slammed him against the concrete, pinning him.

"I'm going to kill you, you bastard!"

Through clenched teeth, he hissed at her, "We're in the same fucking boat."

She dismissed his words. A coward and a liar—she sure knew how to pick 'em. Yvette's fangs itched, and she made no effort to disguise them. As they descended and pushed past her lips, she snarled at him. But instead of seeing fear in his eyes, she saw defiance, bright and hot.

"Release us, now!"

"I can't: I'm imprisoned just like you are—so let go of me."

Yvette's eyebrows drew together as she frowned. What the fuck was he talking about?

Without loosening her grip, her eyes scanned the room. She'd been too dazed up to now to take in her surroundings. But there was no time like the present. There was a door built into one wall and a boarded-up window in another. Neither would provide an insurmountable obstacle to escape. Another door at the other end of the room was open; she spotted a toilet behind it.

Could he have told the truth? Yvette shook off the thought. No, he was a liar.

"Don't mind if I find that hard to believe," she snorted. "Last time I checked, you were the one who attacked us."

"He's telling the truth," Kimberly's voice came from behind her.

Yvette glanced back at her charge, trying to assess whether Kimberly was in shock. What kind of crap had Haven fed her while Yvette was unconscious? Turning back to the bastard, she narrowed her eyes.

"I should kill you right here, right now. You know why I won't?"

"Because you still want my dick?"

She slapped him across the face. How dare he trifle with her? "You're still alive because I'm not going to subject Kimberly to such gore. But the second she's safe, I'm coming after you."

"I figured you'd bear a grudge against me." He shrugged, his face giving nothing away.

Yvette ignored his comment. "Where are we?"

"In a warehouse in the outskirts of San Francisco."

"Where exactly?" She pressed her arm tighter across his chest, forcing the air out of his lungs.

"South San Francisco, off the 101."

"How did we get here?"

Haven visibly fought for air, and in the interest of getting an answer to her question, she released her hold by a fraction. When he pulled in a few breaths, she kicked her knee upwards, aiming for his balls. To her surprise, he blocked her by tilting his hips sideways so her knee merely dug into his thigh. She was slower than usual—a fact she attributed to the substance that had knocked her out cold. But just as her sense of smell had come back, she was sure her other senses would catch up soon.

Anger surged inside her. "How?"

"I took the limo."

"And the driver? Where is he? Did you kill him?"

"No! He ran off, I guess."

It was the first good news in a long time. Her colleagues would track him down once they realized she and Kimberly were missing. And with any luck, he could tell them what had happened. Tracing the limo wouldn't be too hard either. She was sure it came with an antitheft device that would lead her colleagues right to its location.

"Where's the limo now?"

Haven's muscles twitched as if he was attempting to shrug. But she still had him pinned to the wall, giving him no room to move. "I parked it outside."

Things were looking up.

"What time is it?"

Haven gave her a surprised look. "Three o'clock."

"Night or day?" Whatever the vapor was she'd inhaled, it had screwed with her sense of time. Impatient by his delayed response, she kicked him in the shin, when really she wanted to aim for something a little higher, and a little softer.

He clenched his jaw. "Bitch!"

"I asked, night—"

"It's night."

Yvette released her hold on him. Another second longer, and she would have rubbed herself all over him like a cat in heat. Damn the man for the way he smelled: all male, all sex. How was a female vamp going to keep her wits about her, being in such close quarters with a virile man like him? The faster she and Kimberly escaped from here, the better. Sure, her colleagues would rescue them within hours, but she didn't have hours. She needed to get out of this place before she did something she would regret later.

Whatever happened to Haven, she didn't care. Which still left one question open.

"Why are you here with us?"

Haven righted his shirt and jacket and glared at her. "Because I had a job to do."

"That's not an answer. If you're in here with us, who's holding us captive?"

Haven took a step toward her, placing his tempting body in too close a proximity to hers. Like tendrils of fire, his body heat leapt from his skin and landed on hers, intent on burning her with its intensity.

"Here's your answer: I was double-crossed by the person who wanted me to kidnap Kimberly, okay? Happy now?"

Angry, he was even sexier than when she'd toyed with him at the party. How pathetic was that?

"A hired gun. Despicable."

"You're not any better than me."

"I don't kidnap people for money! Serves you right that your boss turned on you. Don't expect me to help you now."

Haven felt his blood boil. Yvette pissed him off even faster than his little brother could, and that was quite an achievement. But he wouldn't let her get to him.

"I'm afraid we'll fail if we don't work together."

She looked at him with disdain in her eyes. "Your goal was to kidnap Kimberly—guess your work is done. Now I'll do mine—and mine is to free her. And that's exactly what I'll do."

"How do you propose to do that since we're locked up in here?"

She motioned toward the door. "You really think a flimsy door like that is going to stop me?"

He should tell her what they were up against. It was only fair. "Look, there's no way—"

"Incompetent fool!" she hissed and turned away.

On second thought, maybe he'd let her find out for herself. The woman clearly needed her attitude clipped. Nobody called him incompetent. Nor did he like to be called a fool. Especially not by a female—make that a female *vampire*—who got him hard as hell just by being within a couple of feet of him. "Go ahead."

Suddenly, he felt like Dirty Harry, and Yvette could just make his day for all he cared.

Without her or Kimberly noticing, Haven adjusted his cock and swept his eyes over Yvette's naked back. Oh man, that dress fit her like a second skin, and the ripped seam on one side of it exposed her leg from ankle to upper thigh to his hungry look. Her legs were toned and strong, not overly muscular, but perfectly shaped. Perfect for wrapping them around his hips when he—

He growled inaudibly and shook his head. Thinking like that wouldn't help him get his boner down.

But he couldn't tear himself away from watching her. He was fascinated by her. And one thing was totally different about her now.

While she'd been unconscious, he'd literally been able to see her hair grow. It now cascaded over her back in a thick mane. While he'd certainly thought she was attractive with her short spiky hair, the way the long hair caressed her face and shoulders was just utterly distracting. He had no idea why it was suddenly long; for sure, it was some strange vampire trait. And he wasn't interested at all in knowing about it. That's right. He didn't care one whit.

Just like Kimberly, he now observed Yvette as she approached the door, tested it with her hand, sniffed for who knew what, and then stepped back. A second later, she landed a high karate kick against the lock. But instead of the door splintering under her forceful blow—and he'd never seen a woman so strong—she was propelled backwards and slammed into the concrete wall a dozen feet behind her. Haven flinched instinctively, wondering how much pain she could take.

"What the fuck?" she grumbled.

But she was already up and lunged toward the door again. Haven knew it would be useless and blocked her path. "It's no use."

"Get out of my way!"

"The door is protected by wards."

"Wards?" Recognition slowly seeped into her features. Then she pushed him back, away from her enticing body and drugging scent. "You made a deal with a witch?"

Haven crossed his arms over his chest, feeling the need to defend himself. "I had no choice." He needed to save his brother, whom he still hadn't seen since he'd been imprisoned here. He felt increasingly uneasy about the developments. If he could only figure out what the witch wanted from all of them, then maybe he could devise a plan of how to get out of this mess. But without that—

"There's always a choice. You chose to get involved with a witch. No wonder you were able to knock me out. I should have known. All you are is a weak human, and look where you ended up."

Had his hearing just failed him? "Are you telling me I'm inferior to you?"

"What if I am?"

Haven clenched his teeth, ready to strangle the woman.

"Stop it!" Kimberly's determined voice made his head snap in her direction. "You both are acting like spoiled brats!"

He raised an eyebrow. Had the kettle just called the pot black? Maybe the girl wasn't quite as immature as she'd let on. He took a step away from Yvette. "I can take a hint."

"If it's delivered with a sledgehammer," Yvette muttered under her breath.

He glanced back at her over his shoulder. "I heard that."

"You were supposed to."

"Damn it, didn't I just tell you guys to stop?" Kimberly threw up her hands in capitulation. "What are you? Twelve?"

She did have a point.

"Since you both consider yourselves such great fighters, why don't you use your energy to get us out of here? Frankly, I have no intention of staying here any longer. I'm not into camping, and I need a shower." She sighed, studying her fingernails. "And a manicure."

Before Haven had the chance to make a snide remark about Kimberly's last words, the door opened. Wesley stumbled in, or rather was pushed in by the witch who remained on the other side of the threshold.

"Wesley!" Haven rushed to his brother and hugged him. He appeared a little shell-shocked but seemed to recover quickly.

"Oh, shit, Hav, I'm sorry." The emotion reflected in his downcast eyes.

"I see you haven't killed the vampire yet," Bess droned.

Haven whipped his head first to her and then to Yvette, who stood in the middle of the room ready to attack. "Don't, Yvette. She's too strong."

"Vampire?" Wesley tossed an angry look at Yvette. "Oh, I wish I had a stake!"

"Now, you're talking!" Bess whistled. "Your brother has one."

Haven held a hand against Wesley's chest, trying to stop him from doing anything stupid, which he realized was *exactly* what his brother was about two seconds away from. "She won't hurt us."

"Wait until she's hungry enough," the witch hedged, stirring things up like a potion in a cauldron.

Haven looked at Yvette at that moment and noticed how she flinched. Bess had hit the nail right on its head. Shit, he hadn't thought of that. "How long are you planning to keep us here?" he asked without taking his eyes off Yvette.

"Long enough." Her evil grin was evident in her voice and confirmed that she'd caught onto his line of thinking. Sooner or later, Yvette would get hungry—for blood.

Yvette's defiant glare told him she was a fighter, and the way she'd protected Kimberly indicated she was loyal. But if he'd learned one thing about vampires while fighting them over the years, it was that when their hunger for blood became too severe, they would lose control, and nobody was safe. Yvette might be controlled by her learned behavior now, but what would happen when she was controlled by her survival instinct? Could he allow his scruples to get in the way of rational thinking?

"Guess you'll have to kill her after all." The witch's voice grated on his nerves. Hell, just to defy her, he'd let Yvette live—and *only* for that reason. Not because his body revolted each time he tried to come up with a reason to kill her. Since when did he even need a reason to kill a vampire? The murder of his mother and disappearance of his baby sister should be justification enough to stake her without a second thought.

"Give me the stake," Wesley demanded. "I'll do it if you can't."

"No, you won't!" Kimberly's determined shout stunned him. She leapt up from her cot and pushed in front of Yvette, spreading her arms out protectively to shield her bodyguard. "You think I wanna be locked up with the two of you alone? Like I don't know what guys like you want from a pretty girl like me."

Behind her, even Yvette couldn't seem to control her smirk despite the seriousness of the situation. Haven rolled his eyes; it had never even crossed his mind to touch the girl inappropriately. For some reason, while she was certainly pretty, nothing stirred when he looked at her. Now, the same thing couldn't be said for the way his body reacted to Yvette.

"Thanks, Kimberly. I'm glad we're of one mind here, because I have no intention of leaving you alone with those two." Yvette sent a pointed look his way, but there was little fire behind her words. Not the kind of fire he'd seen in her when she'd first awakened after being unconscious. The fire that had shot from her mouth then had been hotter and more potent than dragon fire. And despite the explosiveness of the situation he'd found himself in when she'd pinned him against the wall, he'd almost looked forward to being singed by her flames. Which was stupid and totally out of character for him; he wasn't the hotheaded one of the family: Wesley was.

"God, this is annoying. You should have killed her when she was unconscious," Bess nagged, letting out an exasperated breath. "Well, never mind. I'm sure you'll come to your senses, but for now, you, Haven, are next."

She stepped over the threshold and crooked her finger. As if pulled by strings, Haven's body moved toward her. "What the—?"

"Don't fight her, Hav," Wesley cautioned. Then he reached for him. "And leave me the stake."

Haven twisted his body and gripped the stake. Not a chance in hell. He wouldn't part with the stake.

8

Hidden behind a row of bushes and set back from the quiet side street it inhabited, the place looked unassuming. Zane turned the spare key in the lock and let himself into Yvette's house. There was no sound. He let his senses swirl around the place, feeling for anything that was alive, but all he detected was the faint scent of Yvette and that dog. Not her dog, she'd said. Right.

Why couldn't she admit that she'd taken in the stray and adopted it? All evidence pointed to it: the feeding bowls with dry food and water, and the doggie door to the backyard. Ridiculous how somebody could be in such denial about wanting to form an attachment to something or someone.

Zane explored the little two-bedroom house. Its decorations seemed warm and comforting and in stark contrast to Yvette's outer shell—not at all what he'd thought he'd find. Somehow he'd expected a black-and-white modern, sparsely furnished house. What he saw all around him was quintessential *Town and Country*: pillows, warm colors, ornaments, and frilly curtains galore.

No wonder she'd never invited any of her colleagues to her home, even though they'd all pestered her to throw a housewarming party after she'd bought the house a couple of months earlier. If she knew he was sneaking around her home now, she'd probably stake him without ceremony. Not that he could blame her; he'd do the same to anybody who showed up uninvited in his place and poked his nose into his business.

"Dog?" he called out, but the beast didn't reply. Zane couldn't sense it anywhere. Had Yvette taken it with her, or had the animal run away? Just when he thought that the dog could come in handy, like maybe being able to sniff out where Yvette had disappeared to. It seemed to be able to follow her everywhere in the city. Maybe if he could locate the dog, Yvette wouldn't be far.

Zane turned a corner and opened the next door. The bathroom. He flicked on the light switch and looked around. It wasn't what he'd expected either. Instead of a collection of makeup, lipsticks, and creams, the granite counter held a single toothbrush, toothpaste, a pair of scissors, and a plastic bag.

He examined the plastic bag. *St. Jude's Hospital—Cancer Department* it said.

What the hell? Vampires couldn't get sick, and for sure they couldn't get cancer, so why on earth would Yvette have a bag from a hospital's cancer department in her bathroom? He opened it and peeked inside. Strands of long black hair were inside it. He stuck his hand in, pulled out a bunch and sniffed. Not just anybody's hair: Yvette's hair.

Now there was a discovery he didn't make every day: Yvette had long hair! Damn it if that didn't surprise him just a bit.

This meant she'd had long hair when she'd been turned. He'd always assumed the opposite. So why would she go through the pain of cutting it short, which she'd clearly been doing every single day he'd known her. Weren't women supposed to love long hair? What was the point of cutting it? And more importantly, what else was Yvette hiding from her colleagues?

***

Yvette glared back at Wesley, whose body posture reeked with open hostility. "Like your brother said, I won't hurt you." Then she smiled, the little devil on her shoulder rearing its ugly head and making her lips part once more. "Not yet."

Wesley's attempt to hide his flinch was unsuccessful.

God, how she loved to rattle the stupid little pup. Sure, he was almost as tall as Haven, and the family resemblance was evident in their dark hair and blue eyes, but that's where it ended. Where Haven seemed controlled, Wesley was anything but. A young blowhard. She'd have to watch him; otherwise, he'd wreak havoc and destroy their chances of escape. Or better yet, scare him into submission so he wouldn't dare do anything idiotic.

"So, you're his brother?" Kimberly asked, now standing next to her.

In the last few minutes, Yvette's estimation of the girl had gone up a notch, despite her comment that she was afraid the two men might rape her if she was alone with them. She doubted that either of the two had that inclination. They just didn't seem to be the kind—with their looks they didn't need to force a woman. Turning on the charm was all that was needed. She'd been at the receiving end of it when Haven had unleashed said charm on her.

Yvette liked the fact that Kimberly had stood up for her. It was a step in the right direction. Maybe the girl was much more resilient than she'd presumed at first. Having made it this far in the acting world had to mean that the girl had stamina and, hopefully, a backbone.

"Yes, I'm Wesley. Haven's my older brother." Then he tilted his head and flashed a charming grin at her. Kimberly instantly blushed. "You look familiar. Have we met?"

Yvette walked back to the cot and stretched out, leaning her upper body against the wall behind her. She wasn't interested in making small talk, and by the looks of it, Wesley would rather talk to Kimberly than her anyway.

"I'm Kimberly Fairfax. I'm—"

"—the actress!" he completed her sentence before taking a few steps closer.

Yvette kept her eyes on them, ready to interfere if necessary.

"Wow! How cool is *that*?"

Yvette raised an eyebrow. "Yeah, it's really cool being locked up by a witch, not knowing what she wants to do with us. But hey, at least you've found the silver lining." The aftertaste of sarcasm had a decidedly . . . *pleasing* flavor, she always found.

Wesley glared at her. "I'm not talking to you. You're a vampire. I hate vampires."

She pressed her hand against her chest. "You wound me."

He took a few steps toward her. "Creatures like you should be killed on sight." His voice was full of venom.

"Wanna give it a try?" Yvette jumped up, ready to teach the wannabe slayer a lesson. She gestured with her hands for him to come closer. "Go ahead. Let's see if you can do more than hit like some *human* girl."

The angry glint in Wesley's eyes told her she was rattling his cage. Lighting his fuse was child's play. "What, don't have the courage after all? Were you just showing off in front of your big brother?"

She noticed his fists clenching by his sides, his chest heaving with every breath. Oh, yes, she was getting to him. Just another well-placed shove and he'd lose it. And hell, if she didn't need a bit of an outlet for her own frustration. "Wanna hide behind your mama's skirts?"

A flash of grief flared in Wesley's eyes. With a roar, he lunged for her much faster than she'd expected. He slammed his body against her and drove her against the wall. The sturdy surface connecting with her back would have hurt a human's spine and ribs, but Yvette's body was built stronger, more indestructible.

"Don't you *dare* mention my mother."

It appeared she'd hit a sore spot. Just as well: find the enemy's weak points and exploit them. That's what she'd been taught all these years during her training at Scanguards. And she'd been a good student. On the job, she'd perfected every skill they'd taught her. "I'll mention your mother all I want." There was a wound, and while she didn't know how deep it was, rubbing salt on it was an easy way to find out.

Wesley's hands tried to reach for her throat, but Yvette blocked him effortlessly with her forearm. "I'll kill you. You'll pay for killing my mother. You all will."

For a second, she went still. No wonder the pup was all agitated. She looked into his eyes and saw the deep-rooted pain in them. She could take a wild guess at what the cause of his pain was. It wasn't fresh, but it seemed nevertheless severe. "You really think you have the strength to kill me?" Yvette blew out a breath of air, showing him just how much she thought of his fighting abilities.

"I'll kill you," he hissed through clenched teeth.

"For what? For something I didn't do?"

"You're all responsible—all you vampires," he spat.

It got her hackles up. She hated being accused wholesale for something one of her fellow vampires might or might not have done. "You'd better start explaining what you mean by that." Yvette held firm and didn't move. Their bodies were pressed together, but she felt none of the heat and arousal she'd felt with Haven. Nothing stirred in her; all she saw was the boy inside the man, the boy who was hurting.

"You killed her."

"Your mother. I don't even know you mother." Anger at his accusation made her raise her voice. To calm herself down, she took a few steadying breaths, knowing that she'd get nowhere if she lost control over the situation. "What happened to her?" Like she'd been taught, she made her voice calm and even. She could have pushed him off a hundred times and freed herself from him, but she chose not to. Wesley needed to maintain a semblance of being in charge, because inside she could see him crumbling.

"A vampire." His eyes grew distant.

"A vampire killed your mother?" She knew the answer already, but she needed to get him to talk. If she knew the circumstances, she could rebuke his accusations and make him understand that she had nothing to do with it. But he didn't answer.

"Wesley?"

He shook his head as if ridding himself of the memories. Then his eyes stared at her, and the hardness was back, the pain pushed back into dark recesses where it couldn't be found. "That's why you'll die."

Knowing that she'd played her hand for what it was worth, she pushed him off her, propelling him into the middle of the room. "I'm not the vampire you're looking for."

"Doesn't matter: I'll kill each and every one of you until I find the right one."

"That makes you no better than the vampire who killed your mother."

"Don't compare me to the likes of your kind. You're bloodthirsty killers."

She decided not to correct him on his assumption that she'd killed. She hadn't—well, self-defense didn't count—but it was better if he feared her. It would keep him at bay. "And you're not? What makes your killing any different?"

"I kill despicable creatures like you: heartless, soulless creatures."

Yvette gave a bitter laugh. If she were really heartless, then she wouldn't feel the loneliness that had been engulfing her for years. She wouldn't feel the yearning for a family, for a man and a child who loved her. If she had no soul, she wouldn't mourn the loss of her friends who'd died over the years. "You have no idea who I am."

She turned away from him, not wanting him to see the storm inside her. It didn't stop him from insulting her further. "My brother should have staked you."

Without turning, she responded, "Your brother won't hurt me." She was certain about it, more certain than she'd been about anything lately.

"What have you done to him?"

She smiled to herself. It wasn't what she'd done to him, but what *he* wanted to do to *her*. "He wants to fuck me."

"You fucking bitch. He would never touch a vampire like that."

Yvette swiveled on her heels and lashed a glare at him. "I don't think you know your brother when it comes to that."

"You—"

Whatever he wanted to say was drowned out by a scream from Haven. Unexpected panic coiled through her. The scream was one of pure agony, a pain so raw she felt it creep into her bones where it spread like a chill from a frigid arctic wind.

"What did the witch do to you? Wesley? What did she do to you out there?"

Wesley ran to the door and pulled on the door handle, but it didn't move. "I have to get to him! Damn it, I told him not to resist. Why doesn't he ever listen to me?" Raking his hand through his dark mane, he looked distraught.

Yvette gripped his shoulder and turned him to look at her. His anguish was painted on his face. "What did she do to you?"

He swallowed hard. "She went into my mind, probing around in there. It was like . . . like an electrical current was going through my head, as if she was trying to find something with it."

"Torture?"

He shook his head. "No, it didn't hurt that much. But it was humiliating."

Another scream tore through the room. Their gazes flew to the door.

"Then why is he screaming? What is she doing?" Yvette shook Wesley.

He threw her hands off as if only now noticing that she was touching him. "I—I don't know. He can take more pain than anybody I know."

"Then why?" she wondered, more to herself than to Wesley.

"If he's screaming, it means she's hurting him because he's resisting her. It's all my fault."

"Why is it your fault?"

"If I hadn't gotten caught by the witch, Haven wouldn't be in this situation now. He wouldn't have had to rescue me."

Haven had avoided her question about why he'd kidnapped them, even though when Wesley had entered the room, she'd started to suspect Haven's reason for being compelled to make a deal with a witch.

"Go on," Yvette encouraged him. Maybe Wesley could shed some more light on the situation. She told herself that it was merely natural curiosity that made her urge him to tell her what had really happened and not her unreasonable wish that Haven wasn't just another callous vampire hunter. That maybe he'd had a valid reason for kidnapping them, an excuse that would make it easier for her to forgive him.

"I'm not telling you anything."

Yvette heard the light footsteps behind her.

"Then tell me," Kimberly offered and stepped next to her.

Wesley looked down at her, and his face suddenly softened. Not wanting to destroy whatever headway Kimberly was making with getting Wesley to open up, Yvette took a few measured steps to the side.

"My brother would do anything for me. He always has. He's more like a father to me than a brother."

Kimberly nodded and continued looking at him. Putting her hand on his forearm, she gave him an encouraging smile. Maybe the actress did have some skills Yvette hadn't previously noticed. Was it genuine compassion oozing from her now, or was she simply using her acting skills to tease information out of him? Where was the girl who, only minutes earlier, had proclaimed she didn't want to be left alone with Wesley and his brother for fear they might do her bodily harm?

Yvette gave her another look. Kimberly was like a chameleon, constantly changing her colors for whatever the situation needed. If the girl didn't already have a thriving career as an actress, she would have asked Gabriel if he'd take her on and train her as a mediator or hostage negotiator. Despite being human, a person with her ability to change her demeanor would be valuable in many situations. And surprisingly, the revelation that Yvette was a vampire had barely fazed her.

Not wanting to miss any of their conversation, Yvette put her thoughts on the back burner.

"Hav always bailed me out when I got into trouble. Just like this time. The witch, Bess, she tricked me; I didn't know what she was until it was too late. My mother was a witch, you know, but I didn't inherit her powers."

Yvette listened intently. Their mother was a witch? That would make both him and Haven witches too. Could this get any worse? Not only did she have the hots for a human guy who kidnapped her—oh no; he also had to be the son of a witch, and thereby a witch himself. Perfect. She sure knew how to pick 'em!

Only, she hadn't smelled the telltale scent of witch on him. Nor on his brother. How odd!

"Your mother was a witch?" Kimberly echoed.

Wesley held up his hand. "A good one, but not a powerful one. Only a few spells and potions. She used her powers mostly to heal people, to help, you know. She was a good woman."

"And you? Do you do spells?" Kimberly pressed on, clearly fascinated.

He shook his head, and Yvette thought she could see regret in his face. "I don't have any of her powers. Neither does Haven. That's why I couldn't sense that this woman was a witch. That's why her trap worked. She lured me close and then imprisoned me."

Yvette wrinkled her forehead. How was it possible that none of a witch's children inherited her powers? At the very least at her death, her powers would have had to channel into some vessel or other. She knew enough about witchcraft to know that little fact. Was Wesley hiding the truth? Yvette calmed herself and reached out with her mind to feel his aura . . . She sensed nothing in it that would indicate he was a witch. She inhaled, his scent mingling with that of Kimberly . . . It was different from a purely human scent. Not witch. Not human. Something in between.

She shook her head and felt her stomach growl at the same time. Maybe her hunger for blood was screwing with her. Or the effects of the potion that had knocked her out were still lingering. When she'd been in the limousine with Kimberly, the girl had clearly smelled human. One hundred percent. And when Yvette had been pressed against the wall by Wesley earlier, she'd taken in his scent—then it had been entirely human.

Fuck, she needed blood or her entire mind would get fuzzy and unclear. Already now, she was losing her sharp senses.

"She said she knew where I could find some vampires to kill," Wesley continued and tossed Yvette a sideways glance. She simply shrugged. What else was new? Rome wasn't built in one day either. Teaching the pup that not all vampires were bad would take longer than that.

"Why do you kill vampires?" Kimberly asked, her voice carrying the innocence of her years.

Defiance and anger flared in Wesley's eyes. "Because a vampire killed my mother when I was eight."

Yvette looked away. She could understand his hatred. But she couldn't condone the killing of innocent vampires. There was no use in telling him so, however: she wouldn't change his attitude with her words.

"I'm so sorry," Kimberly whispered.

For a moment, there was silence in the room so thick it had *weight*: an expectant heaviness to the air that pressed down, making it hard to draw a breath. But then Wesley seemed to have himself under control again. "When Bess captured me, she sent a message to Hav. She blackmailed him into kidnapping you and told him that she'd free me if you were brought to her. He had no choice."

Kimberly nodded. "What does she want with me?" There was a trembling in her voice now. Instinctively, Yvette took a step toward her. With a sideways glance, Kimberly made a motion indicating she was okay.

"I don't know. I wish I did."

9

Haven felt the stinging pain as the whip sliced through the skin covering his abdomen. A punch in the gut his trained muscles could have absorbed easily, but the biting ends of the leather whip were another story.

"I wouldn't need to do this if you were as accommodating as your little brother," Bess scolded.

"Fuck you!" If she wanted to get inside his head, she'd have to slice him open. Simple as that.

"You should reconsider. The more you resist, the more it's going to hurt."

Haven's eyes drifted around the room, trying to learn what he could about her. This time, he wasn't in the living room she'd invited him into the first time. This latest torture chamber looked and reeked of mold and sweat, blood and tears. She'd tied him to a wooden scaffold with vines that had wrapped around his arms like rope guided by invisible hands. Whatever powers she held, she was strong. Much stronger than his mother had been.

From where—or what—she drew her power, he couldn't figure out, but once he could discover the source, maybe he could destroy or at least weaken said source. From the little he remembered from his mother's craft, he knew that every witch's powers were anchored somewhere. If he could find that anchor, he could start to rock the boat.

"What do you want?"

"Your compliance."

"Not gonna happen." He spat at her feet, underscoring that he wasn't the compliant sort of guy.

"I figured you'd be the stubborn one. But don't worry, I'll get there even without your help." She flicked her wrist once more, letting the leather lash against his exposed chest. When he'd fought her mental invasion of his mind, she'd first stripped him of his dinner jacket, then ruined the shirt by slashing it in half. So much for getting his deposit on the rented suit back.

Blood oozed liberally from the gashes and trailed in rivulets over his chest and stomach. He'd been in worse shape and survived. "Over my dead body."

There was a flicker in her eyes, and he realized he'd hit a nerve. She didn't want him dead—no, for some reason, she needed him alive. It was her weak point. She could bloody him and hurt him, but she couldn't kill him. It was a consolation, albeit a small one.

The witch narrowed her eyes, and a moment later he felt a current go through his head once more. She was trying it again, trying to invade his mind to find whatever she was after. But he wouldn't let her. Haven clenched his jaw and tightened his neck muscles, trying to push against her. Visions of his mother's last moments blinked in front of his eyes, and her last words echoed in his head. "Remember to love," she'd reminded him with her last breath. Haven took comfort in her words and felt warmth spread in him. Suddenly, an electric shock surged through his body, and he felt himself rocked by a spasm. The accompanying shot of adrenaline gave him enough extra fuel to intensify the outward push against the violation.

He couldn't explain what he was doing, but he knew it was working. The tendrils of Bess's invading thoughts withdrew from his mind and released him. The electric current receded until his head was clear again. "You bitch!" he hissed.

He would not allow her to get this close again. His mind was his own. *Nobody* had a right to go in there. It was where he kept all his fears and hopes locked up for nobody to ever see, hidden away from reality, from the cold, hard truth that kept nagging at him. A reality he never wanted to face, and hopes he wasn't ready to give up even though with every day that passed, his hope of finding Katie grew slimmer. Nobody had a right to see the turmoil in his mind, the pain he concealed. He'd never even shared this with his brother. And he *damn* well wasn't going to share it with the witch who held them captive.

Because showing what went on inside him would weaken him. And he needed to be strong to get out of this alive.

The whip bit into his skin and jerked him back to the here-and-now. There was no escaping the pain as it seared through him. He tried to block it out, shut himself off from feeling anything, but it was useless. The pain sliced through every cell of his body, weakening his resolve. His heart beat frantically trying to pump blood where it was needed most.

"Fine, you won't let me in, then you'll give me the answer instead."

Haven didn't understand what she meant. She hadn't asked him anything yet.

"Where's the key to your power?"

What the hell? "What power?" he rasped out, his voice showing his body's exhaustion from the beating, his ribs aching from the bruising they'd already taken.

"Your witch power!" Bess hissed impatiently.

"You must be crazy. I have no 'witch power.'" Neither he nor his brother had ever had any of their mother's powers, few as they were. If that was what the witch was after, to tap into his powers and maybe steal them, she was on a train to nowhere.

"Don't lie to me!" She lashed the whip against his chest.

Haven groaned through the pain, grinding his teeth to ward off the worst. "I have no—"

Another lash, aimed higher, cut into his neck. Streaks of white hot pain seared his skin as the whip sliced through the tender flesh. Haven pulled on his restraints in an attempt to escape, but they held firm. Like serpents, they snaked around his arms and tightened further, caressing his skin with as much gentleness as sandpaper.

"You'll tell me now." She stepped closer and swiped her hand over his face, delivering a powerful blow. His lip split, filling his mouth with blood. He spat it at her, ridding himself of the metallic taste that threatened to make him gag.

"You think I would let you beat me if I had any power?"

The witch paused in her next movement, a flash of curiosity crossing her features. "Could it be . . . ?" she mumbled. Then she looked straight at him, an evil grin building on her face. "Your mama never told you, did she? Kept the knowledge to herself, huh? Or maybe, she never had a chance." She paused, suddenly nodding to herself. "You were still a kid back then."

He didn't understand her ramblings, but his lips were too swollen to bother speaking.

Bess let out a nasty chuckle, then lashed the whip at him again. "I had to make sure. You understand that, don't you?" The next lash brought darkness and silence and with it a reprieve from the pain.

***

Yvette heard the footsteps outside in the hallway and the sound of something being dragged along the floor. Instantly alerted, she jumped up from the cot she'd been resting on, nervousness and a feeling of dread creeping through her cells. Certain sounds were never a good sign. She'd learned that long ago. This was one of those sounds.

When the door swung open, the stench of witch permeated. But it wasn't the only smell that tensed her nostrils. Blood was in the air. Yvette's gaze snapped to the witch and the bundle of flesh she'd dragged behind her that now slithered into the room. Briefly, she wondered whether the witch was using her powers to drag Haven's heavy body along the floor rather than her muscles, but Yvette's question died a silent death the moment she saw him.

He was only barely conscious, his chest practically naked with only strips of what used to be a shirt clinging to his bloodstained body. His lips were bleeding, his neck and shoulders crisscrossed with cuts and bruises, but that wasn't the worst. Along his abdomen, three large gashes dug deep into his flesh. Yvette's heart clenched painfully. No matter how much pain Haven could take, he was human. The pain would be excruciating, and the blood loss would weaken him. Without a doubt, he was in agony.

The blood pouring from Haven's many wounds made Yvette's stomach growl, no matter how much she tried to suppress her hunger and hold her breath. Certain things not even she could withstand, despite the iron willpower she possessed.

"Oh, my god!" Kimberly took a few tentative steps toward the door.

"Oh, shit, Hav," Wesley cried out, crouching down next to his brother. "What the fuck did you do to him?" There was murderous fury in the glare he pinned on the witch.

"It's his own fault. Too stubborn for his own good."

Yvette tried to stay back, not wanting to get any closer to the enticing smell of blood, but her stomach growled again. The witch heard it and gave her a nasty smile. "Looks like someone's hungry."

Instantly and simultaneously, Wesley's glare and Kimberly's scared look landed on her. Yvette retreated to the far corner of their prison. Whatever headway she'd made with Kimberly, trusting her not to harm her, she'd lost again.

"Human blood's not really my thing." Yvette suppressed the urge to snarl and flash her fangs at the fucking bitch. It wouldn't do any good, other than scare Kimberly even more, which was the last thing she wanted to do. "I prefer the taste of witch's blood myself. Care to make a donation?" Yvette forced a nonchalant look onto her face.

The witch didn't take the bait, seeing through her as if Yvette was as transparent as a politician's campaign promises. "Haven's blood must be stinging your nostrils by now. How does it feel?"

Yvette didn't dare glance down to the floor where Wesley tended to his half-conscious brother. She kept her eyes firmly on the witch. "Not particularly. I fed just before you captured us, so I'm good for at least two days," she lied.

At the best of times, she could hold out twenty-four hours, but even before that she'd get cranky. Her colleagues had always teased her about it and avoided her when she hadn't fed. She could admit it to herself: she was a royal bitch when she was hungry. And she was getting hungry. Her last feeding had been too many hours ago, and the potion Haven had used to capture her had zapped even more of her energy.

The witch scoffed, and maybe for now Yvette had been able to fool her. Not that it mattered. Soon, her colleagues would be looking for her and Kimberly. She'd missed her regular call-in to Central Command. Gabriel would be notified, and knowing him, he'd start combing the city for her. Somehow they'd find her and get her out of here. It was only a matter of time. She just had to sit tight.

"You think I can't tell how you're holding your breath so you won't smell his blood? You want to suck him dry, don't you?"

Yvette narrowed her eyes and clenched her jaw. "No."

The witch turned her head toward Wesley. "I think you'll have to kill her after all. Or do you want to risk her killing your brother?"

"Scheming bitch! Can't do your dirty work yourself, can you?" Yvette hissed. Maybe the witch's powers weren't quite strong enough against a vampire. Was that the reason why she hadn't tried to kill her yet? It was an avenue to explore. If her powers were only strong enough to hold the humans at bay, Yvette just might have a chance at defeating the witch. If she could get out of this room. The wards seemed strong enough to hold even a vampire captive, but if she could somehow get out from within the wards, maybe she could fight her. The problem with witches was you never knew what they had up their sleeve. She hated that.

Warring emotions danced on Wesley's face as he glanced from her to the witch and back. Mistrust won out. Could she really blame him? After what he'd told Kimberly about his mother, it was natural that he hated vampires. Which meant he hated her.

"Here." The witch tossed Wesley a stake. He caught it in one hand. An agonizing moan from his brother made him turn.

"Hav, didn't I tell you not to fight her?"

"I didn't fight her," Haven pressed out. His voice was labored, the pain clearly evident in it. Yvette stole a look to assess his injuries again. The gashes on his abdomen were still bleeding, and if the blood loss wasn't stopped soon, she feared the worst. Despite the fact that he'd kidnapped her and Kimberly, she couldn't just let him bleed out. Only to spite the witch, of course.

"Time to go, little one." Stepping over the threshold, the witch crooked her finger at Kimberly, whose eyes widened in shock.

"No!" Yvette cried. She couldn't allow her charge to be harmed. She was responsible for her. It was her job. "Don't touch her." She lunged forward toward the witch, but a power blast pushed her back.

"Stay out of it!"

"Somebody help me," Kimberly wailed as she was pulled toward the door by an invisible force.

Wesley ran toward her, but like Yvette, he was pushed back by an invisible blast. "Whatever you do, don't fight her!" he cautioned Kimberly.

When the witch grabbed Kimberly's arm and pulled her over the threshold, the force field holding Yvette and Wesley back dissipated. Both stumbled.

Yvette watched the witch slam the door shut. Could she only exert her powers within the protection of the wards? Could this mean that if they were inside the wards, the witch had to be inside them too in order to use her powers on them? Yvette tucked the assumption away in the back of her mind. There were more pressing things to do right now.

10

Wesley's harsh voice bellowing out a warning to someone brought Haven back to reality. He forced his eyes open and knew he was back in the room where they were being held captive. Nothing had changed. Except for the fact that he was in pain.

He lay on the floor and tried to sit up, but the pain around his midsection made him slump back instantly. His brother was kneeling next to him, the haunted look on his face providing little comfort. When his field of vision widened, Haven saw the stake that Wesley held tightly in his right hand.

"What the—"

"She's hungry, and you're bleeding," Wesley cut him off.

Haven jerked his head and saw Yvette standing several feet away from them, her eyes trained on him. Would she attack him?

"Shut up, Wesley, and don't keep repeating the crap the witch has fed you. I'm fine," Yvette insisted. "I've fed plenty. I don't want your brother's blood."

Haven locked eyes with her and for a moment he believed her, but then he saw a glint in them, like a little flame that started burning, and he knew she was lying. Yvette was hungry. His gaze drifted down her body where her hands clenched into fists. Hungry, and fighting it. Which side was stronger? Her humanity or her animal instincts?

"Shit," he mumbled under his breath.

She'd heard it. He could tell by the way she dropped her lids. God, she was beautiful. A beautiful angel of death, yes, that's what she was. Yet, instead of feeling fear of what was to come, he felt a strange excitement build in his core. Almost as if he was looking forward to her bite. It told him how far gone he was already. Maybe the injuries Bess had inflicted were indeed deeper than he'd thought at first. He knew he was bleeding profusely, but was the blood loss to blame for his addled brain? For the fact that he was craving Yvette's touch even more than he had at the premier party? That he wanted her to come closer and embrace him?

"Wesley, I need to—"

Wesley jumped up at Yvette's words, his raised hand holding the stake as a warning: *stay back*. "You're not getting anywhere near him."

"I won't hurt him. I can help him heal."

A bitter laugh left Wesley's chest. "How stupid do you think I am?"

"Do you want your brother to die?"

"No! And that's exactly why you're not getting anywhere near him."

Bless his little brother. Wesley would protect him even though he knew he was no match for Yvette, the strong and beautiful Yvette, the sinful beauty, the deadly vampire whose touch Haven desired against all reason. Was he already drifting into a delirium?

"I told you I won't hurt him. If I wanted to, I would have done so long before you even got in here. Don't you get that?"

Wesley raised his chin stubbornly. It was a gesture with which Haven was all too familiar; he did that when he wasn't willing to budge, but had no arguments left. Haven had been at the receiving end of it many times while they'd grown up together.

"What do you propose?" Haven asked, each word hurting as his breath deserted his lungs.

Yvette's eyes widened in obvious surprise. She hadn't expected him to ask. "I can seal your wounds so they won't bleed anymore. It'll stop the blood loss."

"How?"

"With my saliva. I can lick the wounds and . . ."

Haven didn't hear the rest of her words. She would lick him? God help him. If the blood loss didn't kill him, her lips and tongue on his naked skin would. Already the thought of it made his body temperature rise. How could he let her do that to him? And in front of his brother and the girl! It wasn't an experience he wanted to have in front of an audience. At the thought of Kimberly, Haven scanned the room. She was gone. An icy coldness shot through his veins.

"Where's Kimberly?"

Yvette frowned. Wesley answered, "The witch took her."

"Shit!" What had he done? He'd delivered an innocent girl to a witch, who would hurt her. Why hadn't he resisted? Why hadn't he come up with a better plan that wouldn't have involved kidnapping the girl?

"I told her to do what she says. She won't resist her, not like you, stupid," Wesley growled.

"I couldn't, I just couldn't . . ." But Wesley wouldn't understand. He'd always taken the easy road, the way of least resistance. Whereas Haven had yet to meet a brick wall he didn't like. And his head wasn't thanking him for it either.

"So, do you agree to it?" Yvette intercepted his thoughts.

Haven looked back at her and let his gaze sweep over her body once more. He didn't have much of a choice. The bleeding wasn't stopping no matter how hard he pressed his hand against the wounds. And already now he felt dizzy. It would only get worse. But he still couldn't trust her.

"Wesley will stand next to you. And if you're trying to hurt me, he'll use the stake."

"Now we're talking." Wesley grinned and rolled the item in question between his fingers.

Yvette merely rolled her eyes. "Idiots!"

With fluid grace she walked toward him, waiting for Wesley to step aside before she dropped to her knees beside him. Her closeness made him feel almost intoxicated. He wrote it off to the pain that coursed through his body and made him weak.

"Show me how it works," Wesley ordered, looking down on them.

Haven saw Yvette's mouth twitch as if she was biting back a snide remark. But then she lowered her face to his and looked into his eyes. "Your lip is split."

His groin tightened at the hint of what she was about to do. Couldn't she start somewhere else on his body, maybe on his hand or arm? Did she have to deliver the death blow with her first strike? But before he could voice his protest—and he wasn't even sure it would have been a protest—her lips closed in on him.

Haven held his breath when her pink tongue snaked out and lapped against his lower lip. Instead of a stinging sensation, he experienced a slight tingling, pleasant and gentle. He exhaled and relaxed his facial muscles. Again, her tongue licked over his lower lip, slower this time and with more pressure.

The strange tingling morphed into a shiver which raced down his body and slammed into his groin. She would definitely kill him—that much was clear. By what means? The jury was still out on that.

When he looked at her, he noticed how her eyes had closed as if she was savoring his taste. There was a drop of his blood on her lip, and fuck it if he didn't find that sexy as hell. And hell was clearly where he was heading if he didn't stop this madness. If he could stop it. If he wanted to.

Yvette pulled back.

"Fucking amazing," Wesley commented as he looked at Haven's lip. "It's like new." His brother grinned down on him. "Quite handy." Then he made a movement toward Yvette. "Okay, do the rest."

If his brother only knew what kind of torture he was going through right now . . . It might look cool and be "handy" as Wesley had said, but to be at the receiving end of it was something entirely different. It was the most amazing sensual caress he'd ever felt.

Yvette's hands divested him of the remainder of his shredded shirt, fully exposing his chest to her view. Her eyes showed the hunger she tried to keep leashed, but Haven saw it nevertheless. What if she fell into bloodlust now that she'd tasted his blood? Was it the same way it was for an alcoholic, who once he'd tasted alcohol again couldn't stop himself? Was that what would happen to her?

From the corner of his eye, he noticed Wesley shift and adjust the hold on his stake. He briefly wondered where he'd gotten it from since Haven's own stake was still in his jacket pocket, and his jacket was nowhere to be seen.

Yvette's hands felt surprisingly warm as she took his hand and lifted it from where he was still pressing it against his wound. He'd always thought that vampires would be cold, being the heartless creatures they were. He'd fought plenty of them in hand-to-hand combat, but had never really noticed their body temperature. There'd never been the time during the fight to really register what they felt like. And he'd never wanted to anyway.

But now Haven had all the time in the world to feel and sense what a vampire's hands were like. And why shouldn't he? The more he learned about these creatures, the better he could fight them in the future. Because nothing would change. Just because he was thrown together with a vampire and had to work with her to get out of the predicament he and his brother were in, didn't mean he'd suddenly become friends with one of their kind. At the very least, hell would have to freeze over first.

"What did she use?" Yvette asked and stroked her fingers along the gashes as if mapping them.

"A whip." It took all his restraint not to moan out the answer. Pressing his jaw tightly together, he tried to ignore the effect her warm fingers had on his body. Like a sensual caress, she explored his injuries.

"They're deep."

Yvette bent over his stomach and lowered her head to his wounds. Her tongue flicked against his flesh, spreading the same tingling sensation as before. With long, sure strokes, she licked along his damaged skin, lapping up the blood as she went. Haven's head dropped back. He was unable to watch, not because it disgusted him, but because her actions got him hotter than a lap dance. With every lick of her tongue, he grew harder. He could only hope that neither his brother nor Yvette noticed how his cock expanded beneath his black pants and strained against the zipper, threatening to destroy the last piece of his rented tuxedo and any remaining hope for his deposit.

Haven closed his eyes, not wanting to be exposed to the embarrassment that would follow if either of them discovered his arousal. His brother's lack of discretion would make the situation uncomfortable at the very least.

"Are you okay?" Wesley asked, concern evident in his voice.

"I'm fine." Fine? Who was he kidding? He was about two steps away from paradise.

While Yvette's mouth kept licking his wounds, her hand slipped to his side as if trying to hold onto something. Her fingers dug into him, and by the intensity with which she gripped him, he suspected she was unaware of her own actions.

Haven let out a ragged breath. How long was she going to torture him like this? Did she even know what kind of effect she had on him? Was this her way of paying him back for kidnapping her?

When she suddenly lifted her head, cold air wafted against his wounds.

"It's not working," Yvette said.

Haven's eyes flew open.

"Why?" Wesley hissed. "Are you just sucking him dry? Is this all a trick?"

Yvette ignored Wes's snide remark and instead looked at Haven. "The wounds are too deep and too large. We need to try something else."

Wesley lifted the stake as if to strike.

"No, Wes!" Haven yelled. He couldn't let his brother hurt her. When Wesley lowered the stake again, Haven let out a relieved breath. Then he looked at Yvette. "Was it a trick to get my blood?"

She shot him an indignant glare, then shook her head. "As I said—"

"Too deep, yeah, I heard you. What now?"

"I can get the wounds to close from the inside," she hedged, darting a cautious look from him to Wesley.

Suspicion rose in him. "How?"

"You have to drink my blood."

For an instant, Haven was unable to speak. His vocal cords constricted.

"Hell, no!" Wesley protested. "You fucking bitch—you're trying to turn him into one of you."

He raised his stake and lunged for her, but Yvette had already jumped up. She dove in the other direction, out of his reach.

As she turned with an amazing speed—a speed he'd seen other vampires use before—she faced his brother with her hands at her hips, and her legs set in a wide stance—as wide as her tight dress with the ripped seam allowed. She was ready to attack.

"It won't turn him," Yvette claimed.

"Sure, you'd say that."

"It's true. A human has to be on the verge of death to be turned. Merely drinking vampire blood when alive doesn't turn you into a vampire." She tossed Wesley another angry glare. "You should be grateful that I'm even offering it. No vampire shares his blood lightly. It's a privilege. I should just let him suffer for what he's gotten Kimberly and me into."

Haven wondered whether he could believe her. Would it truly be safe to take her blood? He shifted his position, the move sending a bolt of pain through his body. Damn, this was worse than he'd thought. He looked down at the large gashes on his stomach. The sight of his angry flesh conjured up nausea and something else: a tiny twinge of fear that the injuries were more severe than he'd thought at first. If he passed out again, who'd take care of Wesley? "Why are you offering, then?"

Yvette growled. "I'm not anymore." To Haven she said, "Your brother has just sealed your fate. Go ahead, see whether you two can stop the bleeding. My work's done." Clearly pissed off, she turned away from them, walked to the cots at the opposite wall and slumped down on one. "Why should I even care?"

Damn him if she didn't look hurt. How was that possible? Haven pulled himself to a sitting position, despite the pain it caused him. Could it be that her humanity was truly stronger than her animal side, and that she really wanted to help him?

"What will your blood do to me?"

"Hav! Are you crazy?"

"Stay out of this, Wes." For once, he wished his brother wouldn't be so protective of him.

"You're assuming I'm still willing to give it to you." Yvette pouted. Nothing of her vamp side was visible. She was all hurt woman right now, her arms crossed over her chest, a defiant glare in her eyes. Did she know that her posture emphasized the plump swells of her breasts, making them a focal point Haven couldn't take his eyes off?

"What if I asked you nicely?" He'd definitely gone over the cliff now. Had he just asked her to give him her blood? What the hell was wrong with him?

Wesley threw up his hands. "You're mad! You're totally mad! If you do this, I'll never speak to you again. *Do you hear me?*"

Haven waved his brother off. Wes was full of hot air. He'd calm down later.

At Wesley's words, Yvette smirked. "Just to piss off your little brother, I'll do it."

His heart shouldn't jump like that just because she'd agreed, yet it did. Excitement coursed through him, even though he had no idea what to expect. What if he gagged on her blood? What if it tasted disgusting?

But there was no turning back now. Yvette was already walking toward him again. When she dropped down next to him, he sensed the warmth of her body and smelled the orange scent of her skin. She moved behind him.

"Lean back."

He eased back until his back connected with her chest.

"Idiot!" Wesley chastised, but he ignored him.

Feeling Yvette's body so close to his was all he could deal with right now. Haven turned his head to the side and watched her as she bit her own wrist. He only caught a quick glimpse of her sharp fangs as they dug into her flesh and pierced the skin, but the sight made him shiver.

Blood instantly oozed from her wrist, and she brought it to his mouth. "Just suckle from it."

"How much?"

"Your body will know when to stop." Her voice was low and husky, so sinful, it made the little hairs on his nape rise. Fear rose with it, but it was drowned out by the soft press of her breasts against his back and the warmth it sent through his body.

Haven set his lips to her open vein and took a tentative lick.

"Eew!" Wesley's disgusted groan barely registered. Instead, a taste of richness coated Haven's tongue. As it reached the back of his throat, an explosion of flavors hit him: oranges, cinnamon, cloves. Spicy and rich, it filled his mouth. He took more, wanting to prolong the experience. He'd always thought blood would taste metallic and stale, but this was so different from anything he'd ever known. Her blood was fresh and young, vibrant and rich at the same time.

Haven couldn't stop the moan that started deep in his chest and burst from his throat. With one hand, he gripped her arm and drew her closer, so she wouldn't pull away from him. He felt her breasts press harder into his back and her head lean against his. Her warm breath blew against his nape.

"Yes," she whispered so low only he could hear it.

The intimacy of her action wasn't lost on him. Giving one's blood to another person, a stranger at that, was a gesture so pure and personal, he could only speculate why she'd offered it.

When her blood reached his stomach, his entire body coiled like a tight spring. He tensed at the foreign feeling.

"Relax." Her coaxing word in his ear soothed. "Let go. I'm here."

There was something strangely comforting in her words. He allowed the tension to flow from his body and took more of her blood into him. Her taste was intoxicating, and coupled with her body close to his, there was nowhere else he'd rather be at this moment.

He drew on her vein, getting addicted to her taste.

"What the fuck?" Wesley's voice reached him, just as Haven noticed Yvette going slack behind him.

11

"The only odd thing I found in Yvette's house was this." Zane tossed the bag with Yvette's hair onto the kitchen island. Everybody was assembled in Samson's house: Samson, the owner and founder of Scanguards; Gabriel; Thomas, their IT genius; Amaury; and Eddie, the youngest of the vampires. In addition to the vampires, Oliver, Samson's human assistant, was with them. As always in a crisis situation, Samson's Nob Hill Victorian had turned into their command center.

From upstairs, Zane's sensitive hearing picked up conversation fragments. He recognized Nina's voice. It appeared that Amaury went nowhere without his headstrong mate. Completely pussy-whipped if anybody asked him, which of course nobody did. Maya's voice mingled with Delilah's a moment later. It figured that Gabriel couldn't leave his wife at home either. Well, at least Maya was a vampire, so she was useful in combat, whereas both Nina and Delilah were human, and if anything, would only prove to be a distraction.

"What is it?" Samson asked and reached for the bag.

"Hair." Zane shifted from one foot to the other. He wasn't sure why he'd even brought the damn thing, but somehow he'd been compelled to. It was something out of the ordinary, and he'd been trained to watch for anything that didn't make sense. Whether it would help them find Yvette in the end was another matter.

Samson pulled out a handful of strands of the black mane. "Whose is it?"

"Yvette's."

Samson sniffed and nodded.

"Yvette cuts her hair?" Amaury wrinkled his forehead. Zane tossed him an indifferent look. His linebacker-sized friend with the black, shoulder-length hair and sparkling blue eyes reached for the bag and inhaled. "Yep. It's her."

"Might be strange, but I doubt this'll get us any information on where she is," Thomas interjected. The biker with the IT-geek brain frowned and ran his hand through his sandy-blond hair.

Eddie, the young vampire he was mentoring and Nina's brother, nodded in agreement. He slapped Thomas on the shoulder. "You're right. Maybe she's just not into long hair."

Almost as tall as Thomas, he was built a little slimmer, yet no less strong. His face had dimples, now that it relaxed into a half-smile. Just like Thomas, he ran his hands through his dark-blond hair. Did he have to imitate everything his mentor did? That was irritating.

Zane cursed silently. Did everyone here have a full head of hair except for him? Was that why he'd brought the bag in the first place? To torture himself?

"What else have we got?" Gabriel asked.

Thomas leaned over the map which was spread out on the kitchen island and pushed the bag with the hair to the side. "The limousine was found here." He pointed to a location in the Richmond district. "Luckily, the company had an antitheft device in the vehicle. So we were able to track it."

"And the driver?"

"Still looking for him. The company was a little vague about who he is. Eddie and I will be paying them a visit in person to see what's going on."

Samson nodded. "Good. Amaury, I want you to go and inspect the limousine. See if you can detect anything, any traces of scents, blood, anything."

"Will take care of it."

"Has Kimberly's agent received any demands for ransom?"

Gabriel shook his head. "I just got off the phone with him. Nothing. He's going to cancel her appearances for the next few days, telling everybody she's come down with a severe flu and is contagious. Hopefully, that'll keep people from asking questions until we know what's going on."

"Sensible," Samson commented. Then he looked at Thomas again. "Any luck with tracing Yvette's cell phone?"

"It's switched off. I'll see what I can do when I get back to my computer."

"What about her dog?" Zane threw into the round and suddenly looked at a bunch of surprised faces.

"Yvette has a dog?" Gabriel asked. "She never mentioned that."

Zane snorted. "Of course she didn't; she can't even admit it to herself."

Samson gave him an impatient look. "Would you care to enlighten us for once, Zane, and stop with your cryptic remarks?" The sternness in his voice underscored his boss's impatience.

Zane knew when to pick a fight. This wasn't one of those times. "She's got this golden lab that's been following her for a few months. Claims it's just a stray, but the evidence in her house says otherwise. She feeds him. She's even built in a doggie door. Hell, the dog even listens to her."

"Well, let's get it. Maybe the dog can find her." Samson's face displayed a ray of hope.

"Dog's gone. I checked the house and the garden: it's nowhere to be found."

"Damn. Do you think she took the dog with her on her assignment?" Samson mused.

"She wouldn't do that," Gabriel interrupted. "That would be completely against all rules."

Zane raised an eyebrow. Yeah, Gabriel was all for strict rules. "And see where your rules have gotten her."

"This is neither the time nor the place to air your grievances," Gabriel snapped.

"When if not now? If you'd let me use mind control on the girl, Yvette wouldn't be the one missing right now." And damn it if he didn't feel a tad bit guilty about that fact. He should be the one in trouble right now, not Yvette. It wasn't Yvette's assignment. It was his. He should have been the one protecting Kimberly, then maybe there wouldn't be *anyone* missing right now. Maybe whatever had happened could have been averted. After all, he was stronger and more lethal than Yvette— and much more ruthless for that matter. If anybody had attacked him and Kimberly after leaving the premier party, he would have been able to defeat them.

"I will not be second guessed on my decision, Zane!"

"It was a mistake to assign her."

"What are you saying? That she isn't a good bodyguard?" Gabriel squared his chest and glared at him. "I'm sure she'll be only too happy to hear what you said once she's back. I'd watch my back if I were you, or Yvette will kick your ass."

Zane narrowed his eyes and clenched his jaw. His hands clenched into fists; he was dying to deal his boss a well-placed punch. But he also knew his place. And it wouldn't serve Yvette if he was taken off this case. His own feelings had to be put aside.

"Once she's back, I welcome the opportunity to get my ass kicked by her." And he wasn't even lying. She was like a little sister to him: a very annoying, very spoiled little sister. And protecting her was just what a big brother did.

The door swung open, and Nina popped her head in. Her short honey curls fell into her face. Instantly, Zane saw a bright smile flash over Amaury's face as his eyes traveled over her with unchecked lust. The two had bonded over four months earlier, and Amaury was *still* looking at her like he did the first time Zane had seen them together. He tried to shake the image from his mind.

"Delilah is asking for you, Samson. The baby is moving."

"Excuse me, guys. I'll be right back." Samson rushed past Nina without a backwards glance.

"And I think the blackout vans are outside," Nina informed them. "I just saw them arrive from upstairs."

"Thanks, Nina," Gabriel answered.

It was almost sunrise, and since they needed to continue their work and be able to move around the city during daylight hours, Scanguards' specially designed vans, which were equipped to take vampires around without exposing them to the sun, would have to be used. Human drivers employed by Scanguards drove the vans and knew about the cargo they were transporting. Only the most trusted of Scanguards' human employees were ever given any inkling of the vampires among their midst. It was safest that way. In emergency situations, they had all driven one of the blackout vans themselves, but in general, it was safer to let a human driver take over.

Nina turned to leave, but stopped as if she'd forgotten something. "And, could somebody please make that dog out there stop barking. It's getting on Delilah's nerves."

Too engrossed in their discussions, Zane hadn't paid any notice to the sounds outside the house. Now he exchanged a look with Gabriel. Could they be so fortunate?

12

The smell of human food was the first thing Yvette sensed when the darkness lifted. Her body felt as if she'd been beaten to a pulp and then jammed into a blender. What the hell had happened to her? Had the witch tortured her like she'd tortured Haven? At the thought of him, she reared up from her supine position and opened her eyes.

She was still in the same room as before, and she was on something soft: a cot. Her eyes instantly sought out Kimberly. Yvette breathed a sigh of relief when she saw her lying on an identical cot next to her, curled up, her eyes closed. On the makeshift bed farthest from her, Wesley was slumbering as well.

She reached out to Kimberly, wanting to reassure herself that she was okay and that the witch hadn't hurt her.

"She's okay," Haven's quiet voice came from the floor. Her eyes snapped in his direction. She watched him as he rose and sat down at the foot of her cot.

"Did the witch—"

He shook his head before she could finish the question. "Kimberly was smarter than I and didn't resist. She's sleeping now." He glanced over to her cot, and Yvette followed his look.

"We all ate. They were tired. But I wanted to make sure you were all right." His eyes scanned her, and she felt oddly aware of her body and the black dress which made her look far more feminine than she was used to.

"What happened?"

Haven gave her an apologetic look. "Do you remember that you gave me your blood?"

Her heart made an excited flip. How could she forget? When he'd suckled from her wrist, she'd felt nearly delirious. She'd never before felt the kind of pleasure that had coursed through her body. "Are you healed?"

Haven smiled and stretched out his arms, presenting his still-naked chest and stomach to her. It looked perfect, unmarred. And sexier than before. The man had a seriously ripped body made for sin.

"You tell me."

"You look . . . good."

When he dropped his arms to his side, his face took on a serious look. "I took too much. You passed out."

"Well, I guess I'm lucky you guys didn't stake me while you had the chance."

Haven nudged closer, casting a quick sideways glance at Kimberly and Wesley, who were still sleeping. "Is that what you think I'd do after you helped me?" he asked through clenched teeth. "That's how low your opinion of me is?"

Yvette glared back at him but kept her voice down. "What do you expect? You kidnapped me, and you made no secret of your hatred for my species."

"And despite the fact that you knew that, you helped me. Why?" His blue eyes bored into her, probing, searching.

"A temporary moment of weakness. Don't worry, it won't happen again," she spat. Ungrateful bastard. Maybe she should have let him suffer.

"Because I won't let you do it again."

Yvette narrowed her eyes. "I see. Feeling dirty because you have vampire blood in your veins now?" How dare he look down at her gift! No vampire gave his blood to just anybody. It was a treasure to be protected. She for one had never shared her blood with anybody— neither during sex, nor to heal.

"No," he hissed and grabbed her upper arms, pressing her back against the wall. "I won't let you put yourself in danger like that anymore. You passed out—because I took too much. You should have stopped me before I weakened you like that."

He was concerned for her health? What the hell was going on? Had she woken up in some alternate reality? "It's none of your business what I do."

"It is when you endanger yourself. We all have to be strong together, or we'll never get out of here. And that includes you. I got you into this mess."

"No need to remind me." Her sarcastic remark didn't even seem to reach him.

"I'll get us out of this."

"Oh, really? And how are you planning that? By playing Rambo? Or MacGyver? Pathetic." What was it with men always having to play the big hero who saved the damsel in distress? Maybe that worked in the movies, but it didn't work here. "I'm stronger than you, so don't give me this crap."

He pressed her harder against the wall, and she could have pushed him away—really, she could, even in her somewhat exhausted state. But something made her remain in his restraints—maybe because he smelled so intoxicating, or maybe because her skin sizzled pleasantly where his fingers dug into her arms.

"You might be stronger when you're well-fed, but right now, you're running on empty."

His smug voice did nothing to make her feel less pissed off with him. Yvette opened her mouth to protest, but he gave a quick shake of his head.

"Don't even deny it. You were hungry even before you gave me your blood. How stupid do you think I am? I've drained you. If anything, you're going to get weaker over the next hours. And we both know that the witch isn't going to bring in a supply of blood for you. She has no interest in you staying alive. And then what?"

Haven's eyes held a challenge, but she couldn't figure out what it was for. Was he accusing her that she would attack one of them as soon as her hunger became too unbearable? "I won't attack any of you, and certainly not Kimberly. She's my charge. I have a duty to her."

"How can you be so sure? When your hunger gets too great, you won't know what you're doing. You'll fall into bloodlust."

So he knew about that. Still, she had to deny it. She pushed against him and shook her head. "No."

"I have a proposition for you."

Yvette raised her chin and leveled a glare at him. What could he possibly do to avoid what she knew would happen in a few hours? "What proposition?"

"You'll feed from me. Now. While the others are sleeping. Nobody needs to know."

The vampire hunter was offering his blood? "But—"

"I ate plenty of food just now. I'm well-fed and healthy again, thanks to you. Now it's time for you to get your strength back. *Quid pro quo.*"

Yvette searched his eyes to understand why he extended this offer. "Why?"

He looked away, avoiding her scrutinizing look. "I hate owing anybody anything, least of all a vampire."

"You don't owe me anything." She locked her jaw, unwilling to accept the crumbs he was offering. She had her pride. "Keep your blood. I don't need it."

"You don't have a choice in this." Haven pushed his body closer to hers.

Yvette shook off his arms. "What are you gonna do? Force me?"

He gave her a wicked grin, and in that moment she knew she'd already lost the battle. "Something like that." Then he gripped her wrists and held them against the wall. When he tilted his head to the side and moved his neck within striking distance of her lips, she took in his drugging scent: clean, male sweat, and the smell of bergamot.

"I'll punch your pretty face to purée," she warned him while trying to stop her fangs from lengthening. It was as impossible as stopping the sun from rising.

"Afterwards," he promised as if he didn't take her seriously.

"You, you—"

His neck connected with her lips as he pressed against her. "You can smell my blood already, can't you?" It wasn't fair that he baited her like that, that he dangled the most enticing scent in front of her twitching nose. "And you're hungry. I won't fight you. Just bite."

Haven knew he'd gone completely crazy, but he also knew this was the only way. She needed to feed and regain her strength, and rather than let her go berserk and attack one of them in a frenzy of bloodlust— something he'd seen from another vampire before; it was terrifying and nearly impossible to stop—he was prepared to take one for the team. Wesley would never agree to it, and Kimberly shouldn't be subjected to such gore. If anybody could get through this relatively unscathed, it was Haven.

He wasn't afraid of the pain. Compared to what Bess had done to him, a bite would barely register more painful than a well-placed punch by a drunken convict. And now that he knew that her bite wouldn't turn him into a vampire, he was willing to make this sacrifice. He owed her that much. But after that, they'd be even. After that, he could go back and hate her with all the pain that he had buried in his heart. She was still a vampire, and a vampire was responsible for the murder of his mother and kidnapping of his sister. A vampire would pay for it.

But for now, he had to pay his debt to her. Yvette had saved him, and it was only right that he'd do the same. And that was the only reason why he was willing to go against his deepest beliefs and give her what she needed.

"Bite me," he repeated. "Before I change my mind."

Her lips pressed against his skin. Then her tongue licked over him. What the—

But he couldn't voice his question, because the next thing he felt was her sharp fangs breaking through his skin and sink into his neck. There was no pain; it was as if the area had been numbed beforehand. Was that why she'd licked him?

Before he could draw any conclusions, Haven's train of thought was suddenly blown off track by the delicious sensations coursing through his body. He'd expected it to hurt, at least a little. At the very least, he'd expected it to be unpleasant, something to endure for the greater good. He'd never in his wildest dreams imagined a vampire's bite to be arousing.

More than that: it was the most erotic situation he'd ever found himself in. Yvette's bite was a full-on assault on all his senses, and his body reacted the only way it could: with a raging hard-on. Her pull on his vein was more passionate than any kiss he'd ever shared with a woman, her body so close to his, he could feel her rapid heartbeat and her heat. The familiar scent of oranges wafted into his nose, and before he knew what he was doing, he buried his hand in her hair and cupped the back of her head to hold her closer.

His other hand snaked around her back and connected with her naked skin. A startled gasp came from her when he drew her into his embrace, but she didn't release her hold on his neck. She continued sucking him greedily, and he had no intention of stopping her. On the contrary, he wanted her to continue.

Haven shifted, trying to find a more comfortable position for his cock—which had grown to massive proportions and was biting into the zipper of his tuxedo pants. Had he worn his tighter-fitting pants, the fabric along the zipper would have already burst under the pressure. Luckily, the rented pants provided a little more space—for how long, he wasn't sure.

His hand roamed over her naked back, grateful that she wore the backless black dress rather than something else. It allowed him to explore her and relish her soft skin. She was hot-blooded, even hotter now than he'd noticed before. Was she enjoying this as much as he was?

When he let his fingers dance along her torso where her naked skin met the fabric of her dress, a moan dislodged from her chest, and her hand came up. Was she going to stop him? But instead of her hand swatting his away, she touched his chest and ran her fingers over the planes of his muscles.

Haven sucked in a deep breath. Her touch, combined with the soft pull on his vein spiked his lust and made him want to throw her down on the cot and bury himself in her to the hilt. "Fuck, baby," he mumbled and slid his thumb under the fabric of her dress, caressing the underside of one breast.

Yvette's nails dug into his chest, but he welcomed the pain, realizing it was the only thing that kept him from ripping the clothes off her body and fucking her senseless. The only thing that left him with any semblance of coherence. As if she knew what she was doing to him and enjoyed her power over him, her other hand went to the waistband of his pants and slid down along the zipper, cupping his straining shaft in her palm.

He let out an involuntary moan and slid his hand further under her dress until he could cup her braless breast. The firm globe lay heavily in his hand, which it filled perfectly. He squeezed it and ran his thumb over her hard nipple.

Yvette squeezed his cock in response, and he lost all control. In the next instant, he tugged on her hair, and she released his neck, licking over the incisions before she severed the contact. When his gaze collided with hers, her eyes were dark with passion and her lips swollen, more plump than before—and far more kissable than he ever could have imagined.

Without thinking, Haven pulled her face to him and pressed his mouth to hers. Her lips parted on a sigh, and he swept his tongue inside. He tried to fight the sensations her body unleashed in him and tried to think of something—anything!—that would distract him from the pliable female in his arms. Even reminding himself that she was a vampire and his enemy didn't diminish the passion in his kiss.

Realizing how useless it was to fight against a tide he could neither stop nor control, he gave up his struggle and explored her wet cavern. Mmm . . . this woman could kiss. Somehow he'd known that. Somehow he'd sensed it when he'd first seen her at the premier party. She knew it too. Her confident response to him said as much. Each of his strokes was countered with one of hers, more demanding and more urgent than the last, as if to challenge him. And hadn't she issued a challenge at that party? Hadn't she openly challenged him and dared him to prove he had what it took to satisfy a woman like her?

He couldn't let this challenge expire unmet. No woman would best him—least of all a vampire female. He'd show her that she couldn't lead him around by his nose. No, he'd show her who was wearing the pants, even if those pants were getting increasingly too tight.

Accepting her challenge, he kneaded her breast more ferociously, then took the hard little nipple between his thumb and forefinger and tugged. Her animalistic moan stopped short in his mouth where he captured it and swallowed it down into his body. He sparred with her tongue as if dueling with a warrior, because that's what she was: a warrior who was fighting him, challenging him; not to stop, but to continue his assault on her curves.

Yvette's curves were worth assaulting. Feminine, despite her toned muscles, and covered with soft, satiny skin, her body's curves fit to his palms as if they were custom made just for him. To feel her ample tit in his hand and stroke her until she moaned uncontrollably was better than anything else he'd felt in a long while. With every moan, his own body heated, his cock throbbing and begging for release.

Haven angled his head to get an even deeper connection, his body urging him to get more of her, to mark her, brand her. To show her that he could give her what she needed, that he was more than man enough to drive her to ecstasy.

One of her hands was still digging into his chest, but the other one moved back to his groin. When it connected with his cock, stroking along his hard length, he groaned. Under his mouth, her lips curled up in a smile.

The wicked little bitch!

She was trying to get him to lose control. But he wouldn't allow it. Not before he could turn her brain into mush and make her forget everything except his touch and his kiss. Trying hard to ignore her caressing hand, he gave her nipple another tug, this time harder. Then he ripped his mouth from hers and lowered his head.

He found her breast through the fabric of her dress and licked over the silk. If it had been white, he'd be able to see her nipple now, but the black fabric didn't give away her womanly secrets. Yet, the effect wasn't lost on her as evidenced by her strangled moan. He repeated his action, licking her hard nipple again and noticed how her hold on his cock loosened. He was winning the battle. Soon, she would submit to him, and he'd be calling the shots.

Yvette couldn't take much more of his passionate caresses. His kiss had been numbing, blocking out everything in the room so she could only sense him and his desire. She'd never responded to a man this openly. She'd always been in control of every situation. When she took her pleasure, it was always on her terms. And she would be the one to set the pace and decide how and when she allowed a man to pleasure her.

This was different. Haven was different.

He didn't ask; he just took. He took, and by taking, he gave her body glimpses of pleasure she had buried deep inside her. Pleasure she hadn't allowed herself to feel for fear she would lose herself, her identity, her heart. Her response to him frightened her, and she should have pushed him away instantly, but his touch was addictive. Like a junkie, she craved more.

Moving her hand to his shoulder, she relished the feel of his sculptured chest and abs, but she wanted—*needed*—him nearer. She pulled him closer to her and felt him suck her breast through her dress.

It wouldn't do. She needed more. She needed him closer, skin on skin. Heartbeat to heartbeat. When his teeth grazed her nipple, she exhaled sharply. A stream of lava raced down her core and into her clit, the liquid heat searing her from the inside. She needed something to ease the need it caused in her. The need to have him, consume him, taste him.

"More," she begged, barely recognizing her own hoarse voice. What had she turned into? What had *he* turned her into?

As if he knew what she needed, his hand slipped to her thigh where her dress had already ridden up. His fingers trailed along her naked skin and moved upwards until they reached her damp panties. One finger rubbed against her, and she let out a relieved sigh. Yes, that was better, so much better. He would take away the ache and make her feel normal again.

"Yes," she encouraged him and dropped her head back against the wall, her neck unable to support the weight any longer. Her lids were too heavy to keep open.

Yvette held her breath as Haven eased his finger underneath the thin fabric and stroked against her wet flesh.

"What the fuck?"

Her entire body stiffened, and her eyes flew open, staring at Haven. But his face was turned to the side, his hands already retreating from her body. She now realized that he wasn't the one who'd spoken.

Her eyes followed his gaze, landing on Wesley, who stood only a few feet away from them, grimacing in disgust. She'd completely forgotten everything around her.

Haven leapt up from the cot, the massive bulge in his pants still making a prominent statement, one his brother didn't miss. Wesley's lips curled downwards. "You, of all people? How could you?"

"Stay out of it, Wes!"

But Wesley couldn't be stopped. He crossed the distance between him and his brother, almost bumping into him.

"You idiot! Don't you see she's manipulating you?" Wesley's disdain for vampires fairly dripped from his voice, but it wasn't his tone that got Yvette's hackles up. It was the words he uttered next. "She's using you."

Yvette jumped up, the wet fabric chafing against her nipple, reminding her all too painfully of Haven's touch. Damn, she'd been stupid to let herself be lulled into a false sense of security with him. He hated vampires just as much as his brother did. "Get your facts straight, Wesley. If anybody is using anyone then it's your brother."

Haven turned and shot her an acid look. "Look who's changing her tune. A minute ago you couldn't get enough of my blood, and now I'm the one who's using you?"

"She bit you?" Wesley hissed and pulled his stake from his jacket pocket.

"He offered it!" Yvette yelled and glared at Haven. "In fact, he forced me to bite him, because he didn't think I could restrain myself from attacking any of you."

Wesley gave his brother an incredulous look. "You gave her your blood? Freely? Who are you? What the hell happened to my brother?"

"Shut up, Wes! If it wasn't for your stupidity, we wouldn't be in this situation in the first place."

"Oh, now it's my fault that you let her bite you?"

"That's not what I said! For once, would you please act rationally? Or do I constantly have to dig you out of every mess you get into?"

"So that's what this is about! Go ahead, blame me for everything! Why did you even try to rescue me if you hate me so much?"

Yvette heard the cracking in Wesley's voice and recognized the strain he was under. He wouldn't last much longer.

"I don't hate you!"

"Yes, you do. You hate me because I couldn't keep Katie safe." A long, tense moment passed between the brothers where none of them spoke. Only the creaking of the third cot could be heard, indicating that Kimberly had been awakened by their heated words. Yvette glanced in her direction and noted the confused look on her face, but the girl said nothing.

Then Wesley looked at Yvette and swept an assessing glance over her body. "God, Haven, you want her? How can you do this when she represents everything we despise?"

"I don't want her." Haven's harshly spoken words stung. Even though Yvette knew that she wanted nothing from him, the rejection still hurt her ego.

"Then how do you explain what I just saw? You were two minutes away from fucking her."

Wesley's assessment couldn't have been more accurate. Another minute or two of Haven's hands on her, and she would have spread her legs for him, not giving a damn about who was watching. Hell, she had completely forgotten where they were.

Haven ran his hand through his thick hair, utter confusion and plain regret flashing over his features. "I don't understand what got into me."

Yvette closed her eyes for a moment. A feeding could bring on instant arousal in both the donor and the vampire who was feeding from him. "Wesley, you shouldn't blame your brother. It's not his fault. It was merely the side effect of feeding."

"Side effect?" Haven lashed a glare at her.

Yvette tried to remain unaffected by the suspicion in his voice, steeling herself for his next reaction. "For a self-proclaimed vampire hunter, you know precious little about us."

"Spit it out, Yvette." His voice was full of venom now. The passionate man who'd driven her wild had vanished into thin air.

She crossed her arms over her chest and widened her stance, realizing too late that her arms created a shelf on which her breasts rose unimpeded and were presented as if she was offering them to him. Which of course she wasn't! But it was too late to change her action, otherwise she would draw needless attention to them. When she looked back at Haven, she realized it was for naught anyway: his gaze had already snapped to her breasts, before he forced it back up to her face.

There were times when she wished she were less endowed. Now was one of those moments.

Yvette cleared her throat. "A vampire's bite induces sexual arousal in the host as well as the vampire."

"Ah, shit!"

She could only echo the sentiment, but for other reasons. While Haven clearly felt deceived by her, Yvette felt regret that the arousal hadn't been real. He'd merely reacted to her because of her bite, not because he was attracted to her—whereas her own arousal, while heightened by the bite, had been real. She still remembered the times she'd fed from humans directly—before she'd started on bottled blood—and while she'd sensed the arousal that came during the feeding, she'd never felt anything of this magnitude.

She'd always been able to control it and rein it in. This time she hadn't. This time, she'd been unable to control the lust; instead, *it* had controlled *her* and whipped her into an uncontrolled frenzy. All she'd been able to think of was that she wanted to feel him inside her. No other thought beyond that had existed.

"You used me," Haven mumbled, his expression a mix of humiliation and regret. "If you ever touch me again, I'll stake you."

Yvette turned away from him, unable to continue looking into his eyes. He hated her. And she knew she had to hate him too. And she would do her best to make sure she succeeded in squashing those pesky little tendrils of sensations that seemed to grow inside her, wanting to morph into feelings and emotions. She wouldn't allow it. Haven was her enemy. She would treat him as such.

13

The dog that had barked outside of Samson's house hadn't been Yvette's, and Zane's hope had deflated quickly. Nobody knew where the beast that had been following Yvette could have gone to. For now, it was a dead end. Luckily, they had other avenues to explore.

Thanks to the tracking device, the limousine that had carried Yvette and Kimberly had been found in the Outer Richmond neighborhood of San Francisco, a sleepy residential area. It was clear that the car had been dumped there. Amaury was currently going through it for any traces of Yvette and Kimberly that might tell them what had happened and where they could be. Luckily, no blood of either one of them had been found.

Zane glared at the driver of the limousine as he pressed him against the car behind him. It was still daylight, but Zane had one of the human Scanguards employees drive him to the house in the outskirts of San Francisco where the man lived. He'd been hiding at home, pretending not to be there, but the human driver had broken into the house, overpowered the occupant, and locked him in a supply cupboard in the garage before driving the blackout van inside so Zane could exit securely.

The large garage appeared to be used for illegal purposes; all windows were boarded up so the neighbors couldn't see what activities were performed inside.

Zane looked at the trembling man again and repeated his question. "Why did you abandon the car and your passengers?"

The man's eyes darted nervously in all directions, fear and mistrust written in their depths. "No can be involve in this." His speech was heavily accented, hinting at Eastern European roots.

"In what?"

"Police. No involve."

Zane grabbed him by the collar of his shirt and inhaled the man's sweat. It reeked of fear. He abhorred the stench. "I'm not the police. I'm worse."

"INS?" he whispered.

"INS?" Zane wrinkled his forehead. The man was afraid of Immigration and that's why he'd run off without notifying anybody? How pathetic. "Listen, I don't care if you have a visa or not, if you're illegal or not. Hell, I don't even care if you pay your taxes. All I want to know is what happened to my friends. Do you get that?"

The man swallowed hard and nodded, his eyes still wide and round as saucers. "You no tell Immigration?"

For an answer, Zane gave the man a brief, rough shake. "Now talk."

"Some guy, he attack them just when they reach limo. I get out and want help, but Miss Yvette, she just going at him, like she some Ninja fighter or something. So I figure she handle him. And it look like she did. But then some strange smoke come, you know, *puff*" —He placed his hands in front of his face and made a theatrical expanding movement with his hands— "and she just collapse."

Zane listened intently. Smoke? "What kind of smoke? Was there a fire?"

"No fire. Was weird. Smoke, no fire. Like maybe what have in nightclub to make fog. Pink color. You know?"

Damn, that sounded like something he just didn't want to deal with. Smoke without a fire was an odd thing, and what the driver described sounded more and more like the kind of smoke that was coming from a witch's kitchen. "Did you get a good look at the guy who attacked them?"

He nodded. "Yes. Tall, big muscle."

That wasn't enough to go by. But Zane knew a surefire way to find out what the guy looked like. "You're coming with me."

"No, I told everything I know." The man struggled against his hold, but it was no more effective than the pathetic struggles of a mouse against a cat.

Zane dragged his victim to the blackout van and opened the door, shoving the man inside despite his protests.

"Get us to Gabriel's house. And make it quick," he ordered his driver and slammed the door shut, embracing the darkness inside the van as he blocked out the scared whimpers of the limo driver.

How Zane hated fearful people—wimps, cowards, chickens, all of them. As if they knew of true fear, true horror. He'd seen it all. He'd lived through it and come out the other side: shattered, broken, but still alive. His heart had died a hundred deaths, but his body was stronger than ever. Zane feared nothing now. Maybe that's why he despised the stink of it so much. And he didn't care if the limo driver feared him now and was afraid of what might happen to him. It didn't matter, not when he knew that the man's memories could help them find Yvette.

His family was all that mattered to him. And if the illegal limo driver could provide them with the information they sought, maybe Zane would even wipe his memory of the events from his mind. If he felt charitable after all was said and done.

By the time they reached Gabriel's house and had pulled into the garage so Zane could safely exit the van with his captive, his mind had somewhat calmed. He knew that Gabriel would be able to extract whatever they needed from the man. Zane envied his boss for his gift— Gabriel could unlock memories—and for that matter, he envied all those colleagues who possessed one, whereas he seemed to be entirely without any special abilities, unless inflicting pain could be called a gift. Even Zane doubted that.

Without delay, he hauled the man upstairs and brought him to Gabriel's office, where his boss was pacing. Gabriel instantly turned to his guests.

"Zane, who's this?"

"The limo driver. He saw the attack on Yvette and Kimberly." Zane didn't want to waste time on relaying what the driver had told him. "He knows what the attacker looks like. It's in his memories." He gave his boss a pointed look.

Gabriel held his eyes for a long while, then nodded. "This is an emergency. We need to know."

Zane understood Gabriel instantly: Gabriel never used his special gift of prying into other people's memories unless it was absolutely necessary, believing that everybody had a right to privacy.

Gabriel looked at the man and gestured to the chair. "Sit. You might as well be comfortable."

"What are you going to doi to me?" Panic was evident in the man's voice and in the way he tried to pull away from Gabriel when he approached. His boss's gruesome scar could be a bit of a turn-off, particularly when it appeared to throb like it did now. Not that the man had any idea that he needn't fear the scarred vampire, whose strong ethics forbade him to harm others.

"It won't hurt, I promise you." Gabriel laid his hands on the man's shoulders and pressed him into the chair. "It won't take long." Then he closed his eyes and fell silent.

The driver's eyes darted between him and Zane, his shoulders hunched, his breathing erratic. Zane could sense how the driver's heartbeat increased, could smell the terror in the sour-sharp rankness of his sweat. Despite his attempt to get out of the chair, he couldn't manage it: Gabriel's hands on his shoulders still pinned him down effortlessly.

Outwardly, nobody could see what Gabriel was doing, but Zane knew how his boss's gift worked. He would slip into the person's mind by bringing himself to the same wavelength, then travel back in the memory bank to the place of the event he was looking for. Once there, the event would play out before him, and it would be as if he saw it through his own eyes in the exact same way as the driver had.

A couple of minutes into the silence, Gabriel opened his eyes and looked straight at Zane. "Witchcraft. Fuck!"

Zane nodded. He'd guessed as much. "Do we need Francine?"

Gabriel gave him a long look, warring emotions dancing on his face. "Unfortunately, yes. If I only knew what she'll take for her help *this* time. I wish the woman took cash."

Zane shrugged. Favors were returned with favors. Because of their longevity, most vampires had more money than they knew what to do with. Money in the end meant very little. Favors were a whole other currency and their world thrived on them. It could be a bitch at times, but it also made you think twice about when to ask someone for a favor.

14

"Why is your hair long?"

Yvette turned at Kimberly's question and watched her tuck her legs underneath her as she sat on her cot. She briefly glanced in Haven's direction. He and his brother were standing in the opposite corner of the room, talking quietly; nevertheless, Haven looked at her from under his long dark lashes. A man shouldn't be allowed to have such sultry-looking eyelashes. With a deliberate jerk of her shoulder, she turned back to Kimberly.

"It grows while I sleep."

Kimberly pursed her lips. "So does mine, but not *twelve inches* in one night."

Yvette let out a long breath, not really interested in going into the reasons for her daily hair cut, but in the interest of keeping her charge at ease, she'd just have to make small talk. "It grows back to the length it was when I was turned. And since I don't like it long, I cut it every day."

"Wow." Kimberly looked at her in fascination. "But why don't you like it long anymore? It's pretty."

Yvette couldn't suppress the bitter smile that crossed her lips. The long hair reminded her of the woman she'd been fifty years ago: the woman, who couldn't make her husband happy, couldn't give him the one thing he wanted. The child he craved. She didn't want to remember those days. Nor was she in the mood to lay herself bare to a stranger. Hell, not even her friends and colleagues at Scanguards knew. "I prefer it short."

"So . . . what's it like to be a vampire?"

Yvette closed her eyes for a moment. Where would she even start? So much was different, yet so much was the same. She had feelings and desires just like a human, yet they were amplified, making unfulfilled desires and unrequited feelings harder to bear and impossible to ignore.

She gave a shrug, unable to answer the question without revealing things she didn't want to share.

"Is it true that you bite people and hurt them?"

What was this? Twenty questions?

From the corner of her eye, Yvette noticed how Haven's head turned toward them. For once, she was grateful for her long hair and deliberately allowed it to fall around her like a curtain, blocking out his seemingly casual glance. Then she forced a smile for Kimberly's sake. "No. I don't hurt people. Hell, I don't even bite people. I drink bottled blood."

The girl peeked toward the brothers, then back to her. She dropped her voice when she continued, "But you bit him, didn't you?" Her eyes darted to the side to indicate who she meant by *him*. Not that it was necessary. "I guess he deserved it."

Yvette gave her a stunned look.

"For kidnapping us, I mean. I would hurt him too if I could."

"Kimberly, a vampire's bite doesn't hurt. It's . . . uh, pleasant."

"Oh," Kimberly said and blushed like a little schoolgirl.

A snort from the corner behind her told her that Haven's hearing was better than she'd thought and that he didn't want to admit just how *pleasant* it had been. Yvette tried to block him out, but his presence was too overwhelming. In fact, something didn't feel right at all. Her senses seemed to be in hyperdrive, now that she'd fed and seemed to have fully recovered from the witch's potion. And not just that—she smelled things that didn't seem possible.

Yvette pulled forward a bit. Now that she was closer to the girl, she picked up the scent of something that hadn't been there earlier: an underlying scent of witch, almost as if the witch had rubbed herself all over the girl . . .

Without thinking, she snatched Kimberly's arm and led it to her nose, sniffing.

The girl let out a gasp. "What are you doing?"

Before she could assure Kimberly that she wasn't going to hurt her, Haven lunged for her. Yvette jumped up from the bed and swiveled on her heels to fend him off before he could grab her. In the split second before he reached her, her mind crazily compared his rush to a charging bull—hell, she could feel faint impact tremors through the floor! Nah, nothing subtle about him—and then he was upon her.

"My blood didn't satisfy you? Now you want hers too?" He looked furious, his eyes wide and glaring, the cords in his neck tense . . . He looked on the verge of delivering a deadly blow.

"I wasn't attacking her." Yvette pushed against him, making him tumble toward the wall behind him. "You sure jump to conclusions pretty fast."

Wesley rushed to his brother's side, stake at the ready. "Don't touch him, you bitch!"

Yvette rolled her eyes.

"I can handle this, Wes," Haven sniped at his brother, got to his feet and marched toward Yvette again, giving his brother a quick sideways glance. "You know what we've discussed."

Oh, she'd heard them talking about how to escape. Stupid ideas, all of them: trying to rush the witch the next time she brought them food. And they wanted Yvette to help them—which was the only reason Wes had agreed to let her live. For now. As if their plan was going to work. All they'd get was another blast of energy.

Yvette was going to stick with her own plan. She had to outwit the witch. Having mulled it over in her head, she was pretty sure that Bess, as she'd heard Haven call her, had to be within her own wards to exert her powers on them. Unfortunately, this eliminated the idea of attacking her while she was in the same room with them because, while within the wards, she'd be able to counterattack. Those attempts would fail. There had to be another way. Only an attack from the outside would work.

"By the way, none of your escape ideas will work," Yvette said casually.

Haven narrowed his eyes at her. "And what do you suggest instead?"

"I, for one, will wait for my colleagues to rescue me." It was the only feasible plan. But Yvette would have to try to warn them about the wards and the kind of powers the witch possessed, so they'd be prepared.

"What colleagues?"

"Scanguards. Ever heard of them? I thought you did your homework before you kidnapped us. Scanguards has the best bodyguards in this country. And many of them are just like me: vampires. A hard bunch to beat."

Haven's eyes flashed in surprise. "What makes you think those heartless creatures will be coming for you?"

The jab hurt. Her friends weren't heartless. Yvette gave an unladylike snort. "Ever heard of the Musketeers? 'All for one, one for all'? That's just how it is among our kind. They'll come." The knowledge gave her strength.

"Well, I'm not waiting for a gang of *vampires* to storm in here— what the fuck do you think we are, suicidal?" Wesley yelled.

Haven looked at her, shaking his head, his body moving toward her. "I've gotta agree with my brother on that one." He was only a few feet from her now. Was he thinking he could overpower her? Distract her by talking, then jump on her? Did he still think she was trying to harm Kimberly?

"Another step closer, and your brother will have to scrape what's left of you off the walls," she warned Haven. Yvette noticed a barely perceivable flinch go through him, and he did a good job at trying to disguise the fact that her words were getting to him. With the way he'd treated her earlier, there was no way she'd walk on eggshells around him. He'd chosen to be hostile, and she was simply reacting to it.

"As if I wanted to get any closer." Despite his words, his tone wasn't as cold as she'd expected. Somehow, hidden in those eight words was a good dose of pent-up emotions. His problem, not hers, she told herself.

"If it's not my body you want, what then?"

"See how she's trying to manipulate you again?" Wesley cut in and took a step forward.

Never taking her eyes off Haven, or moving her head a fraction of an inch, she issued her warning, "If your kid brother does anything stupid, he'll pay for it."

"And if you touch Kimberly again and try to hurt her, then *you*'ll pay for it," the stupid pup replied.

Yvette blinked twice. That's how the latest confrontation had started. She'd touched Kimberly's arm and smelled her skin, then Haven had interrupted her, but now that she was back on the subject, she remembered what she'd wanted to ask Kimberly.

"Kimberly," she called out without letting the two brothers out of her sight.

"What?"

"Tell me what the witch did to you."

"What's that got to do with you trying to attack her?" Haven asked.

"Everything." She didn't even try to contradict him. What was the point? He wouldn't listen. He'd already made up his mind about her. To him she was a bloodthirsty killer with no regard for the feelings of others. His assumption couldn't be further from the truth.

"If you're trying to make excuses—"

"Kimberly stinks of witch." Yvette took in a deep breath, her nostrils flaring in the direction of the brothers. Yes, the stench was definitely coming from their bodies too. It wasn't just something that hung in the air because the witch had been here. "And so do you two."

Being accused of smelling like a witch was the last thing Haven had expected coming out of Yvette's mouth. Not that being called a witch was an insult per se, but the way she expelled the word "witch" from her mouth, made it sound like a four-letter word.

"What's your point?" he hissed, unable to keep his riled-up emotions under control. Yvette got under his skin without even trying very hard. Just keeping away from her and not throwing her onto the nearest flat surface cost him all the strength he had left. And his brother was giving him shit about it. The boner he'd sported earlier hadn't escaped Wesley, who hadn't missed the opportunity to use the knowledge as payback for all the times Haven had accused him of thinking with his dick.

How could he have let himself go like that when Yvette had fed from him? And why the fuck had she not warned him about the side effect it would have? Was she enjoying his humiliation that much?

"The point is the three of you smell like witches *now*. It's faint, but it's there."

Wesley shook his head. "That's bullshit. You're just trying to distract us."

Yvette cut him an annoyed glance, giving Haven a chance to let his eyes rest on her beautiful face. Even angry, she looked sexy.

"To do what?" With a speed so fast Haven's eyes could barely process it, she charged at Wesley and pinned him against the wall. "Listen to me, you arrogant little prick. If I wanted you—or *anybody*— in this room dead, it would have already happened." Her head snapped to the side as she saw Haven approach. "I'm not a killer." Yvette paused and locked eyes with him, and damn it if he didn't know in that instant that she was telling the truth. "Not unless I'm forced to. So don't try my patience."

The slight quiver in her voice was barely audible, but Haven noticed it nevertheless. Was she at her breaking point?

Yvette released Wesley and calmly walked back to where Kimberly was still sitting, looking a little bit shell-shocked.

"Are you okay?" she asked the girl.

Kimberly just gave her a blank stare. "Let me see: I'm locked up with two strange men, one of which kidnapped me; all three of you are constantly fighting; the room is protected by a witch, who's been trying to get into my head; my bodyguard turns out to be a vampire, and now you're telling me I smell like a witch. No, Yvette, I'm not okay," she finished on a sob.

Ready to interfere if necessary, Haven watched Yvette sit down next to her and pull her into an embrace, remembering all too well how comforting her arms could be. "Shh, kiddo, everything will be okay. I promise you." She patted Kimberly's back and stroked her hand over the girl's hair as the tears flowed.

Haven stared at Yvette. He hadn't expected her to show compassion and to comfort Kimberly. Could a vampire feel emotions like these? Were her actions genuine, or was she merely pretending for the girl's benefit?

Haven glanced at Kimberly, feeling sorry for her. She was an innocent, and he was to blame for the predicament she was in. He wanted to reach out to her and help somehow. It was only when Yvette shot him a warning glance that he realized he was approaching them. He nodded to Yvette, trying to indicate that he'd finally understood that she wouldn't hurt her charge.

"I want to go home," Kimberly wailed.

"I know you do. Only a few more hours. Once it's dark again, my colleagues will be here—I know it. They'll find us."

Haven's eyes connected with hers. "How can you be so sure about that?"

"They're my family. Wouldn't you risk everything for your family?" she challenged him.

He tried to hide the pain that sliced through him at the memories. Only half of his family was still left, and if he didn't do something soon, the other half would be gone.

"So your suggestion is we wait for them to free us?" Haven asked. How could she be so passive? He'd seen her fight before and realized she was fearless. What had her sitting back now?

"Like sitting ducks? Stupid! We should make a break for it now," Wesley interrupted, but his voice was calmer now, not as heated as before. He glanced at Haven then back at Yvette.

"Impossible," Yvette claimed. "Don't you think I would have already tried if I could? We can't get past her protective wards. Not even my strength let me kick down the door or break through the boarded-up window. Witchcraft is a bitch. And I'm not messing with it. My colleagues will have to attack her from the outside. It's the only way."

"What guarantee do we have that your vampire friends won't kill us? It can't have escaped your attention that we have no qualms about killing any of your kind." Wesley squared his shoulders.

"Wes!" Haven chastised, suddenly uncomfortable with laying bare his past in front of Yvette.

But Wesley didn't relent. "It's true. Let's not beat about the bush. Just because you're developing scruples."

Which was true. He had scruples, and they built with every minute he spent in Yvette's company. She wasn't at all what he'd known vampires to be. Her fierce loyalty to Kimberly and her continued assurances that she would protect her were facets of Yvette's personality that he couldn't help but admire. The tenderness with which she cradled her charge to give her comfort and allowed her to cry on her shoulder was the last thing he'd expected from a vampire. Yet it was tenderness and compassion he saw in Yvette. Bundled with her strength and determination, she gave off the air of a mother protecting her young.

"They won't hurt you if you don't try to hurt them. But I have to warn you: we have to make sure they know you're no danger to them; otherwise, they'll defend themselves. And considering that you smell like witches, they'll see you as the enemy."

There it was again, her claim that they were witches. "You must be mistaken. Maybe you smell the witch out there. But as I told you earlier, Wes and I never inherited our mother's powers. We're not witches."

Yvette shook her head. "That's impossible; it never skips a generation. And for not even one of the two children of a witch to inherit her powers? That can't be right."

Wes shuffled closer. "Maybe Katie inherited Mom's powers."

"Katie?" Yvette asked.

"Our sister," Haven explained, "the one who was kidnapped by a vampire."

"And never seen again," Wesley added.

Yvette gave him a look full of compassion. "I'm sorry. No wonder you hate us so much."

"It was a long time ago, but I remember it like yesterday." Haven caught Yvette's expectant look. It encouraged him to go on. "Mom was attacked in her own kitchen one night. I tried to help her, but I wasn't strong enough. I was just a kid. The vampire told her she had to give one of us up. I didn't understand at first what that meant, but when he took Katie after he'd killed Mom, I knew. He'd said that he only needed one of the three of us. Just one. And Katie was the easiest to take."

It was still difficult to talk about it. Haven closed his eyes for a moment and took a few steadying breaths. Would Yvette understand now that whatever attraction was between them could never go any further? That he couldn't soil his mother's and sister's memory by getting involved with a vampire?

"Three," Yvette whispered. "Three." Realization bloomed in her eyes as pieces of the puzzle suddenly seemed to click into place. Haven opened his eyes and stared at her. She grabbed Kimberly by the shoulders and held her away from her.

"The Power of Three. That's what the vampire meant." Yvette stared up at Haven. "That's why he said he only had to take one of you. One of the three."

"What?" Wesley asked, his voice as confused as Haven felt. He had no idea what Yvette was talking about.

She jumped up. "Don't you see? The vampire wanted to separate the three of you: Wes, you, and Katie. The three children of a witch."

"And kill Mom," Wesley barked.

Haven shook his head. "No, he didn't want to kill her. He said he would have let her live, but she was fighting him. He killed her because she was trying to bespell him. She died for us, because she couldn't let either of us go."

Yvette nodded. "All he wanted was to break up the three siblings. Destroy the power."

"And what is that supposed to mean?" Haven asked, curious now.

"There's a legend that the three children of a witch will upset the power balance in the underworld, the balance between vampires, witches, and demons. I don't know much about it, but I know that if you and your brother are two of those siblings, then I think I've just come up with the reason the witch captured you. You—" Then Yvette turned her gaze back to Kimberly, who'd risen from her cot. "—and your sister."

15

Haven's incredulous stare bounced from Yvette to Kimberly and then back to Yvette. He vaguely heard his brother gasp in surprise, a sound he would have echoed had he been able to do anything other than gape. He took in Kimberly's slender figure and her blond hair. He and Wes both had dark hair, just like their parents.

"It can't be. Kimberly looks nothing like my parents." He pointed toward her hair. "Nobody in our family has light-colored hair."

Kimberly rose, her movements tentative as if unsure of herself. "I'm not a blonde. They wanted that color for the movie. I haven't changed it back yet."

Haven blinked and tried to see her with different eyes, blocking out her hair. He focused on her facial features: her eyes, the line of her straight nose, her lips, her stubborn chin. Some things looked familiar, others didn't. There was no way to know for sure. He shook his head.

"I don't know." He glanced at Wes, silently asking for reassurance, but his brother merely shrugged.

"It would be too much of a coincidence. We've looked for her for twenty-two years. Why would she—"

"Twenty-two years?" Kimberly asked. "I was dropped off at an orphanage a little over twenty-two years ago. The man who left me there never came back."

"Where was that?"

"In Chicago."

Even though they'd lived in San Francisco at the time Katie had been stolen from them, the vampire could have easily traveled anywhere with her. The police search within California had come up with nothing at the time. And Haven's later investigations, once he was old enough to look for her himself, had been just as fruitless.

"You don't know who your family was?"

The girl shook her head. "DNA was in its infancy back then. The staff at the orphanage thought that my mother might have been a teenager who'd gotten pregnant and that the man who dropped me off was her married lover."

Next to him, Wesley took a tentative step toward Kimberly. A moment later, Haven felt his brother's hand on his arm. "Could it be?" his brother asked, giving him a hopeful glance.

Haven made sure the wall around his heart was firmly in place, except for the few cracks that had started appearing. He shoved that nagging little detail to the back of his mind, refusing to acknowledge it. "Let's not get our hopes up. This could be a wild-goose chase."

"I don't think so," Yvette interrupted. When he tried to contradict her, she held up her hand. "Just listen before you dismiss this. When I met you all individually, I knew you were human. I was alone in the car with Kimberly when we drove to the party. Her scent was human. No doubt in my mind. And then you—" She looked at him. "When we spoke at the party, your scent was human."

Haven felt his face and neck heat. They'd done more than just speak at the party. They'd practically sniffed each other out. The knowledge that she'd inhaled his scent and made a note of what he'd smelled like, excited him when he knew it shouldn't matter. He cleared his throat, trying to push away his errant thoughts. "And?"

Yvette pointed to Wesley. "Same with Wesley, but less so, because when we first came in contact, you guys were here too, you and Kimberly. He still smelled human, but something was a little different. I didn't take notice much, because I wasn't in best form."

Haven gave her a surprised look and noticed how she flinched as if she hadn't wanted to reveal her weakness. So she *had* been hungry, just like he'd thought. "When you need blood badly, it affects your senses?"

"Of course not."

He could see the lie roll off her pretty lips like too much '70s lip gloss.

"I'd only just come around from the poison you used to knock me out. My sense of smell was off."

"Maybe it's still off," Wes scoffed.

Yvette turned her scowl on him. "I'm fully recovered." Her gaze drifted back to Haven, more specifically to his neck, and he recognized that she was thinking of his blood.

Haven suppressed the shiver that tried to race traitorously through his body at her glance, but he couldn't control his pounding heart. Unable to say anything for fear everybody would hear the sudden arousal in his voice, he was grateful when Wes asked the next question.

"So, let's assume your nose is doing its job, then what does it mean? Why would we suddenly all be smelling like witches? Maybe the witch's smell is just rubbing off on us, and it's confusing you."

His brother could have a point. Maybe a vampire's senses could get confused just like a human's. Nobody was infallible. Hell, if a vampire could pass out from loss of blood, maybe they were a lot more vulnerable than he'd always assumed. And when he'd watched over Yvette while she'd been unconscious after giving him her blood, he'd sensed a vulnerability about her that she didn't show when awake. Well, there was actually a moment when she had been without defenses while awake: when he'd kissed her into submission. He'd felt her melt into his embrace, her moans urging him on to take her. The wall around her had been down then.

"What do you think, Hav?" his brother asked. "Hav!"

He jolted out of his reverie. Shit, how long had he spaced out? "Uh, yeah, well."

Wes gave him a strange look, then continued, "See, even my brother agrees. It has something to do with what the witch did to our heads."

"No," Yvette objected. "It's the fact that the three of you are together. Almost as if together, you're witches, apart you're not."

"Ludicrous!" Wes huffed. He raked his hand through his hair.

Something with Yvette's words connected. "Hold it, Wes. I think there's something there." Haven looked at his brother and willed him to listen.

"But you know yourself that we didn't get any of Mom's powers."

He nodded. "Yes, that's what we always thought. But the witch seems to think otherwise. When I resisted her probing in my head, she asked me where the source of my power was."

"But—"

"I know. I told her I had no powers, but she didn't believe me at first. Would I really let her beat the hell out of me if I had any witchcraft to oppose her? You bet I wouldn't."

"Figures." Yvette's lips twitched into the beginning of a smile, which she tried to conceal with a snort, but he caught it nevertheless. When she looked at him like that, and when they engaged in these light, friendly, vocal sparring matches with one another, he could almost forget what she was.

"So the witch is mistaken. We have no powers," Wesley insisted.

Maybe that was what they all thought, but there was one thing the witch had said before he'd passed out that made him suspect that they'd been wrong all these years. "She wondered whether Mom had ever told us."

"Told us what?" Sometimes his little brother could be really thick and slow on the uptake.

"That you do have her power." Yvette pushed her long hair back over her shoulder.

"But then why wouldn't we have known all these years? It makes no sense. I never felt any power."

"It's the first time the three of you have been together since you mother's death. Maybe that's how you all receive your powers, by being together." Yvette shrugged. "I don't know much about this, but I know what I smell. And the three of you are witches. Which means Kimberly has to be Katie."

Dead silence greeted this remark and three sets of eyes stared at Yvette out of identically shocked faces. Haven was the first to recover. "But if that's the case, why would the witch put us all together if that gave us powers? What if we used that power to defeat her?"

Yvette shrugged. "Do you feel any different? I mean, do you feel like you have some power now?"

"How the hell would I know?" Haven grumbled.

"Well, just think of moving something." Yvette looked around, then pointed at the cot. "Move that bed with your mind."

Haven had to restrain himself from rolling his eyes. How would he be able to suddenly move objects? Not even David Copperfield could do that without setting up his trick beforehand.

"Just try it," Yvette urged. "All of you."

Despite the stupidity of the suggestion, Haven concentrated on the cot and willed it to move. Nothing happened. Just like he'd thought.

He had no powers.

"Nothing," Kimberly said.

"Same," Wes confirmed. "We have no powers. Ergo, we're not witches."

Yvette put her finger to her mouth, biting her nail. "I've never been wrong about my sense of smell. Maybe there's a spell or something that you have to do first before you get your powers." She paused, clearly thinking hard. Then her face lit up, and she stared at Haven. "Did the witch ask you where your source of power was?"

"Yes she did, as a matter of fact, but I have no idea what she means by that."

"I think you'll have to tap into something to access your powers. Maybe that's why she feels confident that you can't access the power yourself. Perhaps she was testing you."

"But if I don't know what the source of my power is, then how would she?"

"Maybe she doesn't need to know it. If she wants to steal your powers, and at this point we have to assume that's why she brought the three of you together, then maybe she doesn't need to know. What if she can steal it without that knowledge?"

Haven let the idea take root in his mind. Could the witch really have succeeded in finding Katie when he'd been searching without success all his life? And if she had, if Kimberly was truly Katie, was it true what Yvette suspected? Were the three of them witches with powers yet untapped?

"How would we know for sure? It's not like we can do a blood test here and run our DNA." As much as Haven wanted to believe that they'd finally found Katie, he couldn't allow himself to get his hopes up only to have them come crashing down again.

He directed an encouraging smile at Kimberly, who met his look with round eyes. "I would love for Yvette to be right. I would love for you to be our sister, but there's no proof, just coincidences and assumptions. I need more than that."

Kimberly nodded, disappointment etched into her features. "I understand. It would be nice to have a family. I guess it's just too much to ask." She wrapped her arms around her waist, and he recognized her need to be held and comforted. But he couldn't cross the distance between them and take her into his arms. For all he knew, he was just a stranger, one who'd kidnapped her. As a brother, he could hug her and tell her that everything would be all right. As a stranger, he had no business doing so.

Haven looked back at Yvette, the strain tearing at his strength. "I'm sorry, but I have to be sure."

"There's a way to make sure." Yvette's eyes shifted between him, Wes, and Kimberly.

Intrigued, he took a step closer. "How?"

She locked eyes with him before her lips parted. "I would need to taste the blood of all three of you."

Wesley's reaction was almost instantaneous. "No fucking way!"

Exactly Haven's sentiment, but for a very different reason. Yvette wanted to bite his brother, sink her fangs into him and make him feel the same kind of arousal he'd felt when she'd bitten him? "Over my dead body!"

Yvette rolled her eyes at him as if she thought he was some little kid who was throwing a temper tantrum. Did she not understand the seriousness of the situation here? She couldn't just go around and turn his brother into a pussy-whipped idiot. Was that her intention? To make them both drool over her so they wouldn't give her any more resistance?

Closing the distance between them, Haven faced her, their bodies almost touching. Yvette didn't back away, and he knew she wouldn't. He knew her that well already. She would use all her female wiles to tempt him and then do the same to his brother. And that was one thing he couldn't allow. And for the first time it wasn't because he wanted to protect his brother. No, he wanted to make sure his brother didn't touch her. Just like he wanted no other man to touch her. Yeah, that's how screwed up he was. He wanted the vampire in their midst and would fight any man who trespassed on his territory—and that included his brother.

Yvette noticed the predatory glint in Haven's eyes. She knew what it meant: he was going to fight her on this issue. Had his pea-sized, macho-man brain still not grasped the fact that she wasn't going to hurt Wesley or Kimberly, even if she bit them? Not that she had any intention of doing so. There was no need for her to sink her fangs into either of them. A prick of their thumbs would produce sufficient blood for her to taste and compare to Haven's taste.

Blood of siblings had a similar texture, taste, and scent. It was as foolproof as a DNA test. And once they had established that her assumption was right and that Kimberly was indeed their long-lost sister, then they could go about trying to get out of this place. Maybe with their latent witch powers they could break through the wards.

And maybe then, Yvette would finally be rid of them all. Or at least of Haven, who still looked at her like she'd just swallowed his pet hamster. Was he contemplating how to punish her for not telling him about the sexual side effects of feeding?

Yvette didn't like how close he stood. There wasn't even a foot of space between them. Had the man learned nothing during their earlier encounter? Why else would he stand so close when he had to know that all this accomplished was getting her all hot and bothered and in the mood to press him against the wall and sink her fangs into his delicious neck while she freed his cock and impaled herself on it?

The heat inside her body bubbled to the surface in a warning not to let her mind wander in that direction. Too late. Soon her body would boil over like an unwatched pot of milk and burn its surroundings. And there was nothing she could do about it. It was as inevitable as a runaway truck barreling down a steep slope.

"Listen, all I need is a few drops."

"Your fangs are getting nowhere near my brother's neck," Haven hissed.

How could one human man be so stubborn? "I don't even need to—"

"I said NO! Can't you get that into your head? Don't you think it's sufficient that you turned my head? Now you want to do the same to my brother?"

Had he just said "turned his head"? She must have misunderstood.

"I won't allow it. It's enough that I can't think clearly anymore because of what you've done to me. You'll have to kill me first before I let you do the same to Wes."

What she'd done to him? "You think I'm controlling you because I bit you? There are no lasting aftereffects from a bite. Everything's temporary. Whatever you felt because of it is long gone." Yvette didn't allow the smile that formed inside her to break to the surface. If he still felt an attraction for her then . . . "Whatever you feel is your own doing."

Haven took a step back as if hit by a heavy object. His eyes filled with disbelief, and his mouth opened in protest. Only one word came over his lips. "Shit!"

"So if you'll step aside, I'd like to prick Kimberly's finger so I can test her blood." Yvette looked around his heavy frame, her eyes finding the girl who stood watching their heated exchange. "Is that okay with you, Kimberly? It'll just be a prick like a little blood test at the doctor's office."

Kimberly shrugged. "Sure. If it helps."

Yvette ignored Haven, who still stood motionless in the middle of the room and went around him. Let him think on what she'd told him. Besides, she didn't need his help right now. She could still taste his blood and would have no trouble comparing it to Kimberly's and Wesley's.

When she reached the girl, Wesley pushed in front of her. "Me first."

Yvette raised an eyebrow. How had the pup suddenly gotten so eager? Her questioning look seemed to prompt a response.

"If you hurt me, I won't let you touch Kimberly."

Perfect, another man who wanted to rescue the damsel in distress. This was getting increasingly tiring. "Fine."

16

"I've never scried for a vampire before," Francine claimed in response to Gabriel's question.

Zane looked at the woman—no, make that witch. Fuck how he despised them. They were devious and not to be trusted. He'd yet to meet a witch who fought fair. All they did was use their potions and spells to trick people and overpower them. But Francine, the witch who'd helped both Amaury and Gabriel on previous occasions, had become somewhat of a hanger-on to their group. None of his colleagues seemed to mind her presence, but Zane's nostrils stung with the sickly sweet smell of witchcraft, and he avoided her whenever he could.

Outwardly, Francine looked entirely normal, even human, as she sat there on Samson's sofa, a large tote bag slung loosely over her shoulder, her hand clutching it as if she didn't trust them not to rip whatever treasures she had in there from her grasp. As if anybody wanted to touch her witchy trinkets. It was better to stay away from things he knew he had no defenses against.

"Try it anyway," Gabriel now instructed. "It can't hurt." After a short pause he added, "Can it?"

Francine shook her head. "Of course not. All I'm doing is trying to find her location, but I need something that will help me find her. Something that belongs to her."

"Like a piece of clothing?" Gabriel asked.

"Or some hair?" Zane interrupted, drawing Francine's gaze onto him. Her eyes skidded over him, almost as if she couldn't stand looking at him. The dislike was clearly mutual.

"The hair should work."

Zane stood and went to retrieve the bag with Yvette's hair from the kitchen. Maybe it would come in handy after all and it hadn't been a complete waste of time to bring it. By the time he returned to the living room, Francine had spread a map of San Francisco over the coffee table.

He handed her the bag, careful not to touch her in the process. The last thing he wanted was a witch's stench on him.

Francine peered into the bag. "Is that all Yvette's?"

"Yes." Zane kept his conversation with her to a minimum. There was no need to make small talk with a witch.

"Do I want to know why there's so much of it?" Francine looked away from him and glanced at Gabriel.

But before his boss had a chance to reply, Zane interrupted, "No. Get on with it."

Gabriel's reprimanding glare barely registered as Zane concentrated on watching the witch's movement. It was never a good idea to leave an enemy out of his sight.

Francine took a strand of Yvette's dark hair and pressed it against a crystal, then used a string to tie the two items together, leaving the string longer on one end so the crystal's weight hung heavily on one end of it. It looked almost like a mason's plumb line.

She adjusted in her seat, moving forward on the couch to bend over the map. Her arm stretched out, holding the string with the crystal and Yvette's hair. Then she started swinging it in a slow circle while she chanted softly.

Zane homed in on the words, but they were gibberish to him. For all he knew, the woman could be turning them into toads while they were sitting around like a captive audience. How Gabriel could trust a woman like her, he couldn't understand. No witch could be trusted.

Tense minutes passed as the crystal swung wildly over the entire map of San Francisco, yet it didn't descend onto any specific place. When Francine looked up from her task and gave a shrug, Zane already knew the answer.

"Sorry, but I can't find her."

Zane rose, his frustration forcing him to move, to expend physical energy. He paced.

"It was worth a try," Gabriel said, his voice just as disappointed as Zane felt.

"It's probably got something to do with the fact that she's a vampire. Their auras are different. I don't think the crystal can pick it up. Look at the positive side: at least I'll never be able to find you guys if you don't want to be found," she joked.

"Excuse me if I'm not roaring with laughter," Zane hissed.

"Zane, please." Gabriel gave him a shake of his head. "We're all under stress. But that doesn't mean we have to forget our manners."

He was relieved from answering when the door opened behind him and Samson walked in, a sheet of paper in his hand.

"Got it." He handed the sheet to Gabriel. Then he briefly smiled at the witch. "Hey, Francine. Good to see you."

"Perfect," Gabriel proclaimed, looking at the piece of paper.

"Did I get him right?" Samson asked.

Gabriel nodded. Then he lifted the sheet for all of them to see. "Meet Yvette's attacker."

Zane looked at the drawing Samson had created. He'd always known that Samson was a fantastic painter and sketcher, but he'd outdone himself with the drawing of the man who graced the sheet of paper now. And his photographic memory had clearly helped him in his task.

The man's face had uneven features, piercing blue eyes, dark hair, and a strong jaw line. His lips were full, his nose straight, and all in all he had a rugged look about him. Not classically handsome, but not unattractive either.

"How did you do that?"

Samson smiled. "After Gabriel dove into the driver's memories, he planted them in my mind, so I was able to see him. Then I could draw him."

When Zane looked back toward the paper, he caught Francine's shocked stare, her eyes glued to the picture in Gabriel's hands.

"Francine." She looked at him when he called out her name, and he knew in that instant that she recognized the face. "Who is he?"

All eyes flew to the witch, whose lips trembled. "He looks so much like his late father," she whispered almost to herself.

"Francine," Gabriel prompted. "Tell us who this is."

She swallowed, letting a few more seconds pass, before she answered, "That's Haven, Jennifer's son. I didn't know he was back."

***

"And why should we believe you?" Wesley asked.

Yvette's "taste test" had been positive. Kimberly was Katie. She knew it with one-hundred-percent certainty, but the brothers were still skeptical. "I have no reason to lie. There's nothing in it for me."

"Hmm." Wesley looked at his brother. Haven glanced at Kimberly, clearly torn between his doubts and wanting to believe.

Of course Haven wouldn't believe a vampire. Why would he? He had a low enough opinion of her. Frustration spread in Yvette. Why did she bother to try to help them? She had to be psycho to ask for another smack in the face. "Fine!" Yvette bit out. Then she raised her voice. "Witch! WITCH! Get the fuck in here! NOW!"

From the corner of her eye, she saw Kimberly flinch and cover her ears with her hands.

Yvette's screaming had the desired effect. A few moments later, the door opened. The witch remained on the other side of the threshold, her face distorted in anger.

"What do you want?" She glared first at Yvette, then at the brothers. "You idiots still haven't killed her?! Maybe it's time I did the job myself!"

"A question first, if I may?" Yvette asked, feigning politeness. "Is Kimberly Haven's and Wesley's sister?"

First a flash of surprise crossed the witch's face, then a wicked smile curled around her lips. "You only just figured that out? Gee, if you're all that slow, I guess I won't have much to worry about."

Then she slammed the door shut.

"Believe me now?" Yvette looked at the brothers. Slowly, their disbelief turned to joy, at the same time as Yvette felt disappointment rush through her. Haven believed the witch, but he hadn't believed her. Even though she had expected it given his history with vampires, it still hurt. Deflated, she let herself fall onto the next cot and leaned against the wall.

Yvette had never been to a family reunion—well, at least not in the last fifty years. What she witnessed now nearly brought tears to her eyes. Despite the bare walls and floor of their prison, the room couldn't have been any warmer with the emotions that flowed freely between the three siblings.

Yvette felt a little tingle of envy as she watched the brothers hug their younger sister and bombard her with questions about her childhood at the orphanage, her interests, and her career. They were the picture of a happy family—well, as happy as you could be in captivity.

Kimberly's questions for her brothers weren't any less excited, and while Yvette tried to tune out, she couldn't help but listen to the stories that Haven recounted about his life as a bounty hunter. Yvette wasn't sure, but she had the feeling that he deliberately left any mention of his vampire-slaying activities out of the stories. Maybe he wanted to show his gratitude that in a weird kind of way she'd helped him find his sister.

When Kimberly laughed at one of his stories, Haven's gaze drifted over to Yvette, and he mouthed a silent "thank you" to her. It took all her mental strength not to fall apart. She reclined on the cot and closed her eyes, escaping into darkness. What the three of them had now was more than she ever would. And as much as they deserved this happiness, it made her even more aware of her own loneliness. More than ever, she was the outcast, the one person not belonging.

Trying not to wallow in her self-pity, she forced herself to breathe deeply and relax. They'd only been in captivity for about twelve hours, but she was certain that her colleagues were already working on finding her. However, while it was daylight outside, they wouldn't be able to break her free, even if they'd already discovered her whereabouts. All she could do at this point was wait.

If the Scanguards crew didn't show up by nightfall, she'd have to consider other avenues. And the fact that her three fellow captives were witches could come in handy. Despite the fact that they didn't seem to know about their powers or how to use them, Yvette was sure they possessed them. Somehow they would be able to tap into them.

Then, of course there was the one thing Yvette had discovered about the witch. Bess had to be physically within the wards to hurt them or exercise her powers on them. As long as she stayed outside the wards— on the other side of the threshold—she couldn't do anything to them. It gave her comfort. That meant, for now they were safe within these four walls.

Yvette allowed her tense muscles to relax for the first time since she'd taken on this assignment. Kimberly would be safe with her brothers, and she knew from Haven's recent behavior that he wouldn't stake her either if she napped for a short while. All she needed were a few minutes.

Kimberly's constant chatter provided an easy background noise to drift off to. She couldn't tell how long she was out, but it couldn't have been long. Kimberly was still essentially telling the same story, or maybe it was a variation of it, when Yvette's senses caught something else.

First, a grating noise reached her ears; it sounded like somebody was trying to pry an old door open, the rusted hinges providing the music fitting for a horror movie. The hairs on the back of her neck instantly stood sentry while she tried to get her bearings. Something was wrong about the sound. Disturbing.

Yvette sat up, her spine stiff and alert. A quick glance around the room confirmed that the three siblings were still where they'd been before: sitting on the two other cots, chatting. The sound wasn't coming from them.

She trained her eyes on the door, but nothing moved there, and no sound came from it.

Crank!

There it was again. It came from the outside; that much was sure now.

Yvette yanked her head toward the window at the same time as a ray of sun burst into the room. She froze just long enough to feel a bite of pain from where the sun touched her arm.

"No!" Haven's shout jerked her out of her trance as did another cranking sound. She finally realized what was happening: the fucking witch was prying away the plywood planks to let sunlight into the room, making good on her earlier threat!

"Shit!" Yvette yelled and jumped up, nearly colliding with Haven.

Panic struck her like a lightning strike, then she felt Haven's hand grabbing her.

"Move!" Haven screamed and pulled her with him. She tumbled more than ran with him as he swung the bathroom door open and flung her inside ahead of him, the rays of the sun on their heels. She slammed against the sink before she heard the door close behind them with a loud thud.

Only a single light bulb hanging from the ceiling illuminated the tiny space which wasn't any bigger than a six-person elevator.

Her heart raced and beat into her throat. Behind her, Haven's breathing was just as erratic. When Yvette turned toward him, she didn't even get a chance to thank him for his quick action, because his arms came around her instantly and pulled her tightly to his large chest. One hand on the back of her head, the other around her waist, he squeezed her against him.

"Oh, shit!" he gasped on an exhaled breath. "That bitch!"

Yvette swallowed hard, unable to form any words yet. The shock still sat too deeply in her bones. She'd frozen, even though it had only happened for an instant. She'd never frozen before.

Haven put his hands on her shoulders and pushed her away a few inches. "Are you okay? Did the sun get you anywhere?" His concerned eyes scanned her body, the slight tremble in his voice only underscoring his worry.

Yvette shook off his hands. Having had her face pressed against his naked chest had been temptation enough. She needed to sever her contact with him before it was too late. "I'm fine. Thanks." She wasn't, but she would be.

He nodded briefly, then turned to the door. But he didn't open it. "Wesley?"

"Yeah?" his brother's reply came instantly.

"Take the blankets from the cots and cover the window with them. Make sure you get the sides as well so no light will filter through."

"Okay."

Then Haven turned back to her and crossed the one-foot distance that was between them. There was no getting away from him in the miniscule bathroom. His look was serious when he gazed at her, making her aware again of how much taller and bigger he was. "You can beat the shit out of me later, but right now I have to hold you."

And just like that, he pulled her back into his embrace.

"What—"

"Shh. Not now, Yvette. I almost had a heart attack thinking you'd die right in front of me."

Her heart made a flipping motion as if somebody had installed a trampoline and was jumping up and down on it. This big, bad vampire slayer was worried about her. The man who'd confessed that he'd killed other vampires to avenge his mother had saved her with his quick thinking. And now, he was holding her in the tightest hug she'd ever found herself in as if something bad would happen if he let go. A hairline crack appeared in the door to her heart as her next thought took root.

Haven didn't hate her.

17

Haven tried to calm his galloping heart. Holding Yvette in his arms helped a little, reassuring him that she was alive and well. Had he not watched her while he'd been listening to his sister's stories, he wouldn't have picked up quickly enough that something was wrong. But the instant he'd seen her scan the room for danger, his own senses had picked up the sound and realized what it was.

He'd never moved that quickly in his entire life. He'd acted on pure instinct when he'd grabbed her and practically slammed her into the tiny bathroom to get her out of the way before Bess had pried a corner of the plywood away from the window. He still felt his knees tremble at the thought. But he was in no mood to examine his reaction to the threat that was solely aimed at Yvette. He didn't want to dig too deeply into his reasons for why he was protecting her.

He didn't want to think right now. He only wanted to feel. Her.

Haven eased up on his tight hold and shelved her chin on his hand, tilting her face up to him. The shock and fear in her eyes had dissipated. In its place was surprise.

"Kiss me," he demanded.

And damn it if she didn't move her head closer to his to follow his command without objection. He'd at least expected a little tussle before she'd give in. But maybe she was just as shocked as he was and needed this release as much as he needed it.

"But this time, don't bite me. I want to make sure that what I feel has nothing to do with any side effects." Not that he hadn't enjoyed her bite, but he was desperate to find out why he was so drawn to her. And the only way to figure it out was if she didn't use any of her vampire powers on him. He needed to be sure.

"No biting," she whispered on a shallow breath. "Not even a little?"

His cock hardened at the mere suggestion. Haven shut his eyes for a moment, trying to block her out. Instead, the darkness only intensified Yvette's presence. Her orange scent was all around him, the sound of her heartbeat reverberating against his chest, and her shallow breaths blew warm air against his face. Her hands now moved up his chest, the skin-on-skin contact sending electric shocks of lust through his veins as they traced their way toward his shoulders.

This woman would be his death if he allowed her to get too close.

"No," he finally answered before he opened his eyes and looked into hers. Deep down in those green eyes lay the answers to all his questions. "No, baby, right now, this is just between you and me. No tricks, no powers."

Just plain lust.

Raw.

Untamed.

When her lips met his, he forgot everything that had just happened. Only the sensation of soft lips pressing against him registered in his mind: sinful lips that knew what to do, passionate lips that explored them. Haven parted his lips, and invited her. How he loved the feel of a confident woman who simply took what she wanted. Just as much as he liked to take from her. To drink from her lips, to explore her, to make her respond to him.

When her tongue ran along his lower lip in a sensual caress so soft, a softness of which he'd never thought a vampire capable, he growled in frustration. He couldn't deal with soft right now. Didn't she understand that? He needed fast, hard, pounding. Only then would the shock of almost losing her be wiped away.

But her seductive tongue continued its teasing and only slowly dipped between the seam of his lips. When her taste filled his mouth, he inhaled deeply, taking in her enticing flavors. They hit a nerve inside him, telling his body to prepare for the inevitable. His heart pumped more blood into his cock, bringing his impatient friend near to bursting.

But it seemed Yvette wasn't done with her tender explorations and pressed herself closer to him, angling her head for deeper penetration now. Her body was warm, hot even, and at every spot her body connected with his, passion started its low boil, its slow ascent toward a peak still far in the distance.

Unable to content himself with the slow build, he turned with her in his arms and pressed her against the door, pinning her. The door moaned its protest, but Haven barely heard it. With single-minded determination, he forged his tongue into her mouth and hijacked the kiss. So much for asking *her* to kiss *him*. He wouldn't make that mistake again until they truly had time for this. At present, they didn't. Because he hadn't forgotten where they were. At any time, the witch could intrude, and he needed to get inside Yvette and still his hunger for her before that happened.

Yvette responded instantly to his passionate kiss, stroking her tongue against his, showing him she wouldn't be outdone. Now she was talking. He groaned his approval and lifted his head for a second. "There you go, baby."

An instant later, his lips went back to devour her, his tongue diving deep into her, tasting her, exploring her, at the same time as his hips ground against her. His cock directed his rhythm as it slid against her soft center, moving himself up and down. When her hand slipped to the waistband of his pants, he let out a ragged breath and ripped his mouth from hers.

"Take me out, Yvette."

Her hand went to his button, easing it open, before she went for his zipper.

"You can come out now," Wesley's voice came through the door.

Shit!

He couldn't go out there right now—because Yvette had just taken his cock out of its confinement, her palm resting around him as she too had her head turned toward Wesley's voice.

"Give us a few minutes." He sure hoped his brother would go away and leave him alone.

Haven listened. There was no reply to his request. Good. Then he looked back at Yvette who gave him a questioning look, before she dropped her gaze down to where she was still holding his cock.

A moment later, she stroked him in her fist. He nearly jumped out of his skin at the intense pleasure. "Fuck, baby!" he moaned under his breath.

His hands hiked up her dress which had already ridden up. Now it bunched at her hips, revealing her black g-string. Pushing the fabric aside with one hand, he slipped a finger along her folds, following its path downwards. Her curls were damp, but it was nothing compared to the dew her pussy was drenched in.

Without any resistance, his finger slipped between her folds and drove into her warm slit. Yvette's head dropped back against the door as she let out a breath.

"That's right, baby. That's where I want my cock. Right now. Spread your legs for me." Looking at him from under her lowered lashes, she widened her stance.

Haven pulled his finger out and gripped her hips, lifting her up so her legs spread around his hips, using the door at her back as leverage. Then it hit him.

"Shit, I've got no condom."

She shook her head. "Vampires don't carry disease."

He'd figured as much, but it wasn't what he was worried about. "What about birth control?" The last thing he wanted was to have a child, another person to worry about like he'd worried about his sister. He didn't think he could go through this again. No, it would be better if he never had children who he would be afraid of losing.

When he looked into her eyes, he saw a strange glint there, but he couldn't figure out what it was. "You okay?"

"You won't have to worry about a pregnancy."

Haven liked a woman who took precautions. He dipped his head to her collarbone and nibbled along her skin. God, she smelled good. Good enough to eat. Later, when they had more time, he would learn her entire body with his lips, explore her, taste her, but right now, he needed something else. "Guide me inside."

Using one hand, she pushed her g-string to the side, then positioned his cock at her entrance. The moment she let go and wrapped her arms and legs around him, he plunged inside, the impact of it slamming them both against the door. The rattling of the door's hinges echoed in the small room.

"What are you doing in there?" Wesley's voice penetrated, this time accompanied by a hard knock on the door.

"Go away," Haven yelled back and withdrew from Yvette's sheath only to plunge deeper with his second thrust. Fuck, she was tight.

"If you're not coming out, I'm coming in there!" Wesley's threat made him stop for a second and stare at Yvette.

"Your choice," Yvette said in a low voice only for him to hear. "But if you stop now, there's no guarantee you'll ever get another chance at fucking me." Despite her nonchalant look, Haven knew she wasn't indifferent about the outcome of their little tryst. She wanted this to continue just as much as he did, and she wasn't fooling him or anybody else.

He *tsk*ed. "I've made you spread your legs once, I can do it again," he teased. Her reaction to him had been so passionate, he'd never been so certain in his life that they would continue what they'd started.

Suddenly she pushed against him, his cock dislodging in the process. Her eyes narrowed, and she dropped her legs to the floor before pushing him away from her in earnest. "You arrogant prick! I spread my legs when I want to, not when you decide it."

She tugged on her dress, letting it fall down her thighs. "We're coming out," she yelled toward the door and turned away from him, reaching for the handle.

"No, we're not!" Haven's hand slammed against the door, just as Yvette had turned the handle.

Her furious glare hit him as she pivoted to face him. "You can't keep me in here against my will!"

Haven took one step and pressed her back against the door once more. "Can't I?"

Before she could answer, he captured her lips and kissed her. This time, there was nothing gentle about the kiss, nothing tentative. He'd establish right now that she wasn't going to escape him.

Screw him! Damn Haven that he could make her body turn traitor even when she was mad at him. And she was hopping mad. The arrogant prick thought just because she'd allowed him inside her, he was suddenly in charge. As if he believed himself superior. Like she was simply the weak woman, who'd submit as soon as the big bad bounty hunter and vampire slayer willed it so. Who did he think he was? He had no right to demand anything of her—and she alone would decide if he could fuck her later or not. Haven was not the boss of her.

Unfortunately, he was doing a pretty good job with kissing her into submission. But she wouldn't let him get the upper hand. She would fight with everything she had. She couldn't allow him to have any power over her, because she knew how things like that ended. Particularly in their case: Haven already had a low opinion of her, and his callous words that he could make her spread her legs for him whenever he wanted only confirmed that he had no respect for her. He would use her and then toss her aside like a used candy wrapper. But she wouldn't allow it. No, *she* would be the one tossing *him* aside when the time came, but not until she'd made him completely and utterly besotted with her. Payback was a bitch, and Yvette knew a lot about bitches.

There was only one way to achieve her goal of turning the tables on him: give him ultimate ecstasy and make him hunger for more, then deny him what he wanted most. He wasn't the first man she'd turned into putty in her hands, and he wouldn't be the last.

Ripping her mouth from his, she pulled out of his embrace. His eyes were dark with desire, his lips full and moist. When she dropped her gaze to his groin, she saw his magnificent cock still standing erect. With vampire speed she grabbed his shoulders, turned him and pressed him against the door. Starting now, she'd be in charge.

"What the—"

But Yvette didn't give him a chance to finish his sentence. Instead she dropped to her knees, bringing her mouth level with his cock. A glance up at Haven's face brought her in contact with his surprise, which in an instant turned to red hot desire.

"Yeah, baby," he whispered.

Yvette took his heavy shaft into her palm and stroked along its smooth underside, before she guided it to her mouth and licked over the purple head. Pre-cum had already oozed from him, and she lapped up the salty drops, flattening her tongue over the slit, pressing gently.

Haven's head dropped back against the door as he hissed out a low breath. Yvette let a smile curve her lips. It wouldn't take much to make him pussy-whipped. Her only problem now was how she'd stop herself from enjoying this so much. Because licking pre-cum off him was making her womb clench with desire.

Yvette gripped his cock by the root and, forming a perfect *O* with her lips, she slid down on him to take him into her mouth. He was big, his erection instantly hitting the back of her throat. She relaxed her muscles, trying not to gag and pulled back an inch until she felt Haven's hands on her head.

With light pressure, Haven thrust back into her mouth, his movement accompanied by a deep groan. Several shallow breaths followed as if he was trying to steady himself, but Yvette knew better than to allow him to adjust to the sensations she caused in him. He'd get no reprieve. Using her other hand, she reached for his balls and cradled them, then scraped her fingernails against the sac. It instantly tightened, pulling its rounded contents up toward the root of his thrusting shaft.

She used her tongue and lips to suck him hard, to create a pressure she knew he couldn't withstand for long. And all the while, she enjoyed his taste and the texture of his beautiful flesh. She'd always liked sucking cock because it gave her power over a man and with Haven even more so. His moans and irregular breaths were indication enough that he was nearing the edge of his control. And making him lose control was something she wanted to experience.

Yvette inhaled deeply, allowing his male scent to flood her senses. It reached every cell in her body, making her desire for him almost unbearable. But it wasn't for her own pleasure that she did this; it was for his, so he would go mad with desire for her. Because only if she snapped his control could she hope to gain her own senses back and make him lose the hold he had over her. But hell, if she didn't enjoy every single second of this. It was impossible to tell her body not to react to him.

Haven's hard length pumped faster and faster, and she sucked harder.

"Oh, God!" he grunted.

His cock jerked, his orgasm imminent. Yvette's fangs lengthened, and she took his cock as deep as she could before she set her fangs at the base of it and broke through his skin.

"Fuck!" Haven's surprised grunt barely registered as his blood and cum mixed in her mouth. The combined taste of it sent a bolt of electrical charge into her clit, making her climax instantly.

Yvette relished the sensations traveling through her heated body while she continued sucking his blood and his semen from his cock, which continued pulsating in her mouth.

When she noticed him going slack against the door, she dislodged her fangs and let his shaft slip from her mouth, catching him as his back slid along the door, bringing him to a sitting position. His eyes were closed, but his hands were still on her head, pulling her against him now.

"I've never—" he broke off, taking a deep breath into his lungs. "This was—" Again, he didn't finish his sentence.

Yvette smiled, feeling almost languid from her powerful orgasm— and he hadn't even touched her. She could only imagine what it would be like when he did. But for now, she basked in the fruits of her labor: he was succumbing to her.

"You—" Haven opened his eyes, his gaze falling onto his cock that now lay flaccid against the dark nest of curls. There were remnants of blood at the base, even though the little puncture wounds were disappearing before his eyes. "You bit me!"

18

"I've drawn all the blinds," Oliver's voice came from inside the apartment. "You can come in now."

Zane reached for the doorknob and pushed the door open, entering the dimly lit place before letting the lock snap in behind him. Oliver, Samson's human assistant, did have his uses. Making areas vampire-safe was one of them. Not that Francine, who'd accompanied them, couldn't have done the same thing, but Zane didn't trust her. And while he was many things, he was never careless with his own life. After all, he only had the one.

"Thanks, Oliver, I appreciate it."

He walked past the kid—which clearly he was when you looked at him: fresh-faced, early twenties, barely the appearance of a stubble or the suspicion that he could even grow a beard. His hair was a dark mess with each single strand seemingly sticking in another direction no matter how often he ran his hand through it to tame it into a neat coiffure. The effort was wasted—Oliver's hair did what it wanted to do.

His eyes were clear and bright. He was a good kid—a kid worthy of the privilege of knowing their secrets. And a kid, he suspected from his interactions with him, who wanted to be just like them, like the vampires who worked for Scanguards.

"If I can help with anything—"

"Just watch the door." When disappointment flitted across Oliver's face, Zane added "thanks" and nearly choked on the word. Yuck, he was turning soft.

Haven's apartment had been easy to find. Once the witch had given them his full name, Gabriel had made a few well-placed calls to some trusted sources at the City and the Police Department and been surprised to find out what Haven Montgomery was: a bounty hunter. Apparently a pretty good one too.

That's just what they needed: a bounty hunter who was also a witch. Not that the witch part was evident anywhere in Haven's apartment.

Zane swept the one-bedroom place with his usual cold efficiency, taking in the many boxes in the living room as well as the small bedroom. Either the man had just moved in, or he was ready to move out.

Zane wouldn't let the latter thing happen. He'd nab the asshole before he could get away.

A sigh behind him made him turn. Francine stood in front of the faux fireplace with a framed picture in her hands. Zane approached her and looked over her shoulder.

"What's that?"

Francine shrieked, a sound spreading a feeling of satisfaction in Zane's chest. He still had it: he could even sneak up on a witch, and their senses were said to be superior to those of mere humans. And he might as well make it clear to her that he was watching her every second. If she was planning to trick him, he'd be right on her, because there was no way he believed that Francine would betray a fellow witch, particularly not one she seemed to know personally.

"Who are they?" Zane asked, pointing at the picture with the two boys and the baby which Francine held so tightly her knuckles had turned white.

"Haven and his brother Wesley. And the baby is Katie. So tragic."

"What's so tragic about that?"

"Katie was kidnapped twenty-two years ago and never seen again."

Zane grunted. It wasn't his problem. "What about Haven? What can you tell me about him? What are his powers?"

Francine shrugged and placed the picture back onto the mantel. "I'm not sure he ever received his powers. Nor Wesley for that matter."

"Are you trying to tell me he's not a witch? I don't buy that. He used witchcraft to overpower my colleague. How stupid do you think I am?"

The witch glared at him. "All I'm saying is that I don't know what happened to him. I haven't seen him in over twenty years. I didn't even know he was back."

Zane pulled in a deep breath. "What about his parents? Are you still in contact with them?"

She shook her head. "His father left before Katie was born, and Jennifer was murdered twenty-two years ago." She paused, and her eyes met his. "By a vampire."

Fuck! That wasn't good. Not only was the guy a bounty hunter and a witch, he also had a very good reason to hate vampires and to want to take revenge on them.

"The same vampire who kidnapped Katie."

Two very good reasons.

What better motivation than wanting to avenge one's mother and sister? And Zane knew all about motivation and hate and how it could carry you through the long years of solitude. How it would nurture the drive for revenge, for getting even, how those reasons would fuel the hatred and wipe out anything else in your heart. To destroy those who destroyed your family: it was the greatest motivator Zane had ever known. Haven would be a formidable opponent, who would fight to the death.

"Fuck!" Zane grumbled under his breath. "What about his brother, Wesley?"

"Wherever Haven is, Wesley isn't far. They stick together like glue. Haven was like a father to Wesley."

"What happened to them after their mother's death?" It wasn't compassion that made him ask—compassion was an emotion for pussies—no, he needed to know all he could about his enemy to find his weak spot.

"The boys were sent to a great-uncle in Iowa. He was their only relative."

"And the father?" How could a father abandon his children when they needed him most?

Francine cast her eyes downward in an attempt to avoid his scrutinizing gaze. Was she hiding something? "He wanted nothing to do with them."

There was more to the story, and he knew it. "Why?"

She shrugged. "I don't know."

Zane didn't buy it. "Is he a witch too?"

Francine's eyes flew back to his face. "No. Of course not. Jennifer was the witch. Her husband was fully human."

"Why did he leave them?"

"How would I know? Married people split up all the time." Francine's voice sounded firm on the surface, but Zane picked up a slight tremble at the end of her sentence. The woman was lying to him.

"I'm asking again, and this time I want to know the truth. Why did he leave them?"

Francine turned away and walked toward the kitchen. "It's not important."

Zane stalked behind her. "I say it is."

"Let it be, vampire. Nothing good will come of it."

At the kitchen door, he held her back with a hand on her shoulder. "Tell me now." He tightened his grip and lowered his face to her neck. "Or I'm going to take a bite out of you."

Francine jabbed her elbow back, landing it in his ribs, but his body was so hard, it barely registered.

"You don't want to be at the receiving end of my witchcraft," she warned.

"I can snap your neck much faster than you can cast a spell." Zane wasn't a hundred percent sure his claim was accurate, but hell, he could bluff. He'd never seen Francine exercise her powers on any of his colleagues, so he didn't know what she was capable of. "And I bet you wouldn't want me to tell Gabriel that you're withholding information. Once his trust in someone is shattered, he can be quite ruthless."

Francine pulled her shoulder free of his grip, and he allowed it, realizing from her silence that she was ready to comply. She didn't look at him; instead, she simply stared into the kitchen.

"Haven's father didn't want Katie to be born."

"What?" He couldn't have heard right. "He wanted his wife to abort?"

"When he found out about the prophecy and realized it would be fulfilled, he implored Jennifer to terminate the pregnancy. But she refused."

"Hold it: what prophecy?" Zane never liked the sound of things like prophecies, fate, and other such nonsense.

Francine turned to face him. "The three children of a simple witch will become the most powerful witches of our era and will upset the power balance of the underworld. When Whit, Jennifer's husband, found out about it, he felt betrayed by her. All she wanted from him was those three children, so they would become the Power of Three. So they would rule the underworld."

"Ah, shit!" What the fuck had they gotten into now? If Haven was so powerful, how could they ever rescue Yvette? "If that's true Yvette's as good as dead."

Francine shook her head. "Haven's not a bad man."

Zane let out a bitter laugh. "And what makes him not evil? You said you haven't even seen him in twenty years. The boy you knew doesn't exist anymore. He's a powerful witch, and he'll kill Yvette. If she isn't already dead."

"No, he can't. The prophecy was never fulfilled."

"What?"

"Without Katie, there is no Power of Three. And Katie is gone; I searched for her myself. Jennifer was my friend, and as misguided as she was about wanting to harness her children's power, her children deserved better. I could never find where Katie had been taken. And I wasn't the only one looking for her. For all I know the vampire who took her killed her."

"Why?"

"To make certain that the three siblings would never join to become the Power of Three. Separating them forever is the only way to stop the prophecy."

Was that the light at the end of the tunnel, or just an approaching train? "Does that mean Haven is not as powerful as we think?"

Francine glanced around the kitchen. "From what I can see here, it seems he doesn't even practice witchcraft." She opened a drawer, then a few cabinets. "Nothing in here tells me that he makes potions."

"But Yvette was overpowered with a potion. Some pink smoke or something." Zane stroked his palm over his bald head trying to release the stiffness in his neck and shoulders.

"There's nothing here that would make that kind of potion. There's no residue anywhere." She pointed toward the pots that were stacked next to the stove. "Those pots have never seen a witch's potion. If they had, I would be able to sense it. You can trust me on that, vampire."

Could he? What choice did he have? But one questions still hung in the air.

"Why are you helping us find him?"

"Because I need to know what happened to him, and if he's truly turned bad, then maybe I can help him turn his life around. I feel responsible for not having stopped Jennifer when I still could have. I owe her children."

Zane nodded. At least the witch had some noble reason. "How do we find him?"

"We need something that has his DNA on it so I can scry for him."

"Bathroom," he instantly answered and left the kitchen.

The bathroom was tiny and in dire need of an upgrade. Cracks in the sink and the bathtub revealed that the rental apartment was not in the best shape. Add to that the sketchy neighborhood, and Zane knew that Haven wasn't here to stay. The faster they found him, the better before he slipped through their fingers.

Francine squeezed into the tight space just behind him, a fact Zane didn't appreciate. He was fully capable of finding some hair or fingernails without her help.

"Anything?"

Annoyance made his gut constrict and his fangs lengthen. "I've got it under control." With his broad back, he blocked her from impeding his search any further.

The sink was clear of any hair, and the stained counter showed no fingernail clippings either. Zane bent down and reached for the small trash bin. His nostrils picked up the faint scent of blood. He tipped the bin over and emptied its contents onto the counter. An empty toilet paper roll tumbled onto the floor. Dental floss and the packaging of a tube of toothpaste were intermingled with tissue paper.

"Looks like he cut himself shaving," Zane said and pulled out a tissue with a bright red blood stain. "Can you use that?"

He turned on his heels and held the stained tissue up for Francine to see.

"Perfect." She took it.

"Let's go," he ordered and tried to shuffle her out of the room.

She blocked his exit, looking past his shoulder. "Are you just gonna leave the trash like that?"

Just as he'd started to dislike her less, she had to piss him off. "What am I? The maid?" he hissed and shoved her out of his way.

19

"I can't believe you did this! Letting your dick rule! Stupid!"

Wesley was giving him shit for fucking Yvette in the bathroom. Not that the location had anything to do with it. Besides, Wes didn't even have his facts straight—yet Haven had no intention of correcting his brother's incorrect assumptions. Haven hadn't even fucked Yvette; no, *she* had fucked *him*. Royally. And instead of being pissed at her for biting his dick while she was blowing him like a world champion in oral gymnastics, he was craving more. How perverted was that?

Something was so wrong with that, but his brother was the last person he'd admit it to.

"It's none of your fucking business," Haven growled, sotto voce. "And keep your voice down. She can hear you."

Wesley planted his hands at his waist and glared over Haven's shoulder. "Oh, I want her to hear me."

Haven cringed. After the unbelievably intense pleasure Yvette had given him only minutes earlier, the last thing he wanted to do was make her feel dirty. He'd not even had a chance to tell her how much he'd enjoyed her mouth on him. By the time the knowledge that she'd bitten him had sunk in, she'd already hightailed it out of the bathroom. He hadn't told her that despite his demand not to bite him again, he'd secretly hoped she would. And when she had, the pleasure had been so amazing that he'd had to collect his brain cells off the bathroom floor afterwards.

Even now, he wanted nothing more than to press her against him and kiss her until she passed out from lack of oxygen. If vampires could pass out like that. Yeah, fuck, he'd gotten the best blowjob of his life from a vampire. How unexpected. After chasing and killing her kind for years, karma had suddenly caught up with him. If that wasn't poetic justice!

"Let it go, Wes. What's between Yvette and me has nothing to do with you."

Wes gave him a stern look. "She will be the death of you. And don't tell me I didn't warn you." Then he turned away and sat down next to Kimberly, who'd watched them intently.

Haven directed his gaze toward Yvette, who leaned against the wall farthest from them, feigning interest in her fingernails. But under her lashes, she watched him. When he walked toward her, her body tensed almost unnoticeably.

A foot away from her, he stopped. "We need to talk."

She raised her head in inquiry. "About?" Her eyelashes fluttered innocently. And here he'd thought Kimberly was the actress in the room.

"Do you need me to spell it out?" He kept his voice low, not wanting to be overheard by his brother and sister. Sister—how wonderful that word suddenly felt. He glanced back at them and took in his little sister's appearance for a moment, before turning back to Yvette. "Or have you suddenly gone shy?"

Yvette tilted her chin up and huffed.

"Good. Then tell me something: what happened in there?"

"I don't know what you mean. You're gonna have to be a little more specific."

With a quick sideways glance, he dropped his voice even lower. Placing one hand against the wall behind her, he moved his mouth closer to her ear. "Why suck me like that and then not let me give you the same pleasure in return?"

The quick intake of breath told him that his question had surprised her. Good—the last thing he wanted to be was predictable. Predictable never got the girl.

Got the girl?

What the hell was he thinking?

"You were pissed with me for biting you," Yvette interrupted his thought process.

Haven cleared his throat. Pissed wasn't the right P-word—pleased, pleasured, perfect were more like it. "Right." Where the fuck was he going with this? Why was he trying to seduce her? Yet, he couldn't seem to stop himself. "Did it give you pleasure to bite me while you sucked me? Did you like the taste?" This was clearly his dick talking, but he had no idea how to shut that stupid idiot up.

Yvette's chest rose as she inhaled, her breasts brushing against his chest. "What do you want from me?"

Haven moved his body closer, his erection sliding against her hip as he tilted his body sideways so his brother couldn't observe that he'd gotten another hard-on just by talking to Yvette.

"I want to fuck you until we're both delirious."

Yvette's heart stuttered in excitement. Haven's words and body language told her everything she needed to know: he couldn't stay away from her. And all it had taken was a blowjob and a bite. How simple. He was on the hook. Now she only needed to reel him in, lull him deeper into the deception that she wanted him, and then toss him out like a used tool which had served its purpose.

Everything was working perfectly.

Everything, except for one thing: she had yet to convince herself that she didn't want him and would indeed toss him out to deliver the ultimate humiliation when she was done with him. It shouldn't be so hard. Haven had plenty of strikes against him: he'd kidnapped her and her charge, he was a witch, and on top of it he was an arrogant jerk, who believed she was a heartless creature. Why wasn't that enough to hate him?

But with his words in her ear and his body and scent so close, so tempting, she couldn't concentrate on his bad attributes. She could only think of how good it had felt to touch him and pleasure him.

"Tell me what you felt," he whispered like a sorcerer trying to draw her in with his enchanted spell. And maybe that was what he was doing: using his witch powers on her. She hadn't considered it up till now. But it was the only explanation: by being together with his siblings, he was drawing on his powers. It had to be, or she would never feel herself become so weak and pathetically compliant in his presence.

"Your blood tastes of bergamot, rich and thick." She couldn't stop her words from spilling from her lips. "And your cum is salty, and mingled with your blood, it's better than anything I've ever tasted."

Her body was hot just thinking of it. It heated even more when his warm breath ghosted along her neck.

"Fuck, Yvette. I'm hard just thinking of what we did." Haven exhaled several times as if he was trying to calm himself. "When this is over, you and I, we need some time together. Just you and me and a bed."

She couldn't argue with that. He was playing right into her hands. Like a lovesick puppy, he begged her for more. "I thought you hated vampires."

Haven raked a lusty look over her. "Oh, I hate you. Don't get me wrong. I hate you enough to wanna fuck you until you collapse."

She could deal with that kind of hate. "You, me—" She paused to catch her breath. "—and a flat surface."

But right now, she needed distance from him; otherwise, she'd maul him right in front of his brother and sister.

20

"What guarantee do we have that she's not going to double-cross us?" Zane hissed into Gabriel's ear. They stood in the hallway of Samson's house while the rest of the Scanguards crew and Francine were in the living room. "And how do we know that she really scried for this Haven Montgomery and didn't just give us a bogus location?"

Gabriel shook his head. "We don't know. We'll just have to take a leap of faith."

"That's not good enough."

"Zane, one day you'll have to learn to trust somebody."

Zane narrowed his eyes at his boss. "Today's not that day."

"From where I stand, we don't really have a choice. I know we're up against a possibly very powerful witch—let's assume it's Haven since all evidence points to him—but I trust Francine. If she says she'll help us trap him as long as we don't kill him, I believe her."

"I don't like the 'no-killing' part of that arrangement."

"Careful, Zane. If you go against her wishes on that, be prepared for retribution. Francine might not look it, but she has a great deal of power. And she's smart. We either play it her way and accept her helping us with immobilizing him, or we go in guns blazing. And you know what that means."

Casualties. That's what it meant. Yvette could be hurt, the actress killed. It was a risk. "We're still going in guns blazing."

"Sure, but only with Francine's witch power can we disable him before he can cast anymore spells. *Then*, we go in guns blazing."

"Still don't like it." An uncomfortable tingling on the back of his neck told him they weren't alone anymore. Zane turned to face the witch. "Has nobody ever told you it's impolite to listen in on people's conversations?"

She smiled. "Same as nobody's taught you not to talk bad about other people behind their back."

"You're not people. You're a witch."

"Witches are human."

Like Zane cared either way. He gave Gabriel an exasperated look. "You're the boss."

Gabriel nodded. "We have two hours until sunset." He gestured toward the living room, and the three of them rejoined the others.

There wasn't a seat left in the house. Everybody who could be of any use was assembled: Amaury, Thomas, Eddie, Maya, Nina, Samson, Oliver. Even Delilah sat on the couch, her big belly prominently sticking out. Not that she would get anywhere near the fighting, but Samson always included her in all discussions.

Could six vampires, two humans (one of whom was a woman) and a witch defeat one powerful witch, and free Yvette and Kimberly, without anybody getting killed? Hell yeah! And he bet they could do it without the witch. If Yvette got hurt, they could heal her quickly—that's why they'd take Oliver with them. He'd been an emergency blood donor on other occasions and could act as such again. And if Kimberly was injured, any of the vampires could heal her with his vampire blood. It carried healing properties more powerful than any antibiotic. As long as Kimberly received no fatal wound in the scuffle, she would come out in one piece at the end.

Zane for one would keep a close eye on Francine. One wrong move and he'd have her by the throat.

***

Darkness finally surrounded the large warehouse in the industrial area of South San Francisco. Zane had chosen to ride in the blackout van that carried Gabriel and the witch. He wouldn't leave her out of his sight no matter what his boss said.

With suspicion, he eyed the little potion bottle Francine clutched to her chest. He'd demanded to be the one to carry it, but she'd refused adamantly.

Zane slid the van door open and stepped out into the cool night. Rain was in the air. He could almost taste it. Around him, more shadows appeared. The vampires were all clad in their usual dark clothes to be able to easily blend into the night. Thomas wore his customary biker gear and looked the part.

Because witches were essentially humans, the weapons they had brought this time were meant to harm humans only. The guns were loaded with regular bullets, not silver bullets like they normally were. Nobody wanted to risk injuring Yvette. Instead of silver knives, each vampire was carrying at least one knife with a conventional blade, and a few throwing stars. They'd left their stakes at home, not wanting to risk their opponents getting their hands on the deadly weapon.

They were ready to do battle. And had it been his call, Zane would have stormed into the place and razed it. But Gabriel and the witch had other ideas.

Zane watched closely as Francine stepped out of the van and approached the building. She was dressed in equally dark clothes as his, and without his superior night vision he wouldn't have been able to make her out, because all street lights on the block were out. Thomas had hacked into the city's power grid and made sure no electricity was being fed into the block on which the warehouse stood. Since taking out the power on this block only might have alerted the witch, Thomas had made the decision to widen the radius to several blocks. If Haven looked out the window he'd simply assume that a whole section of the city had lost power and would write it off to a blown transformer, and not associate it with an imminent attack. They still had to be quick, though. The energy-less residents wouldn't just sit and wait indefinitely for the power to come back on; someone would call and their gig would be up.

"You should have let me go with her. What if she betrays us?" he whispered to Gabriel who stood by his side, his eyes glued on Francine, who approached the front entrance of the warehouse.

"If she does, I know it'll take you about one second to reach her. Don't worry; I haven't forgotten how fast you are." There was an almost mocking tone in Gabriel's voice, and Zane didn't appreciate it.

He cursed under his breath. "Why am I even your second-in-command when you never consider any of my suggestions?"

"I always consider all your suggestions," Gabriel disagreed.

Zane tossed him a disbelieving look. "You never adopt any of them."

"Really?" Gabriel gave a crooked smirk, his scar nearly jumping off his face. He pulled out his cell and pressed speed dial before he held it to his ear.

"Gabriel?"

Zane could hear both sides of the short conversation.

"We're in position." Then Gabriel flipped his phone shut and pocketed it.

"What was that?"

"Insurance."

Before Zane could ask what he meant by that, he noticed more figures emerging from behind another building. Still others came out of an alley. Reinforcements.

Zane raised an eyebrow in inquiry.

"They're all Scanguards," Gabriel replied without taking his eyes off Francine and the warehouse. "You didn't think I was going to leave the lives of Yvette and her charge in the hands of one witch and just the six of us?" He *tsk*ed, then chuckled to himself.

"I'm glad you find that funny," Zane snapped. The humor of the situation was lost on him.

Gabriel shrugged. "Francine only knows about the six of us. So if she is trying to communicate with Haven and warn him, he'll think it's just six and prepare accordingly. But if we come at him with a force of another dozen, he'll be overwhelmed. They'll be surrounding the building as soon as Francine is inside."

"And what if she can't get inside?"

"She has sufficient powers to open a door. So, have a little faith."

"And may I ask why you're letting her go in the first place?"

"Haven might recognize her. Since she was friends with his mother and knew him as a child, he might not perceive her as a threat. She's the only one who'll be able to get close enough to him to use the potion to disable him."

Zane hated to admit it, but the theory made sense. But he kept his mouth shut. He wasn't one to praise others. Besides, it was too early to tell if the ploy worked. He closed his eyes for a moment and took in his surroundings with his remaining senses. Over a dozen vampires were in the vicinity as well as one human, Oliver. He recognized several of the other Scanguards vampires, all well-trained bodyguards who would do anything for their colleagues.

While the inner core—Samson, Amaury, Gabriel, Thomas, Eddie, Yvette, and Zane himself—were like a close-knit family, the other dozens of vampires who worked for Scanguards were the relatives who surrounded them. When push came to shove, they could be relied upon.

The sound of a door closing made Zane look back at the building. The witch was gone. She was inside. At Gabriel's signal, everybody moved closer, stealthily gliding through the night. They approached their target without a sound, slowing their breaths, quieting their steps. It was like an army of shadows descended upon the dilapidated warehouse which looked like it had been abandoned and slated for demolition years ago and then forgotten.

They waited for several minutes, giving Francine enough time to do what she needed to— immobilize Haven with the potion. Once he was out of commission, they could storm in and get Yvette and Kimberly out. But instead of going in after Francine, the entrance door suddenly opened—and Francine stepped out!

"What happened?" Zane hissed, startling her.

"Shit, you scared me," she huffed out.

He spotted the potion vial in her hand—it was still full and unbroken. "What the fuck happened?" he growled. Had she ratted them out to their enemy?

"Wards."

"What?"

"He's put wards around several rooms. They act like impenetrable walls, but they contain no mass and are invisible. I can't get in any farther. I could sense he was there, but I'm not sure where. I went as far as some sort of living room, but it was empty. But I could feel the witchcraft in the building. It was all around." She paused and took in a breath. "We need a dog or a cat."

"A what?"

"I thought you had superior hearing, so why do you keep asking me to repeat myself?" she bit out through clenched teeth. It appeared he was getting on her nerves, as she was on his.

"What do you need a dog or cat for?"

She glanced first at him then at Gabriel, who'd sidled up to them. "Animals are unaffected by magic. They can get through wards."

21

"And where are we gonna find a Lassie, who's smart enough to deliver your potion to Yvette with instructions on what to do?" Gabriel ran his hands through his thick, full hair, tearing his pony tail apart before pulling it back into its rubber band.

"Didn't you say she owned a dog that followed commands?" Francine asked.

Zane, Gabriel and Francine stood back near the vans where their voices wouldn't carry to the building.

"Sure, but we can't find the beast. Looks like it ran away. And we won't have time to search for it now. It doesn't even have a tag or a collar."

Francine frowned. "Well, any dog or cat then. Just make it quick before he realizes that he's surrounded by vampires. Witches can smell vampires, you know. Particularly if there's over a dozen." She gave them both a pointed look.

Busted! So much for trying to get something past a witch.

"You have to understand my position, Francine—" Gabriel was rudely interrupted by the hand she abruptly raised in front of her.

"No explanation necessary. I would have been disappointed in you if you hadn't kept it from me. So how many do we have?"

"Eighteen vampires, one human, plus you."

Zane scoffed at Gabriel's word. If he'd been the boss, she wouldn't have gotten that kind of frank information.

"Well, then get a dog or a cat. Preferably a dog. They follow commands more easily."

It took over twenty minutes for one of the vampires to find a suitable dog that ran around the neighborhood and was docile enough to follow the man's coaxing.

Francine tied a ribbon around the vial's neck and affixed it to the poodle's collar.

"And how are you making sure Yvette gets it, and even if she does, how will she know what to do with it?" Zane was still skeptical whether the whole idea had any merit. "And besides, I don't know any dogs that open doors by themselves."

***

Yvette didn't mind the darkness in the room. All lights had gone out over half an hour ago. And she knew what it meant: her friends were coming to get her. A peek outside through the window told her that the entire block was blacked out. Surely, that was Thomas's work.

"Do you see anything?" Haven asked from behind her. Ever since the light had gone out he'd stayed close to her, close enough to touch. Now his hand settled on her waist as he brought his head close to hers to peer out into the black night.

Trying to shake off the sensations his touch ignited in her, she made herself sound businesslike. "My friends are here."

"Ah, shit," Wesley sniped.

"Isn't that a good thing?" Kimberly's voice sounded nervous.

"Yes, that's a good thing," Yvette confirmed, not wanting to alarm the girl.

"Not for us. They'll see us as the enemy."

Unfortunately, Wesley's assumption wasn't without merit.

"Just stay close to me at all times, and I'll make sure they won't hurt you guys."

Her breath hitched when she felt Haven press himself against her back and slide his arm fully across her waist, holding her to him. "How close?" he whispered into her ear only for her to hear. Then he took her earlobe between his lips and sucked it into his mouth.

Yvette's knees would have buckled had he not held her so tightly. "Stop that," she ordered under her breath, hoping neither Wesley nor Kimberly would hear her.

"I'll stop, but just to be clear: when all this is over, you and I have a date. And if you try to run out on me, I'll find you."

While his words were a warning, his hands were pure seduction. One tunneled under her halter-neck and found her naked breast to toy with under cover of darkness, the other slid lower to cover her throbbing sex.

"Don't tell me you're kissing her again," Wesley asked, a disgusted tone in his voice.

Yvette pushed free of Haven's hold. "Of course not!"

"No!" Haven protested just as vehemently.

"It's okay if you are," Kimberly said.

"No, it's not!" Wesley made his opinion known.

"But they look cute together."

Cute? Yvette was glad not to have to suppress her grin. Luckily, she was the only one of the four who could see in the dark. Cute wasn't what she would have called her tryst with Haven, and by the frown on his face, he didn't agree with it either.

"You can't be serious, Katie!" Wesley chastised.

"It's Kimberly, and I am serious. Yvette's very nice, and so is Haven—when he's not kidnapping people."

"We're still in the room," Haven said with a smirk on his lips.

Yvette used the cover of darkness to watch him without his knowledge. The memory of his words and his hands still made her shiver. No, she wouldn't run this time. She'd keep her date with him.

"Sorry, Haven," Kimberly apologized. "But I really don't know why Wesley is so against your and Yvette's relationship."

"We don't have a relationship!" Yvette protested instantly and noticed Haven flinch. Had he flinched at Kimberly's words or Yvette's protestation? She couldn't tell. And it shouldn't even matter. The truth was, they had no relationship. They would fuck and then go their separate ways.

"Gee, you guys are touchy. I'll just shut up then."

Yvette could clearly see the pout on Kimberly's lips and wanted to comfort her. But what would she have said? *Sure, I'll go out with your brother if that makes you feel better?* This wasn't high school.

She turned her attention back to the window, trying to discern the number of shadows she saw moving in the dark. "There are at least a dozen."

"A dozen vampires?" Haven asked.

"Oh, shit—we're so fucked!" Wesley commented.

"Just do what Yvette said, and stay close."

"Easy for you to say!"

"You know what, Wesley? Sometimes you really try my patience. And this is one of those times."

A sound from the outside made Yvette turn her attention back to the window. As she focused her senses, she picked up a sensation she was familiar with. It was the same sensation she felt whenever a dog was near, almost as if she could tune into its thoughts, just like she could virtually feel what her own dog was feeling. Her dog—how strange that sounded. But now that she was separated from it, she missed the annoying stray. Yet, she knew it wasn't her own dog out there, a different breed. And that dog was approaching the building, a tall man by its side.

***

The dog trotted obediently next to him. Zane had never fancied himself to be a pet lover, but considering that they needed the animal to get the potion past the wards, he'd volunteered to guide the dog into the building, still doubtful their plan would work.

Something stank, and it wasn't just the witch's smell that permeated through the building, Zane thought as he reached the door and pushed it open. Why had Haven not attacked yet? By now he surely knew that an army of vampires was surrounding him. Or had he taken the coward's way out and fled already? But then, would the wards still be in place if the witch was gone? Shit, he hadn't asked Francine about that little detail.

Zane walked through the stale air in the corridor, the trusting dog waddling by his side as if he was its owner. He let his nose guide him toward where the witch's smell was the strongest and entered a large room. His eyes scanned the darkness: odd pieces of furniture, some rugs on the concrete floor, bookcases stuffed with odds and ends. Frilly and feminine, not the way Haven's place in the city had looked.

A sense of unease rolled over his back and made the little hairs on his nape stand up. He stopped in his tracks, the dog mimicking his movements without making a sound. Smart animal.

Zane inhaled deeply. The scent was clearly witch, yet it was very different from the scent at Haven's apartment, where everything had smelled entirely human. And he was never wrong when it came to scents. Reminding himself of the smell in Haven's apartment, he tried to merge the smell in his mind with the smell of witch, which added a certain sweetness to any human's scent. But the mix his brain came up with wasn't what he scented in this room.

They were so screwed.

Haven wasn't the only witch in the place. That much was clear. They had to fight not just him, but at least one other. Had the brother that Francine had mentioned joined Haven's fight? Zane had to assume as much.

He dug his hand into his leather jacket and pulled out his cell, pressing speed dial as he flipped it open. The moment the call connected, the cell flew from his hands, ripped from him by an invisible force.

Zane spun on his heels, but there was nobody. The dog whimpered.

"Fuck!"

"Zane?" The faint sound of Gabriel's voice came from the cell phone on the floor.

Zane dove for it, but a blast of energy whipped him back and flung him against a bookcase. The dog barked loudly.

"Gabriel!" Zane shouted, hoping the cell would pick up his voice for his boss to hear. "There's more than one witch!"

The dog's barking drowned out any reply Gabriel might have had for him.

Zane picked himself up. Closing his eyes for a moment, he focused all his energy on his sense of smell, then turned into the direction where it was strongest. Opening his eyes, his night vision picked up a movement. He reached for his gun, pulling it out of the holster so fast, no human would have even seen the movement.

He aimed at the shadow and squeezed his trigger finger before the weapon fell from his hand. His flesh was hot, and had he been human, third-degree burns would have already formed on his palm. The gun had turned red-hot within a split second. Fucking witches!

Zane reached for a throwing star in his pocket and, ignoring the now searing-hot metal of the lethal weapon, threw it. A second later, a blast accompanied by a lightning strike hit him in the gut and catapulted him back, slamming him against a door between the bookshelves. Wood splintered.

The dog jumped in front of him, barking loudly at the person who'd attacked him. At the same time, Zane heard footsteps from the outside. His colleagues were descending on the warehouse.

"Come here, dog!" he ordered, hoping the beast would obey. He needed the vial around its neck to immobilize the witch who was attacking him—and this witch wasn't Haven. It was a female; he could smell it. What he would do to eliminate Haven once he'd used the vial on this witch, he wasn't sure yet. But first things first.

The dog jumped away, clearly frightened by the commotion. "Fuck!" Zane cursed and reached for another throwing star to distract the witch who, despite his night vision, he couldn't make out clearly.

"Zane?" he heard a faint voice through the door whose wood he'd splintered by crashing against it.

Relief flooded through him. At least she was alive. "Yvette, we're coming for you." He pushed his entire weight against the door and broke it, yet he didn't fall. Some invisible force was denying him entry into the room despite the now open door. He realized that this was the ward Francine had spoken of.

Zane had no time to peer into the room to find out what condition Yvette and her charge were in, because another lightning bolt charged toward him. Alerted by the dog's bark, Zane lunged to the side and saw it bounce off the ward surrounding the captives' room.

It appeared not even the witch's own weapon could penetrate the ward, which told him that at least Yvette and Kimberly were safe for now.

Rolling to the side, he lunged for the dog, trying to grab it by its collar. As he reached it and pulled the beast closer to him, a bolt of energy hit him in the side, slicing through his jacket and shirt, burning through his flesh. He cried out in agony and involuntarily released the dog. It scampered away from him, now clearly frightened of him too.

When he made another attempt at catching the dog, it ran full speed into the other room, right through the ward as if it didn't exist.

"The vial!" he yelled. "Yvette, take out the witch with the vial on the dog's collar."

It was all the instructions he could shout to her before another attack hit his leg and made him tumble. As he fell, the vibrations on the concrete floor announced the arrival of his brethren, as they rushed through the corridor.

Sliding his hand into his pocket once more, he gripped his knife and aimed.

22

Through the open door, Yvette saw Zane tumble to the floor just as a poodle slammed into her at full doggie-speed and nearly knocked her off balance. Had Haven not been standing behind her and caught her, she would have landed on her ass.

Yvette bent down to the frightened animal and hugged her arms around it. The dog instantly licked her neck and shoulders. "Easy, boy," she calmed him. "You're safe in here."

Her hands searched the dog's neck, trying to figure out what Zane had been trying to tell her. She felt a small, oblong glass object which hung on a ribbon off the dog's collar. A colored liquid sloshed inside. Putting two and two together, Yvette realized that Francine must have brewed some sort of potion to help them defeat the witch.

Flashes of light came from the other room, temporarily illuminating her prison as the fighting continued.

Her hand closed over the delicate object, but before she could pull it off the dog's collar, a large hand wrapped around her wrist and immobilized her hand.

"No!" Haven hissed. "Don't touch it."

She twisted her hand out of his grip and tried to push him back, but he locked his other arm around her waist and jerked her back.

"We can take out the witch with it!" She reached for the dog again, but this time Haven wrestled her to the ground, making the dog shrink away from them.

"What the fuck are you doing?" she yelled at him.

With his face only inches from hers and his jaw clenched from the effort of holding her down, he finally responded, "What if it kills us too?"

For an instant, her heart stopped.

"If it's meant to kill a witch, it'll kill Wesley and me." He paused. "And Kimberly. Is that what you want?" His eyes bored into her.

"Maybe you don't care much about me or Wesley, but I thought you swore to protect Kimberly. Was that all a lie?"

Yvette closed her eyes for a moment. God, she hadn't been thinking. He was right. If she unleashed whatever was in the vial, she could unintentionally harm the three siblings. The risk was too great.

She stopped pushing against him and allowed her body to go slack, showing him that he didn't need to fight her anymore. "Thanks," she whispered. "I wasn't thinking."

Haven nodded and released her, lending her a hand to get up. "And besides, how are you gonna get it through the ward anyway?"

A flash of light suddenly shone into their prison as if somebody had positioned a car or truck outside so its headlights shone through the window. It threw the room into different shadows.

Yvette looked down at the dog that now stood near the door, its head tilted as if listening to their conversation, when realization hit her. "The dog got through the wards around the room."

Haven's head snapped to the animal. "Shit, how did it do that?"

"Come here, dog," Yvette cooed and crouched down. The animal approached. With her mind she reached out to it, feeling its fear and confusion almost as intensely as if she was inside its body.

In her mind, she formed words her lips didn't utter, words only meant for the dog. It was her unique skill, one none of her vampire colleagues possessed.

Don't fear me; I'm your friend.

The dog moved its paws and came closer. When it stopped before her, she stroked her hands over its fur and buried her face it its neck. The dog licked her.

Good boy. Now you have to help me with something.

The dog pulled away and turned its face up to her as if waiting for instructions.

"What are you doing?" Haven asked behind her.

Yvette turned toward him. "If I can't get the vial out there to kill the witch, the dog will have to do it."

"Didn't I just explain to you that you can't risk that?"

"We'll be protected through the ward. Look!" She pointed toward the door where lightning bolts still bounced off the invisible shield around the room. "Not even her own weapons can make it through. As long as whatever is in the vial is unleashed outside of these wards, you, Wesley, and Kimberly are safe."

An expression of unease came over his features as he clearly contemplated her words. "Are you sure?"

Was she? Was she really one hundred percent sure that it wouldn't harm any of them? A cold shiver ran down her spine at the thought that she could be wrong, that maybe the potion Francine had brewed was stronger than that and could penetrate the wards nevertheless. But what other choice did they have?

Looking out into the other room, she noticed the fighting continue. Only three other vampires besides Zane had crowded into the room. The others seemed to be prevented from entering through the door on the other side. Somehow the witch seemed to have erected another force field. Yvette wondered how long the witch's powers would last if she had to keep both the wards around the room and the force field intact while fighting three vampires plus the injured Zane.

Yvette turned back to the dog and petted its fur before putting her hand under its snout to make it look at her.

Go back out there. Take the vial back to Zane.

The dog's round eyes stared at her as she felt its fear increase. It glanced to the door, then back at her. The dog understood her, but its body went rigid, the fear too great for it to follow her command.

Please. You can do it. Nobody will hurt you.

A soft whine was the dog's answer.

"Yvette." Haven's voice made her look up. She'd forgotten he was still waiting for an answer from her.

"I'm sure. If I can get the dog to take it back out through the ward, my friends can use it to defeat the witch."

Haven shook his head. "What makes you think the dog will do what you say?"

"It will. I just know it."

Won't you?

She looked back at the dog whose intelligent eyes were bouncing between her and Haven.

Please help us. Take the vial to Zane. Go.

A moment later, the animal turned away from her and looked at the open doorway. When it looked back over its shoulder, Yvette simply nodded, feeling the beast's fear dissipate. From the corner of her eye, she noticed Haven stare at her, his mouth dropping open as he watched the dog approach the open door.

"How did you do that?"

"I talked to it."

"You didn't say a word."

"It heard me anyway."

She watched as the dog paused at the door and peered outside into the chaos. The witch fended off her attackers with bolt after lightning bolt, but Yvette noticed how the bolts seemed to become shorter and less luminous, as if they carried less energy. Was she already weakening? Gabriel and two other vampires were fighting against her with throwing stars, sticks, and knives. Their handguns were nowhere to be seen.

Zane's face was twisted in agony; yet, even injured and barely able to sit up, he managed to participate in the fight, launching throwing star after star toward the witch.

Go!

The dog followed her silent command.

23

Zane pushed back the pain in his leg. One of the witch's lightning bolts had shredded his thigh. It would heal eventually, but since he had no human blood to help along the process and certainly no time to fall into a restorative sleep, he might as well continue fighting.

His colleagues were doing a formidable job, pushing her back despite the loss of their handguns—their opponent had almost melted them right out of their hands. From what Zane could see, the witch was weakening, but not sufficient for her combatants to deliver the *coup de grâce*. Only three vampires had made it into the room with him, one of them being Gabriel, but then the witch had erected another ward, making it impossible for more of his brethren to join the fight.

When he noticed a movement, his head snapped toward the open doorway where he'd seen Yvette. Automatically, his hand went to his last throwing star. He'd make this one count. His action arrested in his shoulder as he noticed the dog gingerly walk toward him.

Shit! He'd almost killed the poor animal.

Zane's night vision zoomed in on the dog's collar. The vial still hung on it untouched. Yvette had clearly understood that it was no use unleashing the potion behind the wards. How she'd made sure the dog had come back out into the chaos, he didn't care.

The animal put paw in front of paw to approach him. Too slow for Zane's liking, but not wanting to scare the dog away, he kept as still as he could, at the same time keeping an eye on the fighting to prevent any stray lightning bolts from hitting him.

"Come here, doggie," he cooed and hoped nobody could hear him over the grunts and shouts that filled the room. He'd never survive the embarrassment.

For whatever reason, the dog closed in on him, its eyes locked with Zane's as if it was trying to communicate. When the beast was close enough to touch, Zane reached out his hand, slowly, without haste so as not to make it change its mind. When his hands connected with the dog's fur, he stroked over it, and the dog closed the distance between them.

Zane felt for the collar and pried the vial off it.

A lightning bolt charged toward the dog's head and without thinking, Zane threw himself over the animal, flattening it against the floor. The heat of the bolt passed over his head, close enough to singe his hair had he had any left.

The animal beneath him whimpered. "Shh, boy, it's good."

Zane's fingers tightened around the vial as he lifted himself off the dog and twisted his upper body toward the witch. For an instant, he saw her eyes connect with the object in his hand. A flash of fear crossed her features as she seemed to recognize its significance.

Zane's arm pulled back, ready to toss the vial at her feet so the potion in it would be released, when a lightning bolt blinded him briefly. When he blinked, the witch was gone.

Not a second later, more vampires stormed into the room, the ward that had held them outside suddenly gone. They crowded into the room, armed to the teeth, yelling their battle cries, yet there was nobody left to fight.

"Yvette!" Zane shouted toward the open door. He could scent her now with the ward being gone too. But there was still a lingering scent of witch in the air, and he didn't like it. Had Francine come in with the other vamps?

He scanned the group, but Francine wasn't among them. Yet, the residual scent of witch was stronger now. Were his senses tricking him because adrenaline wasn't flowing as freely in his veins as during the fight? He grimaced in agony as the pain in his leg intensified.

"Thank God!" Yvette's relieved voice made him snap his head back to the room where she'd been kept. She rushed out, her eyes instantly taking in the situation. Relief spread in her face until she noticed Zane lying on the floor.

"Ah, shit, Zane!" She ran toward him and crouched down.

"You okay?" he pressed out through clenched teeth, trying not to cry out when she put her hand on his injured thigh, trying to assess the severity of the wound.

"Better than you. You look like crap."

Suddenly, dizziness spread in his head. Shit, he was going to pass out. No, couldn't do that. Not in front of all his colleagues. And even less in front of Yvette. Couldn't show weakness. He bit the inside of his cheek to distract himself from the pain in his leg.

"We need blood here," Yvette instructed, waving toward Gabriel, who instantly rushed to them even as he issued commands to search for the witch. "Is Oliver with you?"

Gabriel nodded and waved to one of the vamps behind him. "Get him." Then he turned back to Yvette. "We were worried about you."

"I'm fine."

"And your charge? Where's Kimberly?"

Yvette turned her head to the open door behind her. "It's safe to come out now."

Over Yvette's shoulder, Zane saw the girl appear. He recognized her, but something was different. While she clearly looked the same when he'd seen her a few nights earlier, something was very wrong. There was a strange air about her. But he didn't get a chance to figure out what it was, because behind the girl two men appeared.

One he recognized instantly from the picture Samson had drawn: Haven, the man who'd kidnapped Yvette and Kimberly.

It had been a trap.

Zane took a deep breath, reading himself for another fight, when the whiff he took in jolted him.

Shit! Witches! Not just Haven, but all three of them!

"Get 'em!" he yelled at the same time as he brought his arm up, the vial still clutched in his palm. He caught Yvette's stunned look the instant he flicked his wrist back and released the vial like a pitcher delivering a fastball.

"NO!" Yvette's scream pierced the sudden silence as she dove for it, trying to catch it.

But Zane knew his throwing arm to be as wicked as his heart. She had no chance of stopping him. Why she wanted to in the first place, he couldn't comprehend. Stockholm syndrome, he briefly wondered, before he saw the glass shatter at the feet of the three witches. A green vapor rose from the liquid that was released.

A second later, all three collapsed.

Yvette reached them first, but if he'd expected her to lunge for the girl she'd been protecting, he was wrong. She reached for Haven. "Oh God! Zane! What have you done?"

She fell to her knees and lifted his body, pressing his head against her chest. "NO!"

Zane had never seen Yvette cry, and he hoped to God he'd never have to again. Her tears were pink as they streaked her cheeks, and her sobs sliced his heart in half.

She was crying tears for the witch who'd kidnapped her.

24

Haven's head hurt as if he'd been on a three-day bender. Not that that hadn't happened before, but somehow he didn't think it was the reason for his throbbing, watermelon-sized headache. What the fuck had happened to him? Last thing he remembered was Yvette telling him and his siblings that it was safe to come out. The fighting had already stopped and the witch inexplicably disappeared in the midst of it.

Forcing his heavy eyelids open, he took in his surroundings. An unfamiliar room greeted him. Richly furnished, in contrast to the sparseness of his earlier prison. The mattress underneath him was soft.

Haven jolted upright. He still wore the same clothes as before—pants, no shirt, because the witch had shredded that with her whip. Somebody had taken his boots off.

A sound next to him made him spin his head. Relief washed through him: Wesley was slowly waking beside him. Haven shook his shoulder.

"Wes!"

His brother's eyes flew open. Instantly he sat up and looked around. "Fuck, where are we? What happened?"

Haven shook his head. "I don't know." He gave the room another look, before he realized something was amiss. "Shit! Where's Kimberly?" He jumped off the bed, Wesley right on his heels.

"Kimberly!" he called out as he headed for the door and turned the knob. As it swung open, Haven found himself confronted by a hulk-sized guy with long, dark hair.

"Shit!" Haven cursed. "What have you bastards done with Kimberly?" He didn't have to be a brainiac to figure out that the guy who was blocking the door was a vampire: one of Yvette's colleagues for sure. At the thought of her, he felt a stab in his chest. Had she sold them out after all? Had she lied when she'd promised them they'd be safe? Why that thought hurt so much, he didn't want to examine. He should have expected as much. After all, she was a vampire. A vampire who'd seduced him. A woman he wanted again.

"Kimberly's fine," the big guy responded. "Why don't you guys get cleaned up, then you can come down to meet everybody."

Haven narrowed his eyes. "Who are you?"

The guy grinned. "Amaury's the name." Then his facial muscles tensed. "Yvette is my friend." There was an underlying threat in his words.

"Where is she?"

"At home."

Deflated, Haven's shoulders dropped. She'd run out on him and served him up to the wolves. Why had he ever started to trust her?

A strange smile curled around Amaury's lips. "She'll be back." He turned away from the door, then thought otherwise and looked back at them over his shoulder. "She was a little shaken. Thought Zane had killed you." Then he pointed toward the inside of the room. "There's an ensuite bathroom. Come downstairs when you're ready."

Haven closed the door and turned back to Wes, who stood right behind him.

"He's one of the vampires, isn't he?" Wesley asked.

Absentmindedly, Haven nodded. But he couldn't form words, because he was still digesting Amaury's claim. Yvette was shaken because she thought that someone had killed him? Did this mean she cared? About him?

"Shit, Hav! What are we gonna do now?"

"I'll take a shower."

"How can you think of something so mundane right now?"

Very easily. If Yvette was coming back here, he didn't want to stink like a pig. He hadn't showered in two days. He wanted to give her no reason to pull back from him.

"If that vampire wanted to hurt us, he would have already done it while we were unconscious." Maybe Yvette's promise was good after all. He sure hoped so for all their sakes.

Twenty minutes later, he and Wes were ready to hit the lion's den. The corridor was empty when they left the room behind them. From what Haven had seen so far, they were in an old Victorian home. From the window, he'd looked out into the neighborhood and seen the lights in the dark. They were somewhere in Nob Hill or Russian Hill, the posh areas of San Francisco. Figured the bloodsuckers had money.

Descending the dark mahogany staircase, Haven took in his surroundings. Yes, the place was elegant and well kept. Voices drifted to him when he reached the foot of the stairs. He glanced to his side.

"You ready?"

Wes shrugged then looked at the heavy entrance door. "If Kimberly was with us, I'd make a run for it."

"I know. But we can't leave her here."

His brother nodded. "That's the only reason I'm going in there." He tilted his head toward the door from which the voices emanated.

"Ditto," Haven lied. He cared for his sister, naturally. But he also wanted to see Yvette. Not just wanted, needed. To understand what was going on between them. What he'd felt when locked up with her couldn't simply be attributed to lust. Sure, they'd gone at it like a bunch of randy rabbits, but he knew there was something else between them.

"You gonna stand there forever or are you planning on running?" a voice came from down the long dark corridor.

Haven turned his head and squinted, trying to make out the tall figure of a man as he approached. He was lean, his head shaved bald, his eyes glaring at him and Wes. His mouth was pressed into a thin line; there was something dangerous wafting around him. Haven suppressed the shiver of unease that rolled down his spine. Instinct told him not to show any weakness to the stranger.

"What's it to you?"

The bald man—make that vampire, considering the nasty snarl he now unleashed—took another step toward them. "I wanna warn you. Either of you mess with us, and I'll crush you with one hand. Very, very slowly." From the way he issued his threat, Haven was sure that the jerk would get a hell lot of pleasure out of it too.

"And you wanna tell me who's making that threat?" Haven ignored Wes's hand on his arm, clearly trying to hold him back from saying anything stupid. "Or shall I just call you asshole?"

Before he could blink, the vamp was on him—he hadn't even seen him move!

Haven was choked by fingers like steel traps.

"ZANE!" The commanding voice made the asshole release his death grip on Haven's throat.

Haven coughed and pulled in a breath of air. Shit, that bastard was strong—and fast. He'd had no chance to react: the vampire was that snake-quick.

From the now-open door, a man walked out: equally tall and dark, yet with short black hair. He scowled at Zane. "If you can't be civil with our guests, I can take you off the team."

Zane narrowed his eyes, then stepped back farther. Through clenched teeth, he issued only one word. "Understood." Then he walked into the living room without another glance at Haven or Wesley.

Whatever the "team" was, clearly the bald asshole didn't want to be removed from it. Haven's gaze drifted back to the man who'd intervened.

"Samson Woodford," he introduced himself and stretched out his hand.

Without thinking, Haven shook it. "Haven Montgomery."

"I know." Then he shook Wesley's hand. "Yvette already filled us in." He nodded toward the living room behind him. "Come inside."

The elegant Victorian living room was jam-packed. Were all those people vampires? Haven counted the heads: six men and several women. His eyes searched the room.

"Kimberly!" he called out with relief as he saw her. She jumped up from the couch and threw herself into his outstretched arms. "Did they hurt you?" He held her away from him to search for any injuries, but everything looked good. She'd showered, by the looks of it, and was now dressed in jeans and a T-shirt.

"We were worried," Wes said from beside him and wrestled Kimberly from Haven to squeeze her tightly.

"I'm all right." She glanced back at Haven. "They've been very nice to me."

Haven nodded, then looked back at the strangers facing him. Again he searched the room: four women, but Yvette wasn't among them. Disappointment spread. Amaury had said she'd come back. Haven looked at the hulk of a man and gave him a questioning look, but Amaury said nothing. And Haven was too proud to ask where Yvette was.

"Take a seat, please," Samson offered and pointed at one of the couches.

"I'd rather stand." Most of the men in the room stood. He didn't want to have to look up to them. It was bad enough that they all looked intimidating. Big guys, all of them: one with a ponytail and gruesome scar on his cheek, a blond one in biker gear, the evil Zane, a sunny-boy all fresh faced and innocent looking; he was probably the least intimidating of the bunch, Amaury, and Samson. The women sat: each of them beautiful in their own right. Were they all vampires? He glanced at them, trying not to be too obvious in his perusal, in case any of the vampires took issue.

When he moved his eyes from one woman to the next, they suddenly landed on a rounded shape that was oddly out of place. Holy shit, one of the women was pregnant! Heavily so. By the looks of it she was ready to pop. A pregnant vampire? Instantly his thoughts went back to Yvette and her assurance that he didn't have to worry about pregnancy.

"I believe introductions are in order," Samson said, his voice even, as if it happened every day that he welcomed a vampire hunter into his house. "You've met Amaury and Zane."

At the mention of his name, Zane simply pressed his lips together even tighter. Haven ignored him and followed Samson's pointing hand as he introduced the remainder of his colleagues.

"Gabriel, my second in command." The scarred guy. He nodded.

"Thomas, our IT specialist." Ah, the biker. Who would have thought?

"Eddie, he's our youngest." Sunny-boy. Figured.

"Amaury's wife Nina," he introduced a stunning blonde.

"Gabriel's wife Maya." The dark beauty tossed her long hair over her shoulder and nodded.

"My wife, Delilah," he introduced the pregnant woman. She gave him a ravishing smile.

"Excuse me if I don't get up to shake your hand, but the baby is getting a little heavy."

Instantly, Samson moved to her side, concern on his face. "Why don't you lie down, sweetness? You look tired."

She waved him off. "You fuss too much. I'm fine. But I could do with some food."

Samson stood and called out toward another open door which lay behind the dining area. "Oliver?" A second later, a young man appeared.

"Yes, Samson?"

"Bring some food for my wife and the guests." Then he turned. "Nina, are you hungry too?"

Haven watched the exchange with surprise. Food? What was going on here? He knew for certain that vampires didn't eat food. If he'd ever had any doubts about it, being in close quarters with Yvette had dispelled all of those. Were they going to drink blood right in front of him and Wesley? Haven's lips turned down in disgust.

"A sandwich would do," Nina replied.

Haven gave her a surprised look. "Sandwich?" he echoed.

Samson looked back at him and smiled. "Excuse the oversight, but maybe I should have made it clear that not all of us are vampires."

Haven raised his eyebrows.

"You're kidding," Wesley let out.

"My wife and Nina are human."

The clearing of a throat made Samson look at the last woman he hadn't introduced yet. "I'm sorry, Francine. My apologies for not introducing you. This is Francine. She's a witch."

Haven's head swam with information he needed to digest. Two of the vampires were married to human women? And one of them was pregnant? Hell, if he'd ever had an information overload, it was now. How was this possible? How could a human woman marry a bloodsucker?

And how common was this? Vampires sleeping with humans? Did this mean that him wanting to fuck Yvette wasn't quite as perverse as he thought it was?

Haven gazed at the woman who'd been introduced at the very end: Francine. She looked familiar. He knew her from somewhere, but the memory of her face was blurry. "Have we met?" he asked her.

Francine smiled. "I was wondering whether you'd remember me. I was a friend of your mother. You were ten or eleven back then."

Haven closed his eyes for a moment, letting the memories flood his mind. Yes, Francine had visited her mother. The last time he remembered seeing her was shortly before Katie was born. "You and she . . . you argued."

Francine's face turned serious. "Let's not talk about that now. I'm happy to see that you finally found Katie."

Instinctively, his gaze wandered to his sister, who now sat next to the pregnant Delilah. She seemed to be comfortable and completely at ease in her surroundings, despite the knowledge that the men around her were vampires. "It was that witch who found her, but nevertheless, we have her back."

He felt his brother's hand on his shoulder. "Yes, we do."

Samson crossed his arms over his chest. "Family reunion aside, that's where our problem begins."

"Problem? Listen," Haven started. "I know you're probably all pissed because I abducted Yvette and Kimberly, but I had no choice. That witch, Bess she called herself, was holding Wesley captive. I couldn't let him rot there."

"We know all that," Samson said calmly. "That's not the problem. Not anymore anyway. Nobody was killed in the fight. But it's not the end of it."

"You freed us from the witch. Thank you for that. Now, since there are no hard feelings, I'd like to have a word with Yvette and then get out of here. No offense."

"None taken," Samson conceded. "But you're not leaving. None of you three."

Shock coursed through Haven. Had he simply exchanged one prison for another?

25

Haven drew in a breath and glared at Samson, taking two steps toward him, before Zane blocked his approach. The bald vampire flashed his fangs. Vaguely, Haven heard Kimberly gasp and sensed Wesley move to his side. But he couldn't take his eyes off the hostile vamp.

"Get out of my fucking way!"

"Zane!" Samson admonished.

Tense seconds passed before Zane rolled his shoulders and followed his boss's command.

"Excuse my associate, but he has an aversion to witches," Samson explained.

Great! And if Yvette could be believed, he and his siblings were witches. This didn't bode well for his immediate future. Haven cast a quick glance at his sister and noticed how the pregnant Delilah patted Kimberly's hand as if to reassure her, a warm smile playing around her lips.

The assembled group was a study in contradiction. On one hand, Amaury and Delilah were treating him, Wesley and Kimberly politely, on the other hand, Zane showed open hostility, while Samson was keeping them prisoner. Where the rest of the vamps stood, he couldn't determine yet. And as to where Francine fit in . . . he was entirely in the dark.

"I'd like an explanation of what you want from us," Haven demanded, tossing Samson a challenging look while at the same time widening his stance. Yet deep down he knew fighting them would be a suicide mission. And he couldn't risk the lives of his brother and sister. He'd jumped from the frying pan into the fire.

Samson nodded, a contemplative look on his face. "And you deserve one. Let me assure you that we have no interest in harming you, but we need to protect ourselves, and unleashing the Power of Three will upset the balance of power in our world. We can't allow that."

"Hold it right there." Haven held up his hand. "I still don't know what you're talking about. As I told Yvette before, we have no powers. We might smell like witches, but we have no powers."

"Not yet." Francine rose from her seat.

Frustrated, Haven huffed. "And what the fuck does that mean?" He glared at Francine. "How about you tell me what you know and stop with the cryptic remarks."

Francine exchanged a look with Samson. After a few seconds, he nodded. "Go ahead. If we want their cooperation, they'll have to know everything."

"You might want to sit down for this, Haven. You too, Wesley. It's a long story."

Haven looked at his brother, who shrugged and headed for the sofa, where Kimberly made space so he could squeeze in next to her. He kissed her forehead. "You okay?"

Kimberly nodded. "They won't hurt us."

Haven wished he had the same confidence his little sister displayed, but the hostility rolling off Zane was still palpable, and if push came to shove, he knew the bald vampire would kill him in an instant.

"I'm good." Haven looked at the witch, indicating that he preferred to stand.

"Fine then. As you know, I knew your mother, Jennifer. She was a dear friend, but we had different views when it came to our powers. Hers were minor: some spells, some potions, but she couldn't control any elements. Only powerful witches control the elements. She wanted more. She wanted real power. And she knew how to get it."

For a moment, Francine closed her eyes as if it was too painful a memory.

"She chose your father not because she loved him, but because of the royal blood that pumped through his veins."

Haven listened closely. He'd never heard anything about his father being an aristocrat. Not that he cared to know anything about him that he didn't already know: he'd left them before Katie was born. Just up and left as if he'd never loved his sons. Haven clenched his fists at the memories. The hatred for what his father had done had never waned.

"Not the kind of royal you might assume. Not a European aristocrat, but a descendent of one of the first witches."

"Our father was a witch too?" Wesley gasped.

Francine shook her head. "No. His grandmother had given up her powers so her offspring wouldn't be witches."

"How can you just give up your powers?" Kimberly asked, eyes wide.

"It's not an easy undertaking, but there's a ritual by which you can release your powers and trap them in another vessel. That's what she did. But it didn't destroy the bloodline. The blood flowing through your father's veins was still royal, and that was all your mother needed."

She sighed. "There's a prophecy. The three children of an ordinary witch unable to control any elements will receive the Power of Three if they come from royal blood. The Power of Three overrides every other power. Nothing is stronger. Nothing is more tempting, more alluring than that power. Few would ever be able to resist. The holders of the Power of Three will rule this world. Jennifer wanted to fulfill this prophecy, and she did everything she could to reach her goal. By giving birth to Katie, she had the three children she needed."

Haven swallowed hard. "She and Dad fought a lot before Katie was born."

"Your father didn't want the third child. By then he'd realized what she was trying to do, and he wanted to stop it. But Jennifer was already pregnant, and she refused to get an abortion."

A tiny sob tore from Kimberly's chest. Haven's gaze snapped to her, and he saw how Wesley put his arm around her and pressed her head against his chest. "Katie ... Kimberly, we always loved you," he whispered to her.

Haven was glad that Wesley was comforting her. Knowing that your father didn't want you to be born had to hurt. Even more than knowing that your father didn't love you enough to stay. His heart went out to her.

"I'm sorry, Katie, but that's the cold hard truth. Your father wanted to prevent the prophecy. But he couldn't. Jennifer wouldn't be swayed. Now she only had to wait until Katie reached her first birthday—"

"But I'm twenty-two now. Why didn't we get our powers?" Kimberly asked.

"Every witch has some powers when he or she is born. They get honed until adulthood before they mature into true gifts. But your mother expunged your ordinary witch powers at birth so that they wouldn't interfere with what she'd planned for later."

"And what's that?" Haven asked, not at all liking what Francine was telling them. It painted his mother in a bad light, and he didn't want her memory tarnished.

"Once Katie was old enough, Jennifer would have performed the ritual to harness your Power of Three."

"Doesn't make sense," Wesley chimed in. "You just said she took away our powers at birth."

"That's correct, but the power that still ran through your veins because of your royal blood was still there. And that was all she needed."

"Then why take away our other powers?" Haven asked, totally confused by now.

"She didn't want you to fight her."

"Fight her for what?" He would have never fought his mother. Hell, he'd fought to save her—and failed.

"The ritual she had to perform would have left one of you dead; there's not enough life force left after she extracts the Power of Three from you and takes it into herself for all of you to live. That was her plan: to be the most powerful witch who ever existed."

Wesley jumped up from the couch at the same time as Haven took a step toward Francine. "You're lying! Admit you're lying! Mom would have never hurt us like that!"

"Fucking bitch! You're no friend of Mom's!" Wesley yelled.

"Calm yourselves," Samson interrupted.

Haven glared at him. How could anybody believe such drivel?

"I'm afraid what Francine is telling you is true. Everything points to it: you didn't smell like witches when Yvette first met you; you started taking on the scent of witch when the three of you were thrown together; the other witch wanted to do what your mother had planned. It all makes sense."

Haven shook his head, still refusing to believe. "Then why throw us together, if that turns us into witches? Wouldn't our captor have been worried we'd defeat her with our powers?"

"No," Francine replied. "Because without the ritual you have no power. Yes, you started smelling like witches when you were imprisoned together, because finally the unity was restored, but there's another step to get your powers."

Something still didn't make sense. "The witch tortured us, trying to find our powers. Why would she do that if she knew we had none at this point?"

"A precaution. A test. For her to be safe performing the ritual, she needed to be certain that you had no powers, otherwise you could fight her and make sure she couldn't take the Power of Three from you. If that happened during the ritual, the three of you would be so powerful, you'd destroy her."

Shocked, Haven leaned back against the wall, bracing himself. Was that the truth? Was it possible? "She asked me what the source of my powers was. What does that mean?"

"It's a way for you to access your powers and recall them."

"I don't understand."

"The powers your mother took away. They're in another vessel. If you had the key to it, you could get them back. That's what she wanted to know, if you had the key."

Frustration built in his chest. "Would you please say that in English?"

Francine sighed. "I'm not sure how to explain this, but if you knew what you had to concentrate on in order to access those powers, then you could call them back to you. You were a child back then. I doubt you would have ever realized what the key was. You were too young, and while your mother would have known, I'm not sure she would have told you."

Francine swiped her hand over her mouth, looking like she suddenly remembered something. "Even though—" She looked straight at Haven. "To make sure you could defend yourself in an emergency or if anything happened to her, she would have given you a hint."

Haven searched his memory, but didn't even know where to start. Fragments of conversations with his mother played in his mind, bringing back memories long buried. But it was useless. There was no key.

"What was Bess waiting for? Why didn't she perform the ritual right when she'd captured us?" Haven asked, trying to wrap his brain around all the news.

"She has to wait for the next full moon."

"Do you understand now why we can't let you leave?" Samson asked, his eyes a fraction more solemn than earlier. "If that witch recaptures you, she'll perform the ritual and harness the Power of Three." He looked into the round and pointed at his friends and colleagues. "We would all be in danger. No creature can be allowed to obtain such absolute power. She'll annihilate us."

Haven pushed off the wall, looking first at Samson then sweeping his gaze to the others in the room. "Does that mean you'll kill us instead?"

"The only person who'll die is the witch!" The female voice coming from behind him sent equal measures of surprise and delight through his bones.

26

Yvette slammed shut the door to the living room behind her, a gesture simply made for effect since the room could have done with some airing. There was decidedly too much testosterone floating in the air.

Seeing Haven up and well filled her with relief, but she didn't show it. Already her colleagues had given her dirty looks when she'd cried thinking Zane had killed Haven. Only when Francine had joined them and explained that the potion she'd produced would simply knock any witch out for at least twelve hours, did her tears dry.

How utterly humiliating. Ugh! Showing such weakness in front of her colleagues had been a mistake. But when she'd seen Haven fall, all she'd been able to feel was the pain of losing him. It had sliced her heart in half, and she'd realized that her feelings for him had nothing to do with hatred.

What would she do now? Did she even have a choice when her body screamed to run into Haven's arms? Sure, he'd fuck her like he'd promised. But then he'd come to his senses: he hated vampires. He'd never fall in love with her.

Putting on a brave face, Yvette looked at her colleagues. She felt better after having been home. Unfortunately, her dog was gone. And because of the approaching daylight, she hadn't been able to go out and search for it. All she'd been able to do was send out her thoughts to it and hope the stupid dog would hear her and come back. She'd slept, then showered and changed into leather pants and a tight-knit turtleneck sweater—and cut her hair. She was the tough woman again. Nobody could get through her armor now.

"Yvette, you've been through enough. Why don't you take a few days off?" Samson asked. "We can handle this."

"Thanks, but no thanks. I have an account to settle with that fucking witch." From the corner of her eye, she noticed Haven looking her up and down, his gaze heated. Under his perusal she felt her body temperature soar and for once was glad that vampires couldn't blush, because she would have made a ripe cherry look pale in comparison.

Samson nodded. "Very well."

Unable to bring herself to approach Haven to ask him how he felt, she looked at Kimberly. "How are you feeling? I hope the potion Francine brewed doesn't have any aftereffects."

"I felt a little dizzy when I woke up. But it's okay now."

"You brewed that potion, Francine?" Haven barked at the witch. "Why unleash it on us?" He gestured toward his siblings.

"Zane thought you were the enemy," Yvette explained, for the first time fully looking at Haven. God, he looked sexy. He'd obviously showered and shaved, and despite the scent of witch that clung to him, his sexy male scent overpowered everything else. It brought back memories of their encounter in the bathroom. Another heat wave traveled through her core, threatening to melt her from the inside.

Haven glared at Zane. "Figures!"

Her colleague simply frowned and twisted his lips into a thin line. "I didn't get a chance to explain—"

"I'm not blaming you, Yvette. I'm blaming him." Haven jerked his thumb toward Zane, but didn't take his eyes off her. His voice softened when he continued. "I'm glad you're well."

Yvette nodded past the lump in her throat, suddenly feeling like the quintessential wallflower clumsily talking to the quarterback in the corridor of her high school. This wasn't good. She couldn't allow herself to dissolve into a puddle of need when she was around him. Pathetic! That's what she was: completely and utterly pathetic.

"Thanks," she managed to say before tearing her gaze from him and focusing on the other people in the room. She cleared her throat, forcing more strength into her voice. "So, what's the plan?"

Samson gave a nod to Gabriel, who stood. As Director of Scanguards' San Francisco operations, he would run point on any major undertaking. "Samson and I discussed a few scenarios, and we've agreed on the most feasible one. We'll separate the siblings and—"

"Whoa—hold it! You're not separating us," Haven interrupted, his voice tense.

Gabriel held up his hand. "Sorry, but we can't risk you three getting captured again together. It's safer this way. And it won't be forever, only until we've eliminated the threat."

"How long?" Haven pressed.

"A few days, maybe a week. Thanks to Francine and the fact that we know the witch's name, we already have an idea who she is and how we can find her. Our people are looking for her. Once we have her, you'll be safe again."

"Safe? I think you're overlooking something."

"Believe us; once we've eliminated her, you and your brother and sister will be safe."

Haven shook his head. "Yeah. From her."

At his words, Yvette suddenly realized what he meant. He was right. They weren't safe. They would never be safe.

"How about all the other witches out there who know about the prophecy? What makes you think they won't come after us too?"

When Yvette heard the collective curses of her colleagues, she knew they understood the threat as well as she did.

"The only way to eliminate her and any other witch who might try to steal the Power of Three is if Wesley, Kimberly and I harness it ourselves."

At Haven's suggestion, all her colleagues jumped up, their angry voices talking and shouting over each other.

"Out of the question!"

"Fuck, no!"

"Over my fucking dead body!"

"I won't allow it."

"No way!"

"SILENCE!" Samson yelled and everybody shut up instantly. He looked into the round and then at Haven. "I'm afraid we can't let you do that. Any attempt at harnessing the Power of Three, and I'll give the order to kill one of you."

Yvette looked into Samson's eyes, realizing how hard the words were for him. Samson wasn't a killer, but he had to protect his friends and his family. She understood that.

"Oh, I see," Haven snapped. "You want the power for yourselves, don't you? So you're the ones who rule!"

"Even if I wanted the power, which I don't, there's no way I could take it." Samson looked at Francine. "Explain it to him."

"Only a human body can harness the power of a witch. No demon. No vampire. Samson is right. Even if he wanted the power, his vampire body wouldn't be able to contain it. No witch power can survive in a nonhuman body."

Relief crossed Haven's handsome features, the frown on his face lessening, the tense jaw relaxing somewhat.

"Then why not let us harness it and make sure it's safe forever? Or will one of us die if we do it?"

Samson shook his head. "No, only if the power is stolen from you, then the weakest of you will die. However, no side can be allowed to have ultimate power."

"We promise we won't harm you," Kimberly claimed.

Samson gave her a soft smile. "You say that now. But once you have the Power of Three you'll want to use it. The temptation will be too powerful to resist. Even if you believe now that you'll never harm us, you will. We can't risk it."

Francine nodded. "Samson is right. Even resisting the power when it's close is virtually impossible. Once it's within your grasp, you'll want to have it. And you'll want to use it for your own purposes. You have to have a pure heart to be able to resist. And let's face it, nobody really has that."

Kimberly pouted at the explanation.

"Then what are we supposed to do?" Haven asked, looking deflated.

His blue eyes searched for Yvette. A pleasant tingling swept through her body when their gazes connected. She wanted to give him assurances that he had nothing to fear from her friends, but with an audience around her who was watching her every step she felt paralyzed and couldn't bring herself to give him the words he was looking for.

Gabriel cleared his throat, forcing her to break eye contact with Haven. "Okay, here's the plan: we separate the three of you. Kimberly will stay here at Samson's house under the protection of Samson and Amaury. Wesley will come with me, Maya and Oliver. We'll protect him at my house. That leaves Haven. He'll be protected at Thomas's house. Zane and Eddie will be there too."

Yvette noticed that her name had conveniently been left out of the equation. "I'm staying at Thomas's house too."

Gabriel raised an eyebrow. "That won't be necessary."

Yvette took a step toward her boss. "If you think I'll leave Haven under the supervision of Zane, you don't know me at all. He's tried to kill him once." She gave her bald colleague a sideways glance. "No offense, Zane, but you're a loose cannon."

Zane only answered with a low growl.

"Zane knows not to harm our guests," Gabriel assured her.

"Don't mind if I check on that myself?" She wouldn't be talked out of this.

"Fine. One more bodyguard won't hurt."

When Yvette turned away from her boss, she caught Haven's eye. Had he guessed that the only reason she wanted to be at Thomas's house was so she could steal some alone-time with Haven? Was she that transparent to him?

***

Haven pulled Francine aside as she stepped into the hallway in Samson's house. "A word."

She nodded and smiled at him. "Has anybody ever told you how much you look like your father?"

Not wanting to revisit his feelings about his father, Haven tried to fight against the memories. He understood now why he and his mother had fought before Katie's birth. But he wasn't ready to forgive his father for leaving them. Had he not loved him and Wes at all?

"Why didn't he fight her? Why didn't he take us with him?"

Francine's look was full of pity. Haven averted his eyes, not wanting to show how the memories of his father affected him.

"Jennifer threatened him."

Renewed anger started to boil up in him. "He could have fought for Wes and me."

Francine placed her hand on his forearm and squeezed. "He did. He lost."

"But he left us!"

She shook her head. "He didn't leave you." She paused and sighed. "He loved you and Wes. Even more than he loved her."

Confusion made itself at home in Haven's chest. "But you said so yourself: you told all of them in there that he left us." He gestured toward the living room where the vampires were preparing for the tasks ahead.

"I had to lie. Wes and Katie can't handle the truth. But you, you're stronger. You've always been stronger, even as a boy."

He knew the answer to his question before he even asked it, yet the words still tumbled over his lips. "What did she do to him?"

"She killed him."

Haven felt his knees buckle and gripped the banister, his knuckles turning white under the strain. "No, it can't be true." But in his heart he knew the truth.

"She was obsessed with the lust for power. She hid it well for a long time. But I could see it. Once it gripped her, she couldn't let go. It was like a curse. Like a sickness that takes hold and strangles you. Once you're afflicted, it's only a matter of time until you succumb. She never had a chance." Francine's eyes were moist with unshed tears. "I hope you and you brother and sister never succumb to it. You have to stop it before it's too late."

Haven shook his head, his thoughts jumbled. His mother had betrayed them all and robbed him of his father. How could he ever get past that? And for all these years, he'd hated his father when he didn't deserve it. He'd fought for them, given his life to protect them. Shame spread in Haven's heart about the feelings he'd harbored there for so many years. He wished he could ask him for forgiveness.

"I have no taste for the Power of Three. I don't want it."

"You say that now because you don't know yet what it's like to be within reach of it." Her eyes shone with the glint of a child beneath the Christmas tree. "But once you can feel it, taste it, sense it . . ."

"I don't want it." The Power of Three was the reason why his father was dead, why his sister had grown up without them. He could never embrace a force so destructive.

"Then you have to destroy it."

"But—"

"You'll find a way." She let go of his arm and made a motion to turn.

"Wait—there was one question I wanted to ask you."

She looked at him, tilting her chin up. "Yes?"

"You spoke of the key to the power my mother took away. How would I find it?"

Francine remained silent for a few moments, before she answered with a question of her own. "Did she die instantly when the vampire attacked her, or did she have a chance to say anything?"

"She chanted a spell."

Francine shook her head. "That's not what I meant. When she knew she was dying, you were there with her. Did she say anything?"

Haven's mind traveled back to that fateful night in his mother's kitchen. She'd mumbled something, but the words were beyond his reach. "I don't remember."

"That's a shame, Haven, because despite everything I said about your mother, once she knew she had lost, she would have given you the key so you could defend yourself in the future. You have to try and remember it."

Remember it. Those words triggered something in him . . . He reached for it, but wasn't quick enough, the echo of his mother's final words escaping him once more.

27

By the time all talk of how to find and defeat the hostile witch had ended and Haven had said his goodbyes to Wes and Kimberly, daylight was approaching again. A blackout van took him and his captors to the Twin Peaks neighborhood, where Thomas's house was located.

Haven was painfully aware of Yvette's presence in the van. Sitting close to her, yet not nearly close enough, his body heated with desire. They hadn't exchanged a single private word since they'd escaped their prison, and if he had to wait much longer before he could touch her, he'd go up in flames.

He let his eyes dance over her body. Clad in tight black-leather pants, she looked as hot and sexy as in her halter dress, but he would have preferred her in a dress. It would take precious seconds to tear those pants off her, whereas a dress he could simply push up and he'd be home in an instant.

Haven shifted in his seat, hiding his growing erection. He'd long given up trying to suppress his body's reactions to her, knowing it was no use. She turned him on, and there were just no two ways about it. He had to make the best of it.

Thomas drove the van into a garage. The moment the garage door came down behind them, everybody scampered out. Haven looked around. Apart from an unpretentious SUV, several motorcycles lined the large space. Somebody clearly had a love for bikes. It explained Thomas's leather outfit.

"Come, I'll show you my digs," Thomas said lightheartedly and waved Haven to follow him up a narrow staircase.

Without looking behind him, he knew Yvette was following, close enough to touch. He'd never been so aware of another person.

At the top of the stairs, Thomas opened a door. Sunlight streamed in and hit Haven in the face, blinding him for a moment. He caught a glimpse of a window—no blinds or shades covering it. Panic struck him, his heart leapt into his throat and lodged there, hammering furiously.

"Shit!"

Knowing he had not a second to lose, he swiveled on the stairs, grabbed hold of Yvette behind him and slammed her against the wall, covering her body with his, hoping none of the sunlight touched her. He pressed her head into his chest, feeling her hot breath against him. Her hands dug into his shirt.

"Baby," he whispered. "You okay?"

The roaring laughter from further down the stairs made him snap his head around. Zane stood there slapping himself on his thigh, laughing in wide-mouthed glee. Somehow he'd thought the guy wasn't capable of laughing, but it appeared Haven had underestimated the vamp. Next to him, Eddie chuckled too.

"You've quite a protector there, Yvette," Zane teased.

From the open doorway, Thomas reappeared. "Haven, I think you can let her go. What you see isn't natural light. It's safe."

Looking at Thomas standing there, the light silhouetting him, he had no choice but to believe him. Thomas would have been burned to cinders if the light really were sunlight. Reluctantly, Haven released Yvette.

"I'm sorry," he whispered. "I didn't know—"

"Don't be." Finally, she addressed him directly. "It's the thought that counts." Yvette was still clutching his shirt, and he hoped she didn't notice that he made no attempt at separating his body from hers. When he looked into her eyes, the need to kiss her overwhelmed him. It had been too many hours since he'd tasted her. As if pulled by invisible strings, he lowered his lips to hers.

"Are you coming or what?" Thomas asked, breaking the spell.

Haven backed off and turned. When he reached the top of the stairs, he took in the view. He'd entered the living area of Thomas's house. It was surrounded by floor-to-ceiling windows. And none of them were covered with drapes, affording a stunning view of San Francisco. A stunning *daytime* view.

"Quite realistic, isn't it?" his host asked and waved at the windows.

"I thought you guys burn in sunlight."

"We do. But that's not sunlight. What you see is a movie screen: live feed. And the light is artificial, but very natural looking. I designed it all myself. You can't get that at Video Only." Thomas grinned.

Haven nodded and turned back to Yvette and her colleagues, who'd crowed into the room behind him.

"Don't know about you guys, but I'm beat," Eddie declared. Then he turned to Thomas. "I guess Haven can take the guest room, and Yvette can have my room. I'll just bunk with you."

A quick flash of panic appeared in Thomas's eyes before he quickly hid it. "Sure, no problem." He looked at Zane. "You okay taking the living room?"

Zane nodded. "I'm not planning on sleeping."

Haven glanced at the bald vampire, picking up the implied warning. Yeah, he understood: Zane was keeping watch on *him* rather than standing sentry in case the witch showed up. Mistrustful bugger.

"I'll show you to your room," Eddie said behind him.

Haven sought Yvette's eyes to send her a silent message that they still had to talk. Nothing in her impassive face showed that she understood or agreed. Not wanting to give Zane any reason to be any more suspicious than he already was, he turned to Eddie.

"Sure, thanks."

"The bedrooms are all in the back of the house. No windows."

Eddie opened a door, and they stepped into a corridor which was lit with the same natural-looking light as the living area. Several doors lined the hallway.

"This is it." Eddie pushed open the door to the guest room and stepped inside. Haven followed into the comfortably furnished room. A large queen-size bed, bedside tables, and a dresser were made of the same wood. In one corner of the room was a large armchair with a reading lamp. The room was bathed in a warm glow coming from lighting strips hidden behind cornices on the walls.

"Thanks."

"You have your own bathroom." Eddie pointed at a sliding door.

"So this is your and Thomas's house?"

Eddie laughed and slapped him on the shoulder like they were old buddies. "I wish. No, it's Thomas's. I just live here. He's my mentor."

"Your mentor?" Haven had first assumed since they lived together that they were boyfriends, even though neither of the two acted in any way campy. But when Eddie had offered Yvette his own room, he figured if they were lovers, they'd share a bedroom.

"I'm new to the vampire thing." Eddie grinned, showing his dimples. "Thomas has agreed to help me work through the change, teach me stuff, you know."

Haven nodded, even though he didn't really understand what Eddie meant. "Like biting?" As if a vampire needed to be taught. He was sure instinct told him just how.

"You're funny, you know that?" Eddie's goodnaturedness didn't wane. "Trust me, I know how to bite. Comes with the territory. But Thomas teaches me to control my powers and instincts, so that I don't accidentally hurt people. It's kind of hard to understand your own strength at first."

Haven was aware of that strength only too intimately. Yvette had used it on him, but he was also aware of how gently she had taken his cock in her mouth and sucked him when she could have easily ripped him apart. The thought of Yvette brought back the reason why he'd started to make small talk with Eddie in the first place: he needed to find out where his room was.

"That's nice of Thomas to let you stay with him. So, you got your own room here." Haven motioned his head toward the open door. He hoped Eddie didn't see through his pathetic attempt at subterfuge.

A flash in Eddie's eyes told him that the young vampire was just as smart as the rest of the bunch. And the grin that followed confirmed that he wasn't as concerned with keeping him from Yvette as Zane seemed to be. "Down the hall, last door to the left."

"Thanks, listen, I—"

Eddie held up his hand. "Two things: stay under Zane's radar, and don't hurt Yvette. She's had a rough few days."

"I know. I was there."

Eddie shook his head. "No, you don't understand. First she thought you were dead, and then we had to tell her that her dog's gone, simply disappeared. She's close to breaking."

Yvette had a dog? Did that mean she formed emotional attachments? Was she capable of that? "She was upset?"

Eddie darted a quick look toward the door as if making sure they were still alone. "You seem like a nice guy, trying to shield her when you thought the sun was streaming in."

Haven cringed, wishing to wipe that embarrassing moment from his memory. It had exposed his feelings for her, feelings he didn't want to admit to himself, let alone to a bunch of vampires. "Just a reflex."

A quick shake of his head meant that Eddie didn't believe him. "Odd reflex for a vampire hunter. Hey, I'm not one to judge. Just saying, be nice to her. I don't wanna see her cry again. It hits me in the gut."

Eddie turned and left, pulling the door shut behind him.

Yvette had cried? Over him?

Haven raked his hand through his hair. What was he supposed to do now? Had this whole thing suddenly stopped being about sex and sexual attraction? Because if it had, then all bets were off. He wasn't getting into a relationship with a vampire, no matter how hot and sexy she was.

Haven kicked off his boots and let himself fall onto the bed, crossing his arms behind his head as he stared up at the ceiling. Maybe it meant nothing. Maybe she'd cried about the disappearance of her dog, and Eddie had gotten it all wrong. Hell, the vampire was still a kid, barely in his early twenties by the looks of his fresh face. What did he know about women?

If Haven went to her room now to have sex with her—and he *was* going to have her; that was as sure as the sunrise—would she take that as an invitation for more? Would Yvette try to drag him into a relationship?

He sat up. Only one way to find out.

28

Yvette paced in Eddie's room, barely taking any notice of its coziness. Eddie had really created a nice homey place for himself. But despite her comfortable surroundings, Yvette felt anything but comfortable.

When Haven had shielded her from what he thought was the sun, everything had come flooding back to her: the events in the tiny bathroom of their prison, Haven's hands on her skin, his mouth on hers, his blood on her lips. The need to consume him had started boiling up in her again, now stronger than before. At the same time, the fear she'd felt at losing him was back.

Now that the stress of imprisonment was over, would he come to his senses and push her away again? Would he be the vampire hunter once more, the man who despised vampires? Or had Samson gotten through to him and made him understand that vampires were not the bad guys?

As much as she wanted to go to him and simply fuck his brains out until neither of them could think straight, pride prevented her from doing just that. Pride and self-preservation. She hadn't guarded her heart, and it now lay exposed. If Haven found out, he could hurt her with his rejection just as severely as if he drove a stake through it. And why wouldn't he?

She'd done nothing to endear herself to him. During the entire time of their imprisonment they'd fought. And she'd even bitten him, twice. Once with his permission, and later without, and actually against his express wishes. He had every right to be upset with her. And in the end, she hadn't even been able to protect him and his siblings from Zane's assault. It was only thanks to Francine that they were still alive. Had she made a lethal potion rather than just a debilitating one—Yvette shuddered at the thought.

Whatever Haven had made her promise while imprisoned—that they'd have a date—she wouldn't hold him to it now. It was better if he knew that whatever they had planned wouldn't work. She would tell him as much. Determined to explain to him that nothing would come of their attraction for each other, she opened the door and stepped into the corridor.

It was better she took this step now, before he came to her and told her he didn't want her. At least then she'd have the upper hand again. She would toss him away before he would do the same to her.

Yvette took a deep breath when she stopped in front of the guest room. Calming her thundering heart, she persuaded herself of the importance of her actions. When the door suddenly opened, she was caught by surprise.

The sight of Yvette outside his door made Haven's heart lurch, then it settled into an erratic rhythm. Quickly glancing down the corridor and finding it empty, he pulled her inside the room and shut the door behind her.

He'd wanted to talk to her, explain that things couldn't possibly go any further, but with Yvette so close, he couldn't remember any of his reasoning of why they shouldn't have a fling, or maybe a short relationship. There was only one thing he could think of, and he executed the thought straightaway.

Haven pressed Yvette against the wall, trapping her between two hard surfaces: the wall and his body. And at present he wasn't sure the wall was the harder one of the two. Her low moan indicated that she could feel his erection pressing against her.

"I was just coming to see you," he whispered against her lips.

"To do what?" Her gaze connected with his, her lids lowered to half mast, an invitation as good as any he'd ever get from her.

"Collect on our arrangement: you, me, a flat surface."

Shit, he'd promised himself to talk to her first, to explain that this couldn't go any further, that he wasn't the kind of guy to stick around. But his dick couldn't wait that long.

"We need to talk," Yvette said.

"Later." He sank his lips onto hers, half expecting her to push him back, half knowing she wouldn't. He pulled her upper lip into his mouth and stroked his tongue over it. A sound akin to a whimper was her answer.

"I hate you." There was no heat behind her words.

"Then let's hate each other thoroughly." Because he couldn't admit to her that what was happening to him couldn't be further from hate. Which didn't mean he had to admit anything.

It was safer not to. He'd spent the last twenty-two years hating her species. He couldn't suddenly turn around and acknowledge that hate wasn't driving him anymore.

Yvette's hands, frantically ripping his clothes off his body, pulled him back to the present.

"Can't wait to start hating me?"

"Shut up, Haven, and get busy before I change my mind."

A small smile escaped him. She wouldn't change her mind. The smell of her arousal was so strong now that he was sure the other vampires in the house had picked it up, too. But if she didn't give a rat's ass about who could hear or smell them, neither did he. Let them all know that he was man enough to take on a woman like Yvette: strong, independent, and so full of barely-leashed passion he knew she would kill him if he denied her anything now. But he wouldn't deny her.

Haven took her mouth, nudging her lips open for his tongue to invade. Her taste drugged him instantly and made him mad with desire. He dove inside and sought out her tongue. She sparred with him, stroking against him with strong and powerful moves. He moaned his pleasure, unable to contain his excitement. No other woman had ever gotten him this turned on with just a kiss. Hell, he'd been turned on just by her looking at him.

Haven ran his tongue along her teeth, tasting, exploring, mapping her mouth so he would always recognize her. Along her upper teeth, he felt a small sharp corner. He lapped against it, making Yvette moan into his mouth. Her obvious excitement sent a stream of lava through his core. Without even thinking, he licked against the sharp protrusion again and felt it grow.

Yvette ripped her mouth from him. "No. Please, don't."

He stared at her, her eyes red. Fear—he clearly saw it. She was afraid of what he was making her feel. He understood now: he was making her feel something too intense when he'd stroked against her fangs.

"They're too sensitive."

It was like the devil gripped him when he heard her words. Licking her fangs excited her? Haven captured her face in his large palm and pulled her back to him. "That's good." Without giving her a second to protest, he sank his lips back onto hers and invaded her sweet cave. His tongue immediately stroked against one fang. The shudder that went through her as a result went right through his body down to the tip of his cock, the pleasure so intense, he could barely keep his control.

Yvette ripped his shirt off his body and sank her hands onto his chest. His own hands weren't idle: he tugged on her tight top and only released her lips long enough to pull it over her head. Her breasts fell free, and he crushed them against his chest as he pulled her back to continue his sensual onslaught on her fangs.

With every stroke against them, they grew until they reached their full length. To his own surprise, they didn't disgust him. Nor was he frightened that she would hurt him. On the contrary, the knowledge of what her fangs had done to him those times before only heightened his own desire. If she wanted to bite him, he wouldn't object.

"This is crazy," she whispered, her breaths shallow and erratic.

"Yes, but good crazy." He swiped his tongue over her fangs once more. "You like that?"

"Haven, please . . ." But her voice broke as she writhed against him.

He'd never seen her so out of control—he'd never seen *any* woman so out of control!—and he liked the sight, so he continued to lick all along her extended fangs, from their sockets down to the sharp tip and back up. Her moans were the sweetest music he'd ever heard. And the knowledge that he was the conductor made his shaft pulsate with desperate need.

As if Yvette knew what she was doing to him, her hands reached for the waistband of his jeans, easing open the top button. The zipper almost lowered without her touching it, aided by the pressure his cock exerted on his pants. She freed him first of his jeans, then his boxer briefs. Hastily, he stepped out of them, glad that he'd been barefoot and didn't have to deal with untying shoe laces.

When her hand wrapped around his erection, he stilled his movements and broke the kiss. "Baby, careful. I'm liable to go off any second."

"Then we'd better not waste any time."

He'd never seen her use her preternatural speed other than in battle, but within seconds, her own pants lay on the floor, and she stood before him entirely naked. Just the way he liked her. Haven folded her into his arms, pressing her heated body against him, relishing the skin-on-skin contact.

This time when he took her mouth, his kiss was all consuming. With one hand on the back of her head and the other on the soft curve of her ass, he held her to him and devoured her lips, fully aware that she could push him away at any moment. It made his possession of her even sweeter.

He couldn't stop himself from searching out her fangs again, and swiped his tongue against them, reveling in the shudders that went through her body. To know he could reduce her to a puddle of wanton need and lust made his cock grow another inch—not that he wasn't already hard and ready to burst.

With single-minded determination, he maneuvered her toward the bed. When he lowered them onto it, Yvette's thighs opened automatically, making him slide into place as they landed on the sheets. Not granting her a second of reprieve, he thrust his cock into her and seated himself to the hilt.

"Fuck!" he grunted. She was so slick and so tight he thought he'd lose his control straight off.

Yvette felt his hard length fill her in one single stroke. Just in time. She couldn't have waited another second to feel him inside her. He'd turned her on within seconds, and there was no other way to fill that void he'd made her feel. Only now, with his cock inside her, she felt whole.

When Haven had stroked his tongue against her fangs, she'd nearly lost her mind, so intense had the pleasure been. She'd always known that a vampire's fangs were erogenous zones, but she'd never felt such intense sensations. She hadn't expected it either. Haven hated vampires—she'd pegged him for the last man in this world to caress her fangs with his tongue. But even now as he was lodged deep inside her without moving, his mouth descended onto hers again, and he went straight for her fangs, licking, stroking, caressing.

Yvette ripped her mouth away from him, breathing hard. "Are you trying to kill me?" She couldn't take much more of his sensual onslaught.

He gave a devilish grin. "If I wanted to kill you, I would have already done so."

"So what's your plan?"

Haven pulled his hips back, sliding halfway out of her. "Baby, all I can think of right now is that I hope I can last longer than ten seconds, because what I really want is you climaxing around my cock." He rammed his hard shaft back into her with one powerful thrust.

Yvette's lungs expelled a long breath on impact. "You keep that up, and you won't need to last longer than ten seconds." Her body was hot, and her heartbeat had nearly tripled since he'd dragged her into the bedroom. Her clit throbbed uncontrollably despite the fact that he hadn't even touched her there.

She welcomed his thick cock, sliding back and forth, his lips on hers, his tongue thrusting in the same rhythm as his hips. And for the first time in a long time, she allowed herself to simply feel. She gave her mind permission to rest and shut off, so her body could relish the sensations Haven conjured up in her without analyzing them.

Her breathing as frantic as his, she bucked her hips against him. His answer was a slight shift of his angle before his hand slipped between their bodies.

"Sorry, baby, but I can't hold back," he pressed out and stroked his finger over her clit, igniting her in an instant. "Now, baby, now."

She didn't need his urging, because her orgasm was already cresting. A second later, it crashed over the summit and slammed into her. "Haven!"

He groaned and his body jerked, his cock pulsating inside her. She felt the warm spray of his seed fill her as he continued his movements before he let out a long breath.

"Sorry, baby." He kissed her softly. "Next time, I'll do better."

She wanted to say so many things: the fact that she liked how he called her baby, the way he'd licked her fangs, and most of all how he made her feel. But she couldn't get the words past her lips. If she said any of the things she was feeling, she'd make herself even more vulnerable.

"Baby."

She snapped her gaze to his, recognizing the confusion in his eyes.

"A penny for your thoughts."

Trying to distract him from whatever he was thinking, she joked, "That's about as much as they're worth."

"Yvette," he warned. "What are you not telling me?"

A hell of a lot, but she wasn't going to admit any of it. Just as she wasn't going to admit to herself that she was falling for him. "Nothing, Haven."

He shook his head and slipped out of her. As he rolled off, she felt a sense of loss. Haven sat up, dropping his legs over the side of the bed, his back to her. "You came to talk. So talk." The resigned tone in his voice gave her pause. Did he regret what they'd done?

Yvette cleared her throat and pulled at the duvet, trying to cover herself with a portion. "I think we both know that this won't work. It's only about the sex."

"Is it?" he challenged, his voice hard, the tender man from earlier gone.

"Yes. Or have you already forgotten what I am? I'm the very creature you've hated all your life."

"Does that scare you?"

Yvette pulled herself up, confusion spreading inside. "Scare me?" She wasn't scared of anything other than her heart breaking.

Haven looked over his shoulder. "Does it scare you that we have something that goes beyond sex?"

Yvette pulled at the duvet, trying to cover her naked breasts in an attempt to hide her vulnerability. "We have nothing."

"You're a terrible liar, Yvette. Even worse than I am."

"I'm not—" Her protest got stuck in her throat when his gaze locked with hers.

"You cried."

Yvette's heart stopped. "Who told you?" A sense of betrayal cut through her. How could her friends do this to her, expose her like this.

Haven made a dismissive hand movement. "It doesn't matter. You cried when you thought Zane had killed me, which means you feel something."

"I'm not a stone!" she hissed. Of course she felt something. "Or do you think vampires have no heart, no capacity for emotions?" She was angry now, angry at his assumption that she was heartless.

He reached for her, grabbed her arm and pulled her closer. "You misunderstand me. You feel something for me. And I want you to admit that." His eyes bored into her, and his hand around her bicep burned her as if it was a hot iron.

"And why should I?"

"Because I want to be sure that I'm not the only one who feels that this is more than just a quick jump in the sack." He pulled her until she was in his lap, where his cock was still as hard and heavy as before. Haven dipped his head to hers. "Because I want more from you."

29

Haven brushed his lips against Yvette's, knowing he'd definitely gone off the deep end this time. But he didn't care any longer. When Yvette was in his arms, the world seemed right despite everything that had happened. He was still trying to digest the blow he'd been dealt earlier: his own mother had used him and his siblings to gain power. And she'd killed his father over it—the father he'd wrongly hated all these years. The knowledge had uprooted his entire world. If he couldn't even trust in a mother's love anymore, what or whom could he trust?

And maybe that's why he now threw all caution to the wind, trusting the one thing that had never failed him before: his gut. And his gut told him he needed Yvette. What she was—a creature he'd hunted all his life—didn't matter now. Because suddenly his reason for hunting vampires wasn't quite as pure as he'd always thought. The vampire who killed his mother and took Katie had done so to protect his own race from a power that could have destroyed them. Could he really fault him for that? But more importantly, could he forgive his mother for what she'd tried to do?

Despite what Haven had done to members of the vampire race, neither Samson nor any of his colleagues had taken revenge on him and Wesley, even though they easily could have. Wasn't it time now to show the same sort of forgiveness toward them? Or was he just trying to fashion a reason so he could allow himself to be with Yvette?

"Haven, we can't do this," she whispered against his lips. "We'll just hurt each other."

"No, not hurt—heal." Haven captured her soft mouth, pulling her upper lip between his and licked gently. "We can heal each other."

"This is dangerous."

"I know. So, let's be courageous then." He exhaled deeply, then drew in his next breath and with it her scent. "Let me make love to you." It was the first time he had ever uttered those words. No other woman had heard them from him. But with Yvette it was what he wanted, to make love, to join their bodies, to feel.

This time when he slid into her, he went slowly, forgetting the frantic rush toward a climax and allowing the seconds to stretch to minutes. He didn't want to rush anything but explore her so he could learn what she needed from him, how he could pleasure her, and how he'd learn to understand her. Their bodies intertwined and their gazes locked, Haven couldn't imagine ever doing anything else but making love to Yvette.

Her slick heat felt like home, her hands on him like the soothing embrace he'd gone without for too long. The wall around his heart fractured with every smile and every moan from Yvette's lips. And the sparkle in her eyes, the desire that burned there for him was like a battering ram swinging against the gate of his heart to bash it open. He didn't do a thing to stop it.

"Show me your fangs, baby," he encouraged her, wanting to prove to her once more that he wasn't disgusted by what she was.

Yvette pulled back a little, refusal on her lips. "No, I can't . . ."

"If you don't show them to me, I'll lick them and make sure they descend."

Her eyes went wide with shock, but then slowly, she parted her lips. He caught a glimpse of the white of her fangs and felt his cock jerk at the sight.

"God, you're beautiful." Haven never thought he would call a vampire with her fangs extended beautiful and mean it. But he did. "Will you bite me when I come this time?"

"You want that?" Her surprise was evident, as was her instant desire for what he offered.

"I haven't been able to think of anything else since you bit me the first time."

"I haven't either."

Her admission warmed his heart. "Do you like my blood?"

"Yes."

"Does it turn you on the same way it turns me on?"

"More."

"Impossible."

"Vampires have heightened senses."

He'd never thought of that, but it made sense. "What I'd give for those heightened senses right now. But since I don't have them, promise me one thing."

Yvette gave him an expectant look.

"Don't hold back. I want to feel everything you feel." Haven increased his tempo, sliding in and out of her drenched pussy. "Promise?"

"Promise," she repeated.

Then he slanted his lips over hers and took her in a passionate kiss, fully aware of the sharpness of her fangs and the knowledge that she'd soon sink them into his neck. Yet, he couldn't resist trying to steal her control by licking against those sharp teeth once more. Knowing that she'd nearly lost control when he'd licked them earlier was a bigger turn-on than anything else. And driving Yvette insane with desire had just turned into his most important mission.

Haven drank in the moans she released and relished her fingernails digging into his ass as she urged him deeper into her. Sensing how close she was, he tilted his head, offering his neck to her. He didn't know why he trusted her, but he knew with absolute certainty that she wouldn't hurt him.

A bolt of fire charged through his body when her fangs grazed the sensitive skin of his neck and her hand clasped the back of it to hold him to her as if she was afraid he'd change his mind.

"Easy, baby," he whispered in her ear. "I'm not going anywhere. I'm all yours." And hell, if he didn't mean it.

When Yvette broke through his skin and lodged her sharp fangs in his neck, all rational thought fled his brain. His control shattered instantly, his orgasm breaking over him like one monumental tsunami without warning, obliterating everything it its path. Time ceased to exist. The Earth stopped rotating on its axis. But instead of his orgasm ebbing and retreating, it hit him again like another wave crashing into him. And this time he felt an impact even more powerful than before: with Yvette's muscles convulsing around his cock, all sensations intensified, doubled, *tripled*, until everything suddenly culminated in an explosion.

Haven exhaled. He'd never had a more powerful sexual experience in all his life.

Yvette snuggled—yes, snuggled—against Haven's broad chest, sated like she'd never been before. "Are you okay?"

He groaned dramatically. "Okay?" He pressed a kiss on the top of her head. "That would be an understatement." His arms pulled her closer, one hand slipping down to her backside, lazily stroking her. "If that's what it's like when vampires make love, I'm wondering how any of your colleagues ever has any energy left to work or fight."

Yvette smiled and raised her head to look at him. His eyes opened and pinned her with an intense look which instantly turned to desire. Under her thigh, which she'd draped over his midsection, she felt his cock stir. "It's never been like that for me."

"Never?"

Yvette shook her head. "I mean, it's been good, but not . . . that good."

"Does that mean you're giving me some credit for it?" Haven grinned.

"Maybe."

"Or was it like that because you bit me?"

"I've never bit anybody during sex." She'd never wanted to lose control with anybody else. Sex had always been enough. But what she and Haven had done together was more, bigger, better.

Approval flashed in his eyes. "Good." Then he shelved her chin on his palm and dipped his head to hers. "And I only want you to bite me from now on. You understand?"

Was that jealousy she detected in his gruff tone? The devil made her ask, "Why?"

His jaw clenched. "Because those sexy lips and fangs only belong on my body. If you do this to another man, I'm going to kill him."

Before she could come back with a retort, he pressed his lips to hers and kissed her hard. She was breathless when he released her. When she smiled at him, Haven raked his hand through her hair and changed the subject.

"You cut your hair again."

Yvette shrugged. "You don't like it?"

"I do, I like both ways." His hand stroked through her hair as if to prove that he spoke the truth. "I'm just wondering why you do it."

"No particular reason."

A moment later she found herself flat on her back, Haven pinning her down with his hulky body. "Baby, why do you need to lie to me after what we've just experienced together? Don't I deserve better?"

There was no anger in his voice, just a dose of resignation. Yvette lifted her hand, wiping a strand of hair from his forehead. "I'm sorry. I'm just so used to—"

"—pushing others away?"

For a moment, she closed her eyes, trying to banish the memories, but they didn't vanish, not this time. "I'm so used to being strong."

He eased off his weight and rolled to his side, pulling her into his arms in the process. "You're strong, and there's nothing wrong with that. Yvette?"

"Hmm?"

"You've heard a lot about my past today, and I feel bare in front of you. But you're still trying to hide behind that wall. Please, let me in."

"I don't know how." Because letting him in meant opening herself up to pain. What if he hurt her? What if he didn't like the woman who was inside, the one who needed to be loved but was too afraid to admit it?

"You're safe with me."

Safe with the big vampire hunter? As strange as it sounded, the more time she spent with him, the more he seeped into her and infused her with a sense of peace. But would her feelings ever be truly safe with him?

"I trusted you not to hurt me with your bite. Now trust me."

Yvette recognized the sincerity in his eyes and nodded. Then she looked into the distance, pinning her stare at a painting on the far wall so she wouldn't need to look at Haven while she told him who she was.

"I wasn't always like this. I was the perfect wife: I cooked, I kept an immaculate house, I had a drink ready when my husband came home from work. I supported him in everything he did. His friends were envious of what they thought was the perfect life. Well, it wasn't perfect." She let out a bitter laugh, unable to look at Haven's reaction.

"*I* wasn't perfect. I—"

"Don't say that!"

"But it's true. I wasn't the perfect wife, because I couldn't give Robert what he wanted. After the first miscarriage, he was disappointed but still supportive. But after the second, he hated me. He hated me for killing his unborn child."

"Miscarriages happen all the time. That's not killing."

"It felt like it. *He* accused me of not wanting it, because if I'd really wanted the child, I would have done everything to prevent a miscarriage. But my body rejected it. My body was defective . . . is defective. I'm not a real woman, because I can't do what real women can do: bear children."

Haven let out a deep breath. "That's ridiculous. I hope you divorced that idiot!"

Yvette sighed. "He divorced me."

"He didn't deserve you."

"But he was right. I wasn't perfect. I'm still not."

"There are plenty of women who have a healthy child after a couple of miscarriages. If you really want one, it wouldn't be too late."

She shook her head. He didn't understand. "Vampire females are sterile."

Yvette sensed the surprise in his rigid body.

"But . . . Samson's wife . . . she's . . ."

"Delilah is pregnant because she's human. And vampire males can mate with humans. Vampire males can procreate. Females can't."

Haven's hand stroked over her head. "I'm so sorry, baby."

She swallowed, knowing that now that he knew this, he would realize that whatever they had couldn't go any further. Why would he, a healthy human, give up the chance to have children just to be with her? "So, you see, I'm defective."

Suddenly his hand gripped her bicep hard and made her jerk her head toward him.

"Don't say that! It's not true. You're not defective. There's nothing wrong with you. On the contrary, you're the most perfect woman I've ever been with. You're strong, smart, and you're beautiful. And when I'm inside you, you make me feel whole. Better than whole. That alone would be enough. But when you sink your fangs into me and take my blood . . ."

Haven closed his eyes for a moment as if searching for the right words. When he opened them, warmth flooded toward her. "When you do that, you turn my world upside down. You make me forget everything: the pain of all those years looking for Katie, my mother's death." He swallowed. "Even her betrayal."

Yvette touched his cheek with her palm, stroking over his stubbles. Was he really trying to tell her that it didn't matter to him whether she was able to bear children or not?

"The years of looking for Katie and hunting vampires, those years were only fueled by the desire for revenge. I never want to feel that kind of pain again. I practically raised Wes. We were sent to a great-uncle after our mother's death. But Wes always looked up to me for guidance. Now, I'm not so sure what I did was right. I fueled the hatred in him too. I made sure he didn't forget, always keeping the desire for revenge alive. He looked up to me like to a father. I've felt the responsibilities of a father on my shoulders, and losing Katie felt like I'd lost my own child."

He pressed his hand against hers, holding it tighter to his cheek. "I don't ever want that responsibility again. 'Cause I couldn't stand to lose another child."

It took several seconds for Yvette to process his words and what they meant. He didn't want children?

"But, you can't know that. Nobody would—"

Haven put a finger across her lips. "You couldn't be more perfect for me." Then he smiled. "And as for the reason why you cut your hair short. If you were trying to hide your femininity, I'll let you in on a little secret: it's not working. You'll never be able to hide that you're a gorgeous, hot-blooded, passionate woman."

Before the last word had even left his lips, she pressed her mouth against his and kissed him.

30

Zane answered on the first ring of his cell phone.

"We're under attack," Gabriel yelled through the line. "She's trying to get Wesley."

"We're on our way." He disconnected the call and in the same instant speed-dialed Amaury's number while heading for the bedrooms.

"Yeah?" Amaury answered.

"Gabriel's under attack. We're on our way, but you're closer." Zane stalked down the corridor, banging on Thomas's door before opening it.

"I'm on it," Amaury replied, disconnecting the call.

"The witch is after Wesley," Zane informed Thomas, who came running out of the bathroom, clad only in a towel.

"Shit!" Thomas cursed. "I didn't expect her to regroup that quickly."

Eddie's head rose from the pillow. "Damn it!" Dressed in a T-shirt and boxers, he jumped up.

"Get ready!"

Then Zane turned and gave Yvette's door a brief knock, yanking it open without waiting for a reply. The room was empty.

"Ah, shit!" He didn't need to be a brain surgeon to figure out where she was. Did that woman have no sense of self-preservation? Did she have to get involved with a damn witch?

Pissed off, he headed for the guest room and opened the door without knocking. The sight that greeted him was something he would have given just about anything to erase from his memory. A naked Yvette lay on her back with Haven's head between her legs. Not only was that man sucking her like a world champion, their hands were intertwined, indicating a connection that ran deeper than sex.

Luckily, Zane only had to watch the scene for a split second, because Haven had heard the door opening. His head snapped to the side, and he immediately scooted up Yvette's body, covering her nakedness while he pulled on the duvet to hide her completely from Zane's view.

"What the fuck!" Haven growled. "Get out!"

"Zane!" Yvette yelled at the same time. "Can't I have any privacy?"

"No, you can't. Not now. Gabriel's under attack. The witch is trying to get Wesley."

Haven cursed. Shit! While he'd been thinking only of himself and making love to Yvette, his brother was in danger. He should have known that splitting them up wasn't a good idea. They should have all stayed together.

"Get ready, Yvette. Eddie will stay here with Haven," Zane instructed.

"No. I'm coming with you."

But Zane slammed the door shut before the last word had even left Haven's throat.

"No, you're safer here with Eddie. She can't attack two places at once." Yvette slid out from underneath him and searched the room for her clothes. The instant Zane had opened the door, Yvette had tensed, understandably so, but the coldness of her voice startled him nevertheless.

"I'm not letting you all go out there and fight my battles for me."

Haven jumped out of bed after her and grabbed his jeans—well, they were probably Amaury's, but now they were his. Yvette dressed faster than he'd ever seen a woman dress. Would he ever get over her supernatural speed? Did he care to? Nope.

"Forget your pride. It's not about that. We're stronger than you."

Despite everything that had happened between them—or maybe because—he felt a twinge of hurt at her words. Could he live with the fact that Yvette was so much stronger than he was? Would there always be this power battle between them?

He combed his hand through his messy hair. Hell, when had he started to think like that? How had he landed in this ... this relationship? Because that was exactly what it felt like: a relationship. He waited for the sense of claustrophobia to punch him in the gut, but nothing happened. No feeling of being trapped spread. No fear of doing the wrong thing appeared.

Only a sense that what he was doing was right settled in his chest. "Baby, hate to break it to you, but you're not gonna get rid of me that easily."

Her hand on the door knob, she turned her head and tossed him a surprised look. "Who said I was trying to get rid of you?"

Haven threw on his shirt and took two steps toward her. "You put up your wall again the moment Zane came in the room. Fine. You don't have to tell your friends what's between us. Not yet. But you're not gonna shut me out." Then he took her lips in a hard kiss, asserting his claim on her. Damn it to hell, but he wanted her, a vampire.

"Now let's go."

Her red lips looked thoroughly bruised and even more kissable than before, and once all this was over, he'd get right back to them, but it was time to fight the witch.

Haven jerked his boots on and reached for her hand. To his surprise, she slipped her palm into his. "We're stronger together," he murmured.

Yvette nodded.

***

By the time they reached Gabriel's house, the fight was over and Bess was gone.

"Shit, what happened?" Haven looked at the trail of destruction in the foyer of Gabriel's Victorian home. Maya knelt next to Oliver, whose arm sported a long gash. Frantically, Haven searched the room for his brother. "Where's Wes?"

Gabriel's voice came from the stairs leading down to the garage. "He's fine. I managed to lock him in the safe room downstairs before the witch could come close enough." Gabriel appeared in the hallway. Behind him, Wesley emerged, looking no worse for wear.

Relief flooded through Haven as he hugged his brother close. Then he looked at Gabriel. "You can't separate us again. I won't allow it. We're clearly not any safer if you split us up. On the contrary, she'll have fewer of you to fight. And see what happens." He pointed at Oliver, who was being tended by Maya.

Gabriel squared his stance. "I'll talk to Samson. It's his call." He flipped his cell open and dialed. Seconds passed. Haven noticed how suddenly all the other vampires, Amaury, Zane, Thomas, Eddie, and even Yvette, went completely still. A moment later, even Haven could hear it: the call went to voicemail. Samson wasn't picking up.

"Shit!" Amaury suddenly yelled. Panic skidded over his features. "The witch is attacking Samson's house." Then his face distorted in agony. "Nina! Oh God, she's injured."

Confused about how Amaury could know that his wife was hurt, Haven concentrated only on what he knew now: it had been a trap, a diversion. True fear coursed through him. "She's going after Kimberly." And it wasn't hard to guess why: if the witch had Kimberly, Haven and Wes would come after her, simple as that. And they'd be back to square one.

31

The door to Samson's house was wide open. Not a good sign. Amaury ran past Haven and up the stairs as if a horde of stake-wielding madmen was chasing him. Behind him, Gabriel was shouting orders to secure the area.

"Kimberly!" Haven yelled into the house as he ran inside. Nothing moved on the first floor, so he followed Amaury's example and rushed up the stairs. He burst into one of the bedrooms a few steps behind Amaury and skidded to a halt.

The pregnant Delilah lay on the large four-poster bed, her face distorted in pain, her legs spread with her feet flat on the mattress. She breathed rhythmically.

"Maya!" Samson, his face and torso marred with burn marks yet holding his wife's hand called out. "We need you here. The baby's coming!"

Maya rushed into the room in the next instant and immediately headed for the bed. "I'm here." She glanced back to the opposite side of the room, and Haven followed her look.

Amaury had scooped Nina into his lap. Her torso was littered with burn marks and slashes, and she was bleeding profusely.

"No, Maya," Delilah said. "You have to help Nina first."

"Amaury's got her. Don't worry," Maya assured her. "Now let's get that baby out."

Haven glanced back to Amaury and the woman in his arms.

"I shouldn't have left you alone, *chérie*." He noticed how Amaury's fangs lengthened and then, without warning, he pierced his own wrist with them, making blood spurt from it.

Nina gave him a weak smile. "Had to kick that witch's ass."

"'Course you did," he answered and led his wrist to her lips. "Now drink." Fascinated, Haven watched, reminded of how Yvette had healed him in the same way only two days earlier.

When Samson approached him, Haven turned away from the scene and looked at him. Before the vampire said a single word, Haven already knew what was coming.

"I'm sorry. I couldn't prevent her from taking Kimberly. She was attacking Nina. We fought her as best we could, but when she went after my wife . . . I'm sorry, she was too strong for Nina and me." True regret shone in his eyes.

"Kimberly was my responsibility," Haven pressed out, feeling the sharp edge of failure slice into him. He couldn't blame Samson—he'd had to protect his wife and Amaury's. Those were his first priorities, not Kimberly.

A soft hand slid into his palm, and he turned seeing Yvette step beside him. "We'll get her back. I promise you." Her words were little consolation to the grief that overwhelmed him once more. She must have noticed his dejected look, because she did something that he hadn't expected her to do.

In front of all her colleagues and friends, Yvette put her arms around him and kissed him. When she pulled back to look at him, he felt choked up and couldn't say what he wanted to, so he simply said, "Thank you" and hugged her back.

As he released her from their embrace, he caught Wesley's look fixed on them. For once, his brother wasn't scowling. He simply shrugged as if to convey that whatever happened wasn't something he could change. Maybe his little brother had finally figured out that some things were fate, and you didn't mess with fate.

"Can we have some privacy for Delilah here?" Maya asked and made shooing motions with her arms. "We've got a baby to deliver here, so give us some space."

Despite the fact that Nina already looked much better after drinking her vampire husband's blood, Amaury carried her out of the room. "I can walk, you know," she protested.

Amaury simply grunted. "Let it go, Nina. You're not gonna win this one."

Only Maya and Samson remained in the bedroom with Delilah after all others trailed downstairs and assembled in the living room. A sense of *déjà vu* stole over Haven as he looked into the round. So much was the same, yet so much had changed since they'd been assembled in the same room not twenty-four hours earlier.

Haven tugged Yvette closer. "How did Amaury know that his wife was injured?" He kept his voice down, not wanting the others to hear him.

"They're blood-bonded. They can communicate telepathically."

Yvette's whispered words peaked his curiosity. "How so?"

"That's just how it is. A blood-bonded couple has a very deep connection."

"But Nina's human." That a vampire had special powers didn't surprise him, but Samson had clearly said that Amaury's wife was human.

"Doesn't matter. Once she blood-bonded with Amaury, she's connected to him. It'll always be like that for them. They're closer than any human couple could ever be." There was longing in her look.

"But if she's human, and he's a vampire, she'll grow old and die." And she would have to watch her husband stay as young as he was now while she withered away. Haven shook his head. How good could that be? No, a relationship between a human and a vampire—or a witch and a vampire for that matter—had to be doomed from the start.

A soft smile curled around Yvette's luscious lips. "They're blood-bonded. She won't age as long as he's alive. That's the beauty of a blood-bond. He'll never have to turn her. She can remain human and still be with him."

Haven's mouth dropped open as he looked back at Amaury, who now held Nina in his lap as he sat in one of the armchairs, softly caressing her blond locks. He was surprised by the tender gesture from this hulk of a vampire. The emotions between them were clearly visible in every smile and every action. He loved her, and there seemed to be no fear in her despite the fact that Amaury would be able to crush her with one hand.

As he watched Amaury and Nina, Haven's entire belief system came crashing down. None of the things he thought he knew about vampires made sense anymore. What he'd experienced with Yvette, how she'd healed him and later made love to him, had already shown him glimpses of a truth he hadn't wanted to see. And Amaury only cemented those beliefs: vampires were living, breathing, feeling creatures as much capable of love and compassion as humans.

Haven's gut twisted at the thought of the vampires he'd killed. Had he robbed a wife of her husband, a woman of her lover, a child of its father? And despite the fact that the vampires assembled around him knew what he'd done, they'd let him live. If anything, they were better than him.

"What's wrong?" Yvette whispered next to him.

Could she sense his turmoil, the guilt that was flooding him? Haven squeezed her hand. "We need to find Kat—Kimberly."

The voices around them settled as Gabriel motioned everybody to calm down. "We've made mistakes. I'm the first one to admit that."

Nobody contradicted him.

"Our traditional methods of dealing with a threat haven't worked in this case. We can't fight a witch with our usual powers; she's too strong. And we need to act fast. The full moon is tomorrow night, and we can be sure that the witch will make an attempt at snatching both Haven and Wesley from under our noses to perform the ritual. We can't let that happen."

Haven released Yvette's hand and stepped forward. "I disagree."

Several pairs of eyes snapped in his direction.

"She wants me and Wes. So we're gonna deliver what she wants."

"Out of the question!" Yvette snapped. "You're not—"

Haven snatched her wrist and stopped her. "I know you're afraid for my safety, but it's the only way to get Kimberly back. You have to just trust me. I have an idea."

He hated lying to her and to the rest of them, but he knew that if he suggested what he planned on doing, Yvette would be the first to call him crazy—right after his brother hit him over the head with a heavy object.

"What idea?" Yvette asked, worried that whatever he suggested would put him in the path of danger. Not that he'd ever stepped off that road.

Now that she'd admitted to herself that Haven was more important to her than anybody else in her life, she couldn't allow anything to happen to him. She had to protect him, even if that meant protecting him from himself and his heroic ideas.

A feeling of unease settled at the nape of her neck when Haven finally spoke. "I'm not sure whether any of you know what I do for a living, but I'm very good at it. I'm a bounty hunter. I know how to ferret out people who don't want to come crawling out of their holes. It's all about the bait."

Yvette didn't like a word of what he was saying. "Bait" was synonymous with "suicide."

"We have no idea where that witch is hiding out, right?"

Gabriel tried to protest. "We're still looking for her. Our guards are out there, combing the city for her. Unfortunately, without anything with her DNA on it, Francine won't be able to scry for her, otherwise we would have already tried that route."

"That's what I figured. We know she's going to try to get Wes and me before tomorrow's full moon. Otherwise, she'll have to wait an entire month for another opportunity to perform the ritual. Since we can't go and find her, let's try to control what we can. Next time she snatches us, it'll be on our terms."

"Go on," Gabriel encouraged.

"Wes and I will go back to my apartment and wait—"

"No! You can't leave our protection!" Yvette interrupted. If she and her colleagues weren't around him, how could they prevent him from being taken?

"We have to. Because this time she'll attack during daylight hours. That way she knows you can't follow her if you're not prepared. That's why you have to prepare. Once she has us, she'll take us to Kimberly, and you'll have to follow us. You need to stay far enough away for her not to sense you, but close enough to interfere when we need you."

Yvette knew that what he was suggesting was too risky. What if they lost track of them when the witch took them away? "We need a way to trace you."

Thomas nodded. "I can put a GPS tracking device in each one's shoe. It's tiny; she won't be able to find it."

"Good," Gabriel approved. "See to it."

Thomas rose and waved to Eddie. "Eddie, we'll go get a couple of the chips. I'll show you how to program them." Then he looked at Haven and Wes. "Give me your shoes. We'll be back in an hour."

As the door closed behind them, Yvette felt the finality of Haven's decision close in on her. He wanted to offer himself up to save Kimberly, but what if something went wrong? "We weren't able to defeat her last time. What makes you think we can do it this time?"

Haven took her hand and squeezed it. "I think we all know now what powers she has. We're prepared. If we go at her with more manpower, we can weaken her."

With her eyes, she tried to convey to him that he was making a mistake. "Knowing what she can do, and being able to defeat her are two different things."

"We'll enlist Francine's help. She seemed keen enough to help last time. She can hold Bess off with witchcraft while a dozen vampires try to weaken her with traditional weapons. In the meantime, a few of you can free Kimberly, Wes and me," Haven suggested.

Gabriel gave Yvette a confident half-smile. "And this time we'll double the number of vampires fighting her." He looked at Zane. "Draw up a list of our best men and get them ready."

The cry of a baby interrupted Gabriel's orders. He lifted his head. A moment later, he smiled. "Maya wants me to tell you that Delilah's just delivered a healthy baby girl."

***

After congratulating Delilah and Samson on their beautiful baby, Yvette closed the door to the master bedroom and headed for the stairs, leaving the rest of her colleagues to coo over the newborn.

"Yvette."

Haven's voice behind her made her turn. Without another word, he pulled her into the guest room and closed the door behind them.

"I know you're not happy about my plan, but I need you to trust me. Everything will be all right."

Yvette twisted out of his arms. "It's suicide." Did he have no sense of self-preservation?

Haven cupped her shoulders and drew her closer. "It's not. Didn't you say yourself that your friends are the best bodyguards, the best fighters out there?"

"So now you're using my words against me. Figures."

He put his finger under her chin and tilted up her face so she had to look at him, facing his piercing eyes. "Baby, I have no interest in putting my life in danger, but I can't lose Katie again. She's my family. You understand that, don't you?"

Of course, his family would come first. Yvette wasn't family, maybe wasn't even somebody he really cared about. Or was she? "So everything you said earlier, you didn't mean it."

"I meant every word I said." He pulled her against his chest.

She couldn't resist inhaling his scent and losing herself in it.

"When this is over, you and I, we have a date," he whispered into her ear.

"You said that once before."

"And I kept my promise. We had a date. Only next time, it'll be longer."

She raised her head to look at him, hope rising with it.

"Much, much longer. And that's a promise I intend to keep," he added before he took her lips and kissed her as if he were starving. She returned his kiss, clinging to him in the hope that it would never end.

32

Haven shut the door of his apartment and followed his brother into the living room, where he let himself fall onto the well-worn couch. Wes ran his hands through his hair and paced.

"You sure that's a good idea?"

Haven nodded. "Nobody had anything better to offer." Despite his calm voice, he felt anything but. Yvette's last kiss when they'd had to say goodbye had shaken him. It had been full of fear and desperation. He hoped that he'd interpreted her feelings correctly and that she would do the right thing when she had to. As much as he'd wanted to confide his plan in her, he'd stopped himself. In any case, it was only a when-everything-else-fails measure. Even though, deep in his heart he knew it was the only way to make sure the Power of Three would never be unleashed. And ultimately he'd have to take that step.

"What's gonna happen, Hav?"

Haven shrugged. "I don't know. She'll kidnap us, take us to some—"

Wesley stopped in front of him. "No. Not with the witch. With Yvette. You and her, what is it? Just an itch you needed to scratch?" There was a haunted look in Wes's eyes.

Haven broke eye contact and looked out the window. "I don't know where it's gonna go." How could he tell his brother what he really felt when he hadn't even told Yvette? It felt wrong to confess to Wesley when he'd been too much of a coward to tell Yvette what she needed to hear from him.

"Are you in love with her?"

Haven jumped up and walked to the window. "Hell, Wes, I barely know her."

"That's neither here nor there."

"What do you care?"

Wes joined him at the window as they looked out onto the street and its midmorning goings-on. "It can't have escaped your notice that two of those vamps are married to human women."

"So?" Haven didn't like the direction the conversation was going. His brother was about to corner him.

"So, it means that relationships between our two species are possible. Don't play dumb with me. I know it's crossed your mind."

When Haven didn't answer immediately, Wes dug in again. "Hell, you were holding hands with her!"

"And what the fuck is that supposed to mean?"

"When have you ever held hands with a woman?"

"Plenty of times," Haven lied. He couldn't remember a single time. He wasn't the type, and he didn't do relationships. He did one-night stands.

"You know, Hav, I always thought my future sister-in-law would be some tough bounty hunter chick you met at one of your jobs, maybe even some ex-con. That you'd bring home a vampire one day—not even I expected that."

"I'm not bringing home—"

A hand on his shoulder stopped him. "Don't. I guess you could do worse. Yvette doesn't seem half bad. At least it's obvious that she cares about you."

Haven met his brother's look. "I'm sorry, Wes. I know it feels like betraying Mom's memory, but there are things I can't fight." At the thought of his mother, he again felt a stab in his chest. And he clearly wasn't the only one upset about the revelations Francine had made that night at Samson's house. If his brother only knew what else the witch had confessed, the horrible crime his mother had committed . . . but Haven knew he could never tell his brother. It was one secret he'd take with him to the grave.

"I don't want to talk about Mom right now."

Before Wes could turn away, Haven grabbed his arm. "I think we have to. If Francine was telling the truth, and I believe she was, then we were in the wrong all this time. *I* was in the wrong. And *I* dragged you into it when you would have been young enough to forget."

Wes let out a long breath. "You really think I could have forgotten what happened that night even if you hadn't reminded me constantly?

Hav, I was the one who let him have Katie! I didn't run! I didn't keep her safe."

It was the first time Haven realized that Wesley carried the same guilt with him as he did. It was time to let go of it now, to forgive and forget. They would have Katie back. And this time they'd keep her safe. Haven would make sure of it, even if that meant sacrificing himself to stop the prophecy from being fulfilled.

He took Wesley by the shoulders and shook him. "Stop, Wes! It wasn't your fault. And it wasn't my fault. We were kids. We did what we could. What happened was because of Mom. She brought this on us." Mom had robbed them of their father. But he couldn't tell Wes. He would break if he knew. "We lost Katie because of her, because of what she wanted."

He saw tears well up in Wes's eyes and pulled his brother into an embrace. "The past is over."

"How could she do that to us? Didn't she love us?"

Love? Had their mother loved them? Haven contemplated his brother's question, remembering the last time he'd heard his mother speak of love. Had it meant anything?

"I don't know. I don't think we'll ever know." Could anything cut deeper than a mother's betrayal? "But we'll make things right now. I promise you."

Wes nodded. "Yes. We'll make it right."

Haven released his brother from his arms. "We have to destroy the Power of Three. It's brought too much pain to everybody involved. I don't want it."

"I don't either."

"Good, then we're in agreement. But I need your help. There's a second part to the plan which I haven't told anybody about, not even Yvette."

33

Yvette bit her fingernails. She hadn't done *that* since she was human. But waiting in the blackout van for any news on what was happening at Haven's apartment was nerve wracking. Next to her, Zane sat like a stone statue, not moving, not shuffling around, and certainly not fidgeting like she was. As if nothing bothered him. Which was probably the case.

"Hungry?" he suddenly asked and reached into the cooler next to him, pulling out a bottle of blood.

She shook her head.

"Ah, I guess you dined on Haven earlier. What's it like, witch's blood?"

Yvette's patience snapped like a bungee cord. Her fingers wrapped around Zane's neck, pressing him against the headrest. "Shut the fuck up or I'm gonna stake you right here!"

He grabbed her wrist and freed himself, then moved his head from side to side, cracking the vertebrae in his neck. The sound sent a chill down Yvette's spine.

"Touchy. Guess that'll teach me not to interrupt next time he's going down on you."

Zane really didn't know what was good for him.

"Stay out of my private life!" She wrenched her hand free from his grip and narrowed her eyes. "You know what, Zane—if I had one wish, you know what it would be? Do you? It's for you to fall in love with your greatest enemy. And do you know what I'll be doing then? I'll be laughing my ass off."

She crossed her arms over her chest and stared out the tinted windows. "So leave me the fuck alone!"

"I don't do *love*!" Zane snorted.

"Yeah? Well, neither did I. Shit happens." Yvette felt slightly better at the thought that she was rattling Zane's cage. At least it had shut him up. Better than having him poke his nose into her business. What she felt for Haven was private. Nobody needed to know. She'd have to come to terms with it herself first, before others could add their opinions on the matter.

Not that she would allow her friends' opinions to deter her in the end: whatever she decided to do would be her decision and hers alone. It didn't matter what the others thought about her infatuation with a man who was neither human nor vampire, but witch. Had there ever been a successful vampire-witch pairing? She sure knew of no such event occurring. But then again, Haven wasn't really a true witch. He had no powers at this point. Would that make things right?

Yvette exhaled, trying to ease the tension in her body. It didn't really matter what Haven was, because he was just ... Haven. A man who made her forget all the pain of her past. A man who could maybe even accept her the way she was: damaged, not a real woman. And if fate threw her this bone—who was she to toss it away?

A beeping sound pulled her out of her reverie. Her gaze flew to the monitor in front of her. Two green dots blinked as one. Red dots were circling them. "They're on the move."

"Let's go," Zane ordered the human driver. "Keep back. Let's see where she's taking them."

Yvette watched on the monitor as the green dots moved through the city, the red dots being Scanguards blackout vans moving in synch with them, but always staying at least three blocks away from the green dots. It was imperative that the witch didn't realize she was being followed even though she might suspect it. But since it was daylight, she probably felt herself to be safe from the vampires. She wasn't.

Her eyes glued to the monitor showing a map of San Francisco, Yvette followed the movement of the green dots. Heading west at about the same speed as their own van, the other vehicle slugged through heavy midday traffic. It slowly advanced on one of the main arteries before it turned north onto the road leading toward the Golden Gate Bridge. The witch was heading for the countryside.

Yvette thought about it for a moment. If Francine's assumption was right, then the ritual would have to be performed outside under the moon. Marin County, just north of the Golden Gate Bridge, would offer many secluded and wooded areas where such ritual would go unnoticed. Besides, the area was full of new-age junkies, and another witch dancing naked in the moonlight wouldn't rouse any suspicion. Not that Francine had said anything about naked dancing.

As they crossed the Golden Gate Bridge about a mile behind the witch's vehicle, Yvette glanced out the dark window. The view of the city was stunning. But she wasn't on a sightseeing tour. If everything went well, she'd come back here with Haven one night to look down at the lights of the city. Share an embrace. A kiss.

"They're heading for Mount Tam."

Because of thinning traffic up the winding two-lane road toward Mount Tamalpais, they had to fall farther back in order not to be noticed. Nervousness crept up Yvette's gut and settled in her throat. What if they lost them?

She didn't notice that she'd started fidgeting again until Zane put his hand on her arm. "Don't worry. She won't get away." His voice was uncharacteristically soothing, so much so that she gave him a stunned look.

He shrugged as if guessing her surprise. "All evidence to the contrary, I'm not entirely heartless."

She nodded, speechless at his unexpected show of compassion. The slowing of the van made her look back at the monitor. The two green dots now blinked without moving. "They stopped."

"Stay back," Zane instructed the driver. "We don't want her to hear the car engine or see us."

The driver stopped and turned off the engine. Then he turned back to them. "I'll check it out." He pulled a curtain between driver's compartment and passenger area before he opened the van door and stepped out. The UV-proof glass between the driver and passenger area assured that no daylight entered the area Zane and Yvette occupied.

Despite knowing that their driver was one of their best human bodyguards and trained in stealth just as she and Zane were, Yvette couldn't help but worry. "What if the witch detects him?"

"He's human. She won't think anything of it. There are hikers around this mountain all day, and he's dressed the part."

Feeling silly, she didn't answer. Of course, Zane was right. But waiting for sunset had never felt so torturous.

34

The cabin to which Bess had brought them was rudimentary: one large room with a corner area that served as a kitchen and a small bathroom off to another side. It felt damp and cold. Haven hadn't noticed anybody following them, but hoped that the vamps weren't far away. With several more hours of sunlight—even though very little penetrated through the heavily wooded area—no rescue mission would come before sunset.

When he and Wesley entered the cabin with the witch at their back, his eyes immediately searched for Kimberly and found her curled up on the only bed in the room. She jumped up when she saw them.

"Haven, Wesley! You shouldn't have come! Now she has us all," Kimberly wailed.

Wesley pulled her into his embrace. "It's gonna be okay, sis."

"At least you're all right," Haven noted with relief and patted her shoulder.

"Yeah, yeah, yeah," the witch droned behind them. "How I hate sappy family reunions."

Bess was unarmed, except for the ceremonial dagger sheathed at her hip. Haven eyed the weapon covertly. He'd have to get his hands on it later.

"Now sit, and don't bother me," she ordered and pushed a blast of air against him. Haven's balance was uprooted, but he caught himself quickly enough. There was no need for the witch to have any weapons to keep them in check when all she needed were her powers. Haven recalled his last conversation with Wesley before Bess had swept them away and hoped he hadn't miscalculated about how to defeat her.

***

As soon as night fell, Zane and Yvette joined Gabriel under a copse of trees. Francine was with him. The remaining vampires scattered, creating a wide circle around the cabin the human bodyguards had scoped out.

Yvette slipped her earpiece into her right ear. It would allow their team to communicate with each other to coordinate the attack.

"We'll need ten minutes to hike to the cabin, another five to get to the clearing where we believe the ritual will take place," Gabriel explained.

Francine nodded. "Haven, Wes, and Katie will have to stand in a half-circle around the altar. We'll have to wait until Bess starts the ritual chanting. Her concentration will be on the ritual and her cognitive senses dulled. It's the only time she's weaker than normal."

"Francine will use her powers to take out the witch," Gabriel elaborated. "Once she's defeated, any wards she's put up will fall and allow us to get the three out and to safety."

"Understood," Zane confirmed.

Yvette swallowed hard. It sounded so easy, but nevertheless, she knew a million things could go wrong even with Francine's help. "Thank you for helping us, Francine. I'm sure it can't be easy to have to fight one of your own."

A tight smile formed around Francine's lips acknowledging Yvette's words. "Sometimes we have no choice about what we do. Certain things are stronger than us."

Francine's comment conjured up a vision of Haven and her feelings for him. Yes, certain things were more powerful than Yvette was. Once this was over, she'd tell Haven that she loved him, whether that meant exposing her heart and making herself vulnerable or not. If he didn't love her back, it would hurt. But if he did, then she had everything to gain.

They hiked in silence, careful where they stepped so as not to create any noise as they approached. The moon rose, lending more light to their path even though they could have easily done without it. A vampire's night vision was as good as a human's vision during daylight. Everything was sharp and clear. Yvette concentrated on the mission ahead, on the importance of what they had to do: not only to destroy the witch who could upset the power balance in their fragile world, but more importantly, to save the man who had come to mean everything to her. And to preserve the family he had fought so valiantly to keep.

She understood his fears now, because as she hiked up the mountain to their destination, she walked in Haven's shoes. For years, he'd looked for the sister he'd lost and protected the brother he loved. Yvette realized now that family didn't have to mean giving the man you loved a child. Family was everything: a brother, a sister, friends, trusted colleagues. She already had a family, and she'd fought for it too, protected them when she had to just like they'd protected her. Even saved her life. Zane had done that months earlier. And now they were all by her side to save what was dearest to her.

"I love him," she whispered.

Next to her, Zane turned his head and locked eyes with her. "I know." And, hell, if that wasn't a kind smile playing around his mouth.

As they reached the small wooden cabin, they already knew it was empty. Yvette switched on her earpiece, making sure she was connected to the rest of the team. One by one, her colleagues checked in announcing themselves by name. The only one who wasn't going to join their fight was Samson. He'd stayed back with Delilah, torn between his duty as their leader and his love for his wife and child and the need to protect them.

For the first time since finding out that Delilah was pregnant, Yvette felt true joy for the couple. Her feelings of envy had disappeared. She would have a talk with Maya, letting her know that she didn't want to continue with the futile attempts at forcing a pregnancy, when it truly didn't matter anymore. It never really had. Because all she'd ever wanted was somebody who loved her. And if Haven was that somebody, it would be enough. She wouldn't have to give him a child to make him love her. She alone would be enough.

When Gabriel's pace slowed and then came to a stop, Yvette stepped right next to him and followed his gaze into the distance. In the middle of a small clearing past the protective canopy of the trees that sheltered her and her colleagues from view, moonlight flooded onto a large flat stone long and wide enough for a person to lie down on. On three sides, the area was surrounded by trees in which her colleagues were now hidden. But on one side, behind the large stone altar, a formation of rocks formed a near-vertical wall, making it impossible to approach from behind.

The stone altar held several items: lit candles, a dagger, and a caldron. Behind it, the witch stood looking up at the sky as if waiting for the moon to move into the position she needed. Surrounding the altar stood the siblings. They weren't tied up. Noticing them shift ever so slightly, Yvette realized that while they were most likely bound by some ward or spell not to escape, they could move their arms and legs.

Yvette pushed down her worry about Haven and his brother and sister, not wanting to destroy her concentration. She had to fight and needed a clear mind.

Francine followed the witch's gaze to the starry sky. "It's time," she whispered. "So close, I can almost feel it."

In her earpiece, Yvette heard her colleagues confirm that they were in position; Gabriel had brought three dozen vampires and human bodyguards. There would be no escape for the witch tonight.

The chanting broke the silence of the night, forcing the sounds of the forest into the background. Strange words in an ancient language whispered through the air, stirring up the wind to blow out the candles. Only moonlight shone onto the scene now. Her arms stretching high toward the stars, the witch raised her voice, repeating the same chant louder now. A gust of wind blew across the altar, rattling the caldron and the dagger lying next to it.

"Now, Francine," Gabriel urged.

A look of pain and horror crossed Francine's features before she stepped into the clearing, pointing her hands toward the ground beneath her. "I command the earth," she cried, and raised her arms. Her lips trembled with words that didn't carry to Yvette's sensitive ears.

From Francine's fingertips, lights like little electrical charges sparked. A moment later, the earth beneath Yvette's feet trembled with earthquake-like tremors. It only lasted a second, but whatever Francine had tried to do, it was sufficient.

Bolts of lightning shot from Francine's fingers as she charged toward the other witch, targeting her. Her adversary's head snapped toward her, the chant interrupted now, her concentration broken. Collecting her strength for a counterattack, Bess stretched her arms out toward Francine.

Gabriel's command came through Yvette's earpiece. "Move in!"

From all sides, shadows emerged from the trees in stealth-like fashion, descending swiftly onto the clearing as the first bolts of Bess's counterattack illuminated the night.

Yvette sprinted forward, conscious to stay clear of Francine's path. As the two witches sent lightning bolts at each other, Francine moved closer to her adversary. Besieged by not only Francine, but the many vampires closing in on her from three sides, Bess sent charges into all directions while seemingly still preventing the siblings from moving.

Yvette dove as a flash of bright light shot into her direction, and rolled onto the ground, narrowly avoiding the burning flame. The moment she jumped back up, she saw three vampires attacking Bess from the side. As one managed to grab her arm and twist it behind her back, her fighting force was instantly cut in half. Within seconds, the other two vampires had her in a firm grip, disabling her from launching any further fire bolts.

Relieved, Yvette charged toward the scene. From the corner of her eye, she noticed a flash pass her. A split second later, the energy bolt hit Bess squarely in the chest. The vampires who'd restrained her were thrown into the air and landed several feet away.

The stench of burnt hair and flesh traveled through the air as Bess fell to the ground, her body in flames, her cries echoing in the chilly night like the wailing of a child in agony.

Yvette snapped her head into the direction the bolt had come from and stared at Francine. "We had her!" Disbelief rolled over Yvette as she called out, "What were—?"

But a lightning bolt coming from Francine's hands hit the ground in front of Yvette's feet, instinctively making her jerk back.

"No further!" Francine yelled.

Shock, and the sharp warning in Francine's voice, made Yvette freeze instantly. When she looked into Francine's eyes as the woman approached the altar, holding out her arms like a shield, Yvette saw a glint in her eyes that could only mean one thing: Francine had turned against them.

"No, Francine!" Gabriel yelled as he ran toward her. She shot a warning bolt toward him, making him stop in his tracks.

"Move!" Gabriel's whispered command sounded through the earpiece. "Take her down!"

But it was too late. As Yvette and her colleagues advanced on her, they were suddenly repelled by an invisible wall, which separated them from Francine and the altar and the siblings in front of it.

She'd erected a shield.

Angry shouts came from all sides.

"Francine, you don't have to do this!" Gabriel cried.

The predatory look on Francine's face was chilling, but her next words brought the horror home. "I've tried for too long to resist it. No more." Then she looked at the three siblings, her hand reaching toward them. "Don't you see? I tried everything not to submit to the temptation. But the power is too strong. I fought it. I did."

Yvette pressed her body weight against the invisible shield, but the ward stayed in place. Why had Francine betrayed them? How could she, after all she'd done for them earlier? How long had she planned this? And why hadn't they seen this coming?

"Francine," Gabriel urged. He glanced at Yvette, stretching out his arm as if to tell her to calm herself. "Let them go. You can resist this. You're stronger."

Francine shook her head, a sad look on her face. "No. It's too late. The power is too close, too real. I did everything to prevent this, everything! I tried to stop Jennifer from going through with it, but she wouldn't be persuaded. Even when I had Katie kidnapped when she was a baby, it wasn't enough. I wanted to make sure the prophecy would never come to pass. I even made him promise never to tell me where he left her. I made him promise so I wouldn't have a means to find her."

"You kidnapped Katie?" Haven yelled, fisting his hands, clearly trying to move toward her, but he was held back by an invisible force. "Oh, God! I should have known. You and Mom, you fought! You betrayed her!"

"I had to. I couldn't let her harness the Power of Three. I had to stop her, so I sent a vampire to take Katie. I sent Drake to take her—"

The familiar name jolted Yvette. Drake? Was she talking about the shrink several of her colleagues were seeing?

"*Doctor* Drake?" Gabriel asked, his voice tight.

"He wasn't a doctor back then. He took Katie, because I told him he had to. I told him about the prophecy, that he had to protect the balance of power. So he did. And he protected me from the temptation at the same time. With Katie gone, I was able to resist. I hadn't even thought of it for years. I thought I'd conquered it. But now . . ." She trailed off, her gaze moving back to the three siblings. "I need the power. I've denied it for too long. Don't you see that I can't do anything about it?"

Then her eyes shot back to Gabriel, angry and accusing. "You should have never involved me in this. You should have never asked me for help. It's your own fault. You should have never trusted me."

Then Francine lifted the dagger from the altar and began her chant.

35

Haven exchanged a look with Wesley, silently reminding him of their plan. Nothing had really changed: a witch was still performing the ritual, only now it was Francine, not their original captor. It made no difference to him. He'd never suspected her, never thought she'd turn against them, but the moment Bess had burst into flames and died, he'd seen the glint in Francine's eyes that could only mean one thing: a lust for power.

Now that the vamps had lost their ally and could only fight with mortal weapons rather than witchcraft to combat witchcraft, Haven steeled himself for what he had to do. He cast one look into Yvette's direction, watching her struggle, trying to fight the invisible shield Francine had put around them to prevent the vampires from approaching.

Haven knew with absolute certainty that he loved Yvette, and he wanted to cause her no pain, but there was no time to communicate to her what he'd planned. He hoped she would understand when the time came.

As the chanting reached a crescendo, Francine rounded the altar and approached them. She reached for Kimberly's hand, opening up her palm. Then she took the dagger and sliced through the middle of it, leaving a trail of blood. Kimberly cried out in pain. The sound cut through Haven's heart, but he didn't move to help her.

Instead he concentrated on his mother's last words, "Remember to love." Haven understood it now. She'd given him the key with her dying words. Only with love would he be able to draw on his original powers and collect enough strength to execute his plan.

When Francine moved on to Wesley, his brother dutifully stretched out his palm to let himself be cut. As the blood spread on his open hand, Wesley winced, but just like they'd discussed it beforehand, he didn't fight her and only widened his stance to get ready for his part.

Francine took a step toward Haven, her hand holding the dagger which was covered with the blood of his two siblings. She would only need his now. As she reached for his hand and turned it palm up, Haven closed his eyes for one moment, allowing the love to flow through him: love for his brother and sister, and more importantly the love for Yvette. As it surged higher, he felt a charge travel from the soles of his feet upwards through him as if a foreign, alien force took hold of his body.

His first instinct was to fight it, but he suppressed the urge, and instead let his love for Yvette guide him and welcome the invasion. As the sensation spread in him, he opened his eyes, suddenly seeing everything with more clarity. He knew that his original power was back. It was weak, but it would be sufficient to perform one action with cunning speed and stealth.

As Francine set the dagger against his palm, he grabbed it from her unsuspecting hand. At the same time, Wesley kicked out his leg, his foot connecting with the back of Francine's knees, making her topple. She let out a startled scream as she fell to the ground, but already, she tried to get up.

It was all the time Haven needed. He held the dagger in both hands and gritted his teeth. Taking all his courage and drawing on the love that was now firmly lodged in his heart, he drove the blade into his stomach, jerking it in as far as it would go. White-hot fire exploded from ruptured guts, wrenching an agonized scream from his throat. Warm liquid dripped over his hands still holding the dagger's handle. He looked down and watched the blood seep from his body as the reality of what he'd done settled in.

"NOOOOOO!"

Who screamed, he couldn't tell. He only felt strong arms around him as he tumbled to the ground. Wesley's body cushioned his fall. Cold blasted through him. The damp of the night spread. His vision blurred, and his ears felt as if stuffed with cotton wool.

He was going to die so the Power of Three was destroyed forever.

Yvette's feet simply moved forward, propelling her into Haven's direction. She barely noticed that suddenly the force field was down. Haven's action was most likely the reason for it, breaking Francine's concentration even as the witch now staggered back onto her feet.

But whatever the reason for the force field disappearing, Yvette had to get to Haven. Her body moved independently from her brain; all her mind could focus on was that he'd stabbed himself to prevent the ritual from succeeding.

From the corner of her eye, she saw the other vampires close in, Zane next to her, his hand on his knife as he charged forward, a hairsbreadth faster than Yvette. When he was within several yards of the witch, who now seemed to have regained her wits and prepared to launch bolts of energy against them, Zane raised his right arm, flicked his wrist and threw the knife.

It lodged in the middle of Francine's forehead. Like a dead tree, she fell.

Yvette derived no satisfaction from her death and merely glanced at her body, not halting her dead run toward Haven. When she reached him, she dropped to the ground and ripped him from his brother's arms, cradling his head in her lap.

Haven's eyes opened. "I knew you'd come . . ." His voice was weak and low.

"Haven. Please. You have to hold on." She pressed her hand against his gaping stomach wound, trying to stop the flow of blood, but there was too much. Like a river it flowed from him.

"I love you," he whispered, barely audible, the strength leaving his body. His face pale and bloodless, his eyes still carried the same passion he'd shown her earlier.

"Nooooo! Don't go! *Don't leave me!*" She was beyond foolish pride now. All she knew was that she couldn't live without him.

A hand on her shoulder made her snap her head to the side. Wesley. His face tearstained, his lips trembling, he gave her a pleading look. "You have to turn him."

A sob escaped her. Turn him? Make him into the one creature he despised? "I can't do that to him. He'll hate me." She would never survive his hate when all she craved was his love.

Wesley smiled through his tears. "No. He'll never hate you. Look." He pointed at Haven, and she gazed down into his face. His eyes still open, as if holding on for a few more seconds, his lips moved again.

Yvette lowered her head to him, trying to make out his words.

"Make me . . . like you . . ." His eyes searched hers. "Love me . . ."

229

"Oh God, forgive me for what I'm about to do."

Then she stroked her hand over his face, feeling the clammy coldness of his skin. He had little time left. "I love you."

Her fangs lengthened, pushing past her lips. A moment later, she dropped her head to his neck and pierced his skin, driving her sharp fangs deep into his flesh. His body trembled, fighting the invasion for a second or two before he stilled against her. As she pulled on his vein and took his rich blood into her, she clutched his body to her chest and listened for his weakening heartbeat until it stuttered to a halt.

**

Zane pulled his knife from Francine's head and wiped the blood off on his pants before tucking it back into its sheath at his hip. He'd never trusted the bitch, and by the looks of it, he'd been the only one who hadn't been taken in by her. So it was only right that he was the one who'd killed her. Yet only a sliver of satisfaction spread in his chest. Her speech had given him the chills: she'd been tempted by the power. And he knew better than anyone how hard it was to fight that kind of temptation. Not to simply unleash the power and wreak havoc. To sit back and wait, he knew of that too.

When Wesley rose as Yvette now fed her own blood to the dying Haven, and cradled his crying sister in his arms, Zane approached. For some strange reason, he felt the need to reassure the scared siblings.

"He'll make it."

Wesley nodded. "It's what he wanted."

"To be a vampire?" Zane couldn't have been more surprised about the revelation. The vampire hunter wanted to be a vampire? When he hated them so much?

"No. I mean, yes. But, no. That wasn't his motive. But he knew that if he gave up his human life, he'd destroy the Power of Three for good. That's why he did it."

Haven had just risen in Zane's esteem by about a thousand percent. "He sacrificed himself."

"For us. For all of us." Wesley looked down at his brother. "God, I hope he won't regret it."

"We'll make him welcome. I'm proud to have a new brother with such courage."

Zane wiped his hand on his shirt and held it out to Wesley. "Two new brothers and a sister."

Hesitantly, Wesley put his hand into Zane's. Zane squeezed it. "You'll always have our protection."

Kimberly left her brother's embrace and stepped toward Zane. With a sideways glance toward Yvette, she smiled through her tears. "They love each other."

Zane felt himself compelled to replace his usual scowl with a friendly smile. "That's why he won't regret it."

36

Haven's head swam. His dreams projected in the most vivid of colors he'd ever seen. A multitude of scents invaded, and his brain worked like a computer, analyzing them, comparing and processing them. Among the smells was one he felt drawn to more than any other: oranges. Home. Finally home.

He forced his heavy eyelids open. Images burst into conscious being. Despite the semidarkness, he had no trouble seeing every detail. A room, one he'd never been in. Decorated by a woman, the feminine touches leaving no doubt about that. The softness of a bed underneath him. Soft cotton sheets brushed against his naked skin.

Haven sat up in a fluid motion, the light duvet dropping to his stomach. It reminded him of something. Far away, like in a different lifetime, he remembered pain. A blade. Blood. His gaze traveled down his stomach, where the ghost of a memory lingered. But nothing marred his perfect skin.

As he touched his belly, a flood of memories rushed back. He saw Francine as she performed the ritual. Then the dagger was in his hand. The pain came a second later as his hands plunged the sharp blade into his stomach. And after that, he remembered only one thing: Yvette, feeling her arms around him, then her fangs in his neck, draining him.

Instinctively, his hand went to his neck, but there, too, his skin was unblemished.

Yet he knew what had happened. He was one of *them* now. He felt it with his body and his heart. Every fiber of his new body was alert, every pore of his skin poised to take in impressions, sensations, and stimuli. Not in his wildest dreams could he ever have imagined how alive he would feel.

Haven took his first conscious breath as a vampire and inhaled an utterly enticing scent, one he knew from his earlier life. Only now, it was more pronounced, more intense, and ultimately impossible to resist. Underneath the covers, his body responded. Pulling back the covers, he slid out of bed, not the least bit surprised that his cock jutted out like a tent pole.

His ears picked up the sound of water running: a shower. With single-minded determination he crossed the room and followed the sound. The door to the bathroom was ajar. He pushed it open without making a noise and stepped inside the steam-filled room. The large soaking tub to his right was empty, but next to it was the large glass-enclosed shower. And in it, Yvette stood under the spray, her back turned to him.

Haven's heart raced as he opened the glass door and slipped in. Yvette turned in the same instant, startled.

"You're awake."

"I'm alive." Alive and hungry. The thirst in his throat burned like a furnace.

Her eyes roamed his face. "Do you remember what happened?"

Haven nodded. "Every second of it." His gaze drifted to the pale column of her throat. "I'm hungry."

"I left you a bottle of blood on the nightstand."

While he instinctively knew that he needed the nourishment she'd left for him, he wanted something else first, to still a different hunger. "Later."

"Haven . . . I . . . I had no choice."

He put his finger onto her lips, stopping her from saying anything else.

"It was the only way."

Yvette's breath ghosted against his finger as she parted her lips. "I couldn't let you die."

"I'm afraid I'll have to punish you for that. You see, Yvette, you turned me into a vampire, now you're stuck with me." He let his eyes drift down her nude form. She was even more beautiful than he remembered.

"Why did you do it?" The anguished sound in her voice gave him pause.

"It was the only solution to destroy the power. No witchcraft can live in a vampire's body. Francine said so herself."

"You should have discussed it with me."

"And have you stop me?" He shook his head. "No, baby; you would have tried to talk me out of it."

"But what if I hadn't gotten to you in time?"

Unshed tears stood sentry in her eyes. Haven stroked his hand over her cheek. "But you did. I'm alive. And I've never felt better in my entire life."

"But you've hated vampires all your life, how could you—"

"You've taught me that vampires have a heart. They're not soulless creatures." Then he looked down at himself and noticed how she followed his gaze. "And by the looks of it, vampires have an increased sex drive." Or was it because Yvette was near him?

Yvette's breath hitched. "I love you."

Her words made everything right in his life. Haven pulled her against his naked body and felt his skin sizzle at the touch. The sensations the contact with her skin produced were more intense than when he'd been human. "I was hoping you'd say that." He gently brushed his lips against hers. "Because I'll never let you go. You understand that, don't you? There won't be any running away."

"How're you gonna make sure of that?" Her coquettish smile told him that she was ready to play.

"Only one way to do that . . ." Haven dipped his head and brushed his lips against hers, inhaling her scent. "God, you smell even better than I remember."

"Everything will be different now," she whispered against his lips.

"Different good?"

"Better. More intense."

Haven slid his hand down her back to the swells of her ass and drew her against his aching cock.

Yvette's breath hitched at the contact. "And bigger."

He couldn't suppress a smile from forming on his lips. "If I'd known that, I would have considered this change earlier."

"You shouldn't joke about it."

"Why not?"

She pulled back and slammed her fist into his shoulder. "Because you scared the shit out of me when you stabbed yourself! Don't you ever dare do anything like that again!"

"And how are you gonna make sure I never do that?" Haven sent her own words back at her, chuckling softly.

"There's one way I'd always know what you're planning," Yvette hedged, lowering her lids as if unsure about how to go on.

Haven didn't have to ask what she was thinking of. A memory from the day before crept into his consciousness: of Amaury knowing when Nina was hurt, and of Maya telling Gabriel telepathically that Delilah had delivered a baby girl. He understood.

"You want a blood-bond."

Yvette pulled back slightly, trying to twist out of his hold. "It's too soon to talk about something like that. And besides, maybe what you want is different."

Haven didn't loosen his grip. And now that he was a vampire, he was as strong as Yvette. She'd never again be able to escape him. "Too early, huh?"

"I was just joking. Really."

"Uh, huh." Then he forced her head up with his hand, gripping her chin between thumb and forefinger. "I thought we were past that phase."

"Which phase?"

"Where you lie to me, and I call you on it."

"I wasn't—"

He *tsk*ed. "Baby, I'm asking you again. Do you want a blood-bond?"

She averted her gaze, but he pulled her face back to him. "Because I want one. And I'd be very disappointed if you turned me down."

Yvette's eyes lit up like a Christmas tree. Against his chest, he felt her heartbeat race. "Oh, Haven, are you sure? Because if we're bonded . . . it'll be forever."

Forever was just what he had in mind. Haven stroked his hand over her cheek. "Baby, I wouldn't be asking if I wasn't sure. Or would you like me to repeat my proposal on bent knees? I guess proposing in a shower is a little unorthodox, but I—"

She shook her head, cutting him off with her next words. "I love you."

Then she flung her arms around him and pressed herself against him.

"I take that as a 'yes.'"

"Yes." Her breath caressed his ear, sending a shiver down his body, the shockwave of it traveling all the way to his cock.

Impatient to make her his forever, he asked, "When?"

"Now."

Now couldn't come fast enough. "You have to tell me what to do."

She loosened her embrace and looked at him. "We'll make love and drink each other's blood when our bodies are joined."

Haven groaned. This was better than he'd ever imagined the ritual to be. At best, he'd thought that there'd be a ceremony akin to a wedding, with other vampires present, while they exchanged blood by cutting their hands in the American Indian tradition. But this, well, this was more than just an unexpected treat. He realized that this was what he'd dreamed of ever since he'd met Yvette, without even knowing what it meant. Ever since he'd first tasted her blood.

The moment he sank his lips onto Yvette's and captured her, he realized he'd finally found peace. He was finally free to love the woman in his arms, and he would do so for eternity. She'd freed him from the shackles of revenge and hatred and shown him that love could dwell in any being.

Haven angled his head and swept his tongue between her parted lips, reacquainting himself with her intoxicating taste. Only this time, everything was more intense, more real. Yet despite the intensity, he couldn't imagine ever getting enough of Yvette.

Without effort, he pressed her against the tile wall of the shower and devoured her mouth as if he'd been deprived of food for a week. He licked and nipped, delved and sucked, swept and stroked. And Yvette matched his every action, her body writhing against him, the spray of the warm shower making their bodies slide against each other in a fluid motion.

With every caress, Haven felt the cords of his control strung tighter. His gums itched and burned as if somebody was pressing a branding iron against them. Haven ripped his mouth from Yvette and pulled back, his fingers instantly going to his teeth, before pulling back in shock.

And there they were: fangs. Slowly, but surely descending from their sockets. Sharp, pointy, and dangerous.

His gaze snapped to Yvette's who watched him with rapt fascination. In slow motion, she lifted her hand and touched his cheek, then trailed her fingers to his lips, nudging against them.

"Show me," she whispered.

He hesitated, at first feeling apprehensive about showing her his new self, but then he realized it was stupid. She was like him, and he recalled how beautiful he'd found her when he'd looked at her with her fangs extended.

Haven parted his lips and felt her finger slide back along his teeth. A moment later, a bolt of energy went through him. His cock jerked in concert.

"Fuck!" he ground out. He'd never felt a more intense pleasure than the touch of her finger against his fang.

A wicked smile was her response.

"Is that what I did to you when I licked your fangs?"

Yvette nodded. "Yes. Do you understand now why I tried to stop you?"

"Hell, no!" He grabbed her hand and pulled it away, then drew her closer into his embrace, his swollen cock digging into her stomach. "Lick 'em, baby."

He saw the flash of delight in her eyes just before he sank his lips back on hers. When she swept her tongue into his mouth and ran it along his teeth, Haven was teetering on this edge of his control. No way would he make it back to her bed; he had to take her here and now.

He lifted her and pressed her against the wall, spreading her legs in the process. The instant she licked over one of his fangs, Haven slid into her to the hilt with one thrust, her tight channel engulfing him in wet heat. Her breath caught, her lips dislodging from him.

"Don't stop now, baby," he urged.

"You're killing me, Haven." Her response was more moans than words. "You're new to this. We should take it slow so you won't get overwhelmed."

"Looks to me like you're the one who can't take it. Trust me, taking it slow isn't what I'm looking for." Haven withdrew from her sheath and plunged back in, his balls slapping against her flesh. "The words I'm looking for are hard and fast and deep."

And with each word, he slammed into her.

Yvette's eyes closed on each stroke inward and opened again on each withdrawal. "Oh, God!"

"That's more like it, baby." Then he lowered his head to hers. "Now, weren't you gonna lick my fangs?"

Their gazes connected. In her green eyes, he saw desire and joy. "I never thought you'd turn out to be such a natural. I was worried you'd fight it more. Fight what you are."

Haven brushed his lips against hers, the feather light touch sending pleasant tingles along his skin. "I fought all my life. I want to love now, because it's all that counts in the end. I want to love you and make you mine."

"I'm already yours."

Yvette parted her lips, inviting him in. Even though he wanted to know so much, to ask so many questions, he couldn't resist what she offered right now: total and utter bliss in her arms. Nothing else mattered. There would be time for everything else later, for questions, for figuring out what his new life would be like.

Their bodies moved in synch as they made love, her legs wrapped around his waist, her back pressed against the tiles. Haven barely felt her weight, his new vampire strength allowing him to do things he would have found mildly strenuous as a human. But all he could think of was how their bodies fit perfectly, how her pussy contracted around him, squeezed him, held him. How her generous breasts bounced with each stroke, how her nipples hardened further each time they brushed against his chest.

Never during lovemaking had he ever felt every action so intensely. Every sensation was magnified tenfold, no, a *hundred*fold. And at the same time, he knew he could last longer, drive her higher and make her come harder than he had as a human. The thought of giving his woman more pleasure than before only added to his own desire. All doubts whether he could ever be enough for her were erased. The way she responded to him, the way she held his gaze and the way her love poured out to him, he knew what his new life would be like: happy and full of love. No hatred. No pain.

Yvette's breathing changed, and Haven clearly heard her heartbeat increase. His own balls tightened at the knowledge of how close she was. Her lips parted. "Now. Bite me now."

His eyes snapped to her neck, the vein underneath her skin pulsating. He dropped his head toward it, drawn to it by an invisible force. As he kissed the tender skin, he felt her shiver under his touch. Withdrawing from her pussy, he thrust back into her just as his fangs pierced her skin and lodged deep inside her.

When the first drop of her blood hit his tongue, the taste of it spreading like wildfire, his cock jerked inside her. A moment later, he felt her lips on his shoulder, her teeth grazing him, before she opened her mouth wider and plunged her sharp fangs into his flesh.

Haven's control broke, and his orgasm crashed over him more powerful than any earthquake, any tornado, any tsunami. Every cell in his body exploded, and with every gulp of Yvette's blood entering his body, pleasure escalated.

And then he felt it.

Felt her.

Yvette.

He could sense her, feel what she felt. Sense her love more intensely now. In his mind, he reached out to her.

Yvette, baby, I'm yours now.

My love. Her voice drifted through his mind, yet her lips were still pressed against his shoulder, her fangs still drinking from him as he was from her.

A moment later, he felt the approach of her orgasm and braced himself. When her muscles convulsed around his pistoning cock, another wave of pleasure hit him out of nowhere, sending him over the edge once more.

I'll never let you go, baby.

How are you gonna make sure of that?

He thrust harder, his cock still as hard as before his orgasms. "Like this, baby, like this."

EPILOGUE

One week later

Yvette waited with bated breath for Haven's answer, even though she sensed his decision already. They both sat in Samson's study, facing Samson, who sat in the comfortable armchair across from the Chippendale sofa.

Haven gave her a sideways look before he squeezed her hand and smiled.

Don't look so worried, baby.

Then he looked straight at Samson. "I won't take revenge. Drake did what he had to do to protect his race . . . I think given the circumstances, I would have done the same. He shouldn't be punished for it. My mother was misguided."

Yvette felt his pain when talking about his mother. And now that she was connected to Haven, she also knew what else his mother had done, that she'd killed Haven's father because he'd tried to thwart her plan.

"She was wrong to try and harness the Power of Three. Nobody should be allowed to have such absolute power."

Samson nodded, clearly pleased with the outcome. "I'm glad you made this decision. I'll talk to Drake and make him aware of your generosity."

Haven made an impatient hand movement. "Samson, let's get this straight: this is not generosity on my part. It's penance. I'm sure it hasn't escaped your memory that I killed many vampires. I'm the one who should be punished."

Yvette shot up from her seat. "No! I can't allow that. Samson, you can't allow Haven to be punished."

Samson motioned his hand, making her stop. "Yvette, I have no intention of punishing your mate. So, calm down. I do have a proposition, however."

Yvette allowed Haven to pull her back onto the couch. His arm came around her as he drew her close to his side, the warmth of his body instantly comforting her.

"What are you thinking of?" Haven asked, looking straight at Samson.

"You destroyed the Power of Three by sacrificing your human life. And we're all grateful for that. Nobody would have ever forced you to do that for us."

"I did it for Wes and Katie . . . uh, Kimberly. Guess I'll never get used to her name."

"No matter the reasons, we're in your debt. You're a great fighter, and show great leadership potential. I was wondering whether you'd like to join us at Scanguards."

"You're offering me a *job*?"

Samson nodded. "You can't very well go back to your work as a bounty hunter. But we could use somebody like you."

Yvette's chest filled with pride. To invite Haven to work for Scanguards meant he had his full trust. It meant he truly would be one of them. An equal. A member of the family.

"Think on it for a few days." Then Samson rose, indicating the end of their conversation.

As Yvette and Haven walked in silence into the night, she slipped her hand into Haven's. Only their footsteps echoed on the pavement. Yvette let the last few minutes replay in her head. By the time Haven finally spoke, they were already climbing the steep hills of Telegraph Hill and only a few blocks from her home.

"I don't think I can accept. Not yet, anyway."

"Why?"

"I'm not ready. And I don't deserve it."

"But Samson thinks you do."

Haven smiled at her in the darkness. "I have to believe it first. Yvette, I've killed innocent vampires. I have to forgive myself for that first."

Deep down, she understood. His honor forbade him to accept something he didn't feel worthy of. "I'll help you."

He squeezed her hand and pulled her into the entrance of her home—their home. "And with your help, I'll forgive myself one day." He kissed her, then released her and unlocked the door.

A sound from the inside put her on guard and ready to act. She inhaled. A moment later, she tore past Haven, entering the dark house.

"Dog!"

A soft yelp came from the kitchen. When she entered it, her eyes peered into the darkness. There, on its floor pillow lay her dog. But it wasn't alone.

Behind Yvette, Haven entered the kitchen and flicked the light switch, flooding the room with light.

"Puppies!" Yvette exclaimed as she dropped down to the floor to pet her dog, who licked her neck happily. "She had puppies."

Next to her, Haven crouched down and stroked his hand over the dog's fur. "That's a nice dog you have here, baby. What's her name?"

Through tears, she blinked at Haven. "She has no name." Then the floodgates opened, the stress and strain of the past two weeks finally dissipating. Haven's arms cradled her against his chest as he lifted her into his lap and the dog lapped against her ankle.

"Then we'll just have to pick one, won't we?" He stroked her cheek and lifted her head, kissing her softly on her forehead. "And for the puppies, too."

Haven scooped one of the puppies up in his large palm. Its eyes were closed, and it whined softly. "Look at this one. The color on its head makes it look bald. I think I have the perfect name for this little boy."

He winked mischievously at her, making Yvette laugh through her drying tears.

"Zane's going to kill you if he hears it."

Haven stroked the puppy's snout and addressed it, "What do you think about that, Zane, huh? You're not gonna be afraid of a big, bald vampire, are you?"

THE END

ABOUT THE AUTHOR

Tina Folsom was born in Germany and has been living in English speaking countries for over 20 years, the last 12 of them in San Francisco, where she's married to an American.

Tina has always been a bit of a globe trotter: after living in Lausanne, Switzerland, she briefly worked on a cruise ship in the Mediterranean, then lived a year in Munich, before moving to London. There, she became an accountant. But after 8 years she decided to move overseas.

In New York she studied drama at the American Academy of Dramatic Arts, then moved to Los Angeles a year later to pursue studies in screenwriting. This is also where she met her husband, who she followed to San Francisco three months after first meeting him.

In San Francisco, Tina worked as a tax accountant and even opened her own firm, then went into real estate, however, she missed writing. In 2008 she wrote her first romance and never looked back.

She's always loved vampires and decided that vampire and paranormal romance was her calling. She now has 17 novels in English and several in other languages (Spanish, German, and French) and continues to write, as well as have her existing novels translated.

For more about Tina Folsom:

www.tinawritesromance.com
http://www.facebook.com/TinaFolsomFans
Twitter: @Tina_Folsom
Email: tina@tinawritesromance.com

8230722R00146

Printed in Great Britain
by Amazon.co.uk, Ltd.,
Marston Gate.